Cat Burglar

CARRIE JACOBS

for Mom
from whom I inherited a love of reading and a plethora of neuroses
(at least I didn't get the weird chicken thing)

Chapter One

The entire bathroom Avery left behind in Atlanta was smaller than the shower she was standing in now. She'd come back to Hickory Hollow a year ago to help save her parents' business, but working with family definitely wasn't all rainbows and kittens. She let the hot water wash away the tension of a long, frustrating work day. When the water cooled, she wrapped herself in her favorite fuzzy towel and tried to relax.

The bedroom smelled of honeysuckle, carried in on the breeze, through her open fifth-floor balcony door. Another perk of being back in Hickory Hollow. No air freshener needed.

A blur streaked from the bed to the open door, out onto the balcony.

"Hey!" Avery ran over and yanked the curtain back just in time to see a floofy gray cat abscond through the wrought-iron railing that connected her balcony to the neighbor's… with her favorite bra. "Come back here!"

The cat ignored her and slipped through the neighbor's open glass door, pulling the undergarment inside the apartment.

Avery threw her towel on the floor, yanked on a tank top and yoga pants, then stomped next door, barefoot, and loudly knocked on the door. No answer. "Hello? Anybody home?" she yelled at the door.

"Can I help you?" A man's voice from behind her startled her, which only irritated her more.

"You live here?" she demanded, thrusting her thumb in the direction of the door.

"Yes." He held up the key in his hand and eyed her suspiciously. "Why? Do I know you?"

How had she never noticed him before? He was taller than her, which was notable since she clocked in at almost six feet herself, athletic build, had a stylish amount of scruff on his face, crystal blue eyes… She almost forgot about the thieving cat. Almost. She jerked her head toward her apartment. "I'm your next-door neighbor. 5B."

He stepped around her to unlock the door and go inside. "I'm not sure why you're yelling at me. Or is this how you always introduce yourself to your neighbors?"

Oh, so he was a comedian. "Funny. Your cat snuck into my place and stole my—There it is!" She shoved past him and charged at the cat, who had just deposited her bra on the floor and looked rather pleased with himself. Snatching it from the floor, she shook the pink satin and lace at the neighbor. "Keep your cat away from my apartment."

The corner of his mouth twitched in amusement. "Keep your undergarments away from my cat."

A woman's voice prevented Avery from answering.

"I knew it! I told your father you had a new girlfriend."

Horrified, Avery spun, the bra dangling from her fist. The short, matronly woman looked exactly as she sounded. Very momish in her khaki capri pants and white sneakers with a plain T-shirt and cardigan with a butterfly embroidered on the lapel.

Her neighbor wore a dismayed expression that mirrored her own. "No, Mom—"

"Come here, it's so nice to meet you." The woman set a basket on the small table beside the front door and pulled her down for a massive hug, then pushed back, studying her face as she gripped her arms. "You're just lovely. So natural. Much better than—oh, never mind. Anyway. What's your name?" The woman beamed up at her and gently patted her cheek.

"Uh, Avery." What had she walked into?

"Avery. What a pretty name. I'm Dolly, of course. It's so nice to meet you. Alex has been so busy lately, I just knew there had to be something to it." She grinned and hugged Avery again. "I can't tell you how relieved I am that he's dating again. Where are you from, Avery?"

"I live next door?" What was happening right now? At least now she knew the hot neighbor's name was Alex. And apparently he was single. Not that she cared. Useless trivia.

"Mom, this isn't—"

Dolly's hands fluttered as she talked. "I guess I shouldn't have dropped by unannounced. We were on our way home and wanted to bring you pie." She gestured to the basket that was apparently home to a pie.

"Pie?" Alex was immediately distracted from explaining their non-relationship.

"Your dad and I were at the farmers' market and one of the Amish ladies had homemade apple crumb pies and strawberry cream pies. Avery, do you like pie?"

"Love it." She tried stuffing the bra into the waistband of her yoga pants, but it was no use.

Dolly pulled her phone out of her pocket and tapped at the screen. A moment later, she spoke into it. "Come up here. I just met Alex's new girlfriend. Yes, I know. She lives next door. Uh-huh. Okay." She ended the call and looked up at Alex. "Your dad has to move the car, then he'll be up."

"Oh. Mom, she's not—"

Avery wasn't sure this woman would ever believe they weren't together.

Dolly kept talking. "The strawberries looked really fresh, so we bought ten quarts. I'm going to make preserves. Do you like strawberry preserves?" She directed the question to Avery.

"I guess?" Preserves? Is that like chunky jelly? She wasn't going to ask.

"I'll bring you a jar the next time I come over."

Avery looked at Alex and lifted her shoulders in a what-should-I-do expression. He gave a slight shake of his head that said, "I have no idea."

A slight rap at the door sent Dolly to open it and let in a man, Alex's dad. He was slightly taller than Dolly, slightly wider, and slightly less enthusiastic. He held out his hand and grasped hers. "Nice to meet you…?"

"This is Avery," Dolly announced excitedly.

A warm smile stretched across his face. "Avery. Bert. I'm Alex's dad."

"Nice to meet you, Bert."

"Sorry to interrupt. We didn't know Alex had company."

Dolly shook her head. "She's not company, she's practically family."

Avery coughed, still clutching her bra, probably bending the underwire. "That's very… nice?"

"Presumptuous," Alex corrected. "Mom. Dad. Avery's my neighbor." He stretched the last word out for emphasis.

Dolly and Bert exchanged some sort of knowing look. She pretended to concede. "Okay, dear. Let's have a slice of pie so we can get to know your *neighbor* Avery a little better. Bert, grab that pie and take it in the kitchen."

His parents went into the kitchen, an open room around the corner.

Avery grabbed his arm. "You need to fix this," she hissed.

He lifted his hands in defeat. "Sorry, I don't know how to stop this freight train. We'll figure it out after pie."

The lure of fresh strawberry pie was too much to resist. Besides, Alex owed her at least a nice helping of sugary goodness after his rotten little cat burglar's stunt. "Fine."

They sat around the kitchen table while Dolly dished out generous slices of pie. "So, Avery, Alex hasn't told us a single thing about you. What do you do?"

"I work in my parents' hardware store. I moved back last year to handle their marketing and stuff like that." She'd been handling everything, but no need to share that with strangers.

Bert perked up. "You mean Hannigan's?"

"I do."

Dolly's eyebrows lifted halfway up her forehead. "Oh."

Bert shot her a look and said, "He was laid up in the hospital around the same time I was." He tapped his chest. "I had some blockage and got a couple stents put in around the old ticker. How's your dad doing now? He had a stroke, didn't he?"

Avery swallowed hard, then poked at the last bit of pie with the tines of her fork. "He's much better, thanks. Yes. It was a mild stroke, thank God, so he's recovered very well."

Bert did an abrupt subject change. "How long have you and Alex been an item?"

Avery looked at Alex for help. His parents must reeeeeeally want him to have a girlfriend. He pushed his empty plate back and said, "We're not. I've been trying to tell you. She lives next door. We aren't dating. We just met."

"Oh." Dolly seemed disappointed. Hopefully that meant she finally got it through her head they weren't a couple.

The cat, wretched beast, chose that precise moment to leap onto the table and deposit one of Avery's thongs in the center. He turned and gave her a look of smug satisfaction, then leaped out of reach and dashed under a chair in the living room, where he sat, watching and smirking as he licked his paw. It was the cat equivalent of giving her the finger.

Avery snatched the underwear off the table. They were red, which undoubtedly matched her burning face. "I... Um, *itwasreallynicetomeetyou*." It came out as a single word as she shoved the chair back and hightailed it to the door, keenly aware of the low-pile carpeting under her bare feet.

The cat hissed as she sped past, and she responded with, "Satan!" under her breath before she escaped into the hallway, the slamming of the door echoing behind her.

Safely in her own apartment, the first thing she did was run to the bedroom and slide the balcony door shut and lock it. No way she was allowing the devil cat to have access again.

Once the door was secure, she threw the bra and thong with the clothes to be washed. The brat had gotten into the closet and rummaged through the basket of clean clothes she hadn't bothered to put away. At least he hadn't dug anything dirty out of the hamper, which would have leveled this situation up about a hundred points on the scale of humiliation.

Avery sat on the edge of the bed and shook her head. What a surreal experience. If it wasn't for the red strawberry stain—awesome—on the front of her white tank top, she might chalk it up to being a dream. Her mind flitted to Alex. Her next door neighbor. Who was tall, dark, and handsome. And apparently single.

No! The last thing she needed was to get involved with

someone—anyone—especially someone whose front door was barely ten feet away from hers. Can we say awkward breakup?

She was still contemplating the universe, or at least trying to decide if it was too early to go to bed to end this dreadful day when a knock on the front door startled her out of her thoughts.

Checking the peephole, she was surprised to see Alex in the hallway. After that experience, she figured he'd want to avoid her. She undid the chain and opened the door. "Hey."

"Hey." He held out a foil pie plate with the second, untouched, strawberry pie. "Peace offering?"

She chewed her lip, looking at the pie, considering. "Sure." She pushed the door open.

Alex stepped in and looked around. "Nice place."

Avery tried to see it through his eyes. Almost everything was in its place and fairly pristine. The couch rarely hosted a single butt cheek, but her recliner was worn and well-used. The small side table held a stack of books. Nothing remotely interesting, just a pile of accounting principles and management slash self-help business books.

She led him into the kitchen, not that she would have had to, since her apartment was laid out in an identical mirror image of his. "You don't have to share your pie."

He handed her the pie. "I feel bad. I gave Poof a stern talking to after my parents left. Sorry about that, too, by the way."

"Poof?"

The corner of his mouth lifted in an embarrassed half-smile. "Technically, his name is Empurror Poofington J. Poof."

He said it so earnestly she tried not to smile, but failed. "Empurror Poofington?"

"J. Poof. Yes. My niece Sophie named him. She was seven at the time, and I didn't have the heart to change it."

"Poof fits well enough. He's got enough fur." And he did. Objectively, Poof was a gorgeous cat. Shades of gray stripes in his long hair, with a long, poofy tail. Gorgeous, but rotten.

Alex was hesitant. "I think I got it through to my parents that we're not dating, but I can't be sure. Mom just kind of nodded and gave me that side-eye as she said she believed me."

"She totally didn't." Avery wasn't sure what it would take to convince Alex's parents they weren't an item.

"Probably not. Anyway, enjoy the pie. Sorry for the awkwardness. And sorry for Poof stealing your stuff. I swear I had the balcony door shut, but he opened it somehow."

"It's okay."

He walked back to the door. "See you around."

"Yup." This was rapidly becoming as awkward as the meeting with his parents. "I should put the pie in the fridge. Thanks. Again. For the pie."

"No problem. Well, good night, Avery."

"Okay. Good night. Alex." She swallowed hard, wondering why she got butterflies when he said her name.

He gave her that lopsided smile and it took a minute to realize she was still standing in the open doorway, watching his butt as he walked to his apartment. She slammed the door shut and bonked her forehead against it, cursing herself for noticing the fact that he was attractive. And tall. Heaven knew she had a hard time meeting men who she had to look up at.

"But his cat is a thief," she reminded herself. "It would never work out with a guy who has a cat like that. Especially a cat named Poof. Who names a cat Poof, anyway?"

Or rather, who lets their seven-year-old niece name a cat Poof? Only a kind, devoted uncle would do something like that. Someone great with kids.

Oh, crap.

<h1 style="text-align:center">Chapter Two</h1>

"I hope you're happy," Alex said, as he crossed his arms.

Poof looked up at him, his expression completely unrepentant.

"Stop stealing from the neighbor. Don't go to the neighbor's apartment again. In fact, don't leave *this* apartment again."

Poof sat and wrapped his floofy tail around his legs, then proceeded to lick his front paw.

"Are you listening to me?"

Poof finished licking his paw, then turned and flounced out of the room.

"Wow. Rude," Alex called after him.

In the kitchen, he wiped the drips of strawberry from the table and put the last piece of pie in the fridge. He'd polish it off later. From the counter, his phone lit up and vibrated.

"Hey, Mom."

"I think I left my glasses on the table."

He turned to check. "Nope."

"Oh. Oh, well. Is Avery there? I wanted to apologize. Your dad says I put her on the spot and now I feel bad."

He was sure she did feel bad, but this call was just another fishing expedition for details about a relationship that didn't exist. No matter how much his mom wanted it to. "No, she's not here. I already apologized to her."

"Was she upset? I hope she wasn't upset. I didn't mean to upset her."

Alex could tell his mom was bothered when she started repeating herself, so he reassured her. "No, she was fine. Just embarrassed that Poof dropped her underwear on the kitchen table in front of everyone."

"Hmm."

"What?"

"Nothing. She seems nice."

"Yes. She seems nice. But I don't know for sure, since we just met." He knew what she really wanted. Confirmation that he was completely over Chelsea.

"Hmm."

"Mom. We. Just. Met. Literally five minutes before you showed up."

"I believe you."

"You don't. But you should." Alex pinched the bridge of his nose. Obviously he wasn't getting through to her.

"In any event, I think I might make those preserves tomorrow and bring her some so I can apologize. Do you think she'd like that?"

"I just met her. I have no idea what she'd like."

"Hmm."

"Mom," he tried a stern tone, knowing it was no use.

"I'll drop by tomorrow evening, then. Do you think she'll be home?" Before he could answer, she continued, "I assume that since you live next door, you probably hear her in her apartment around the same time each evening."

"I don't. The walls are pretty thick." It was true. He couldn't hear anything from Avery's apartment, or the one on the other side, so either he had super quiet neighbors, or the building was nicely soundproofed.

"Oh."

"I don't know if she'll be home, but I'm sure if you bring her some preserves and apologize and *leave it at that*, I bet she'll appreciate the gesture."

"Okay. How was work today?"

If there was one topic he didn't want to discuss more than his non-relationship with Avery, it was his crappy job. "About what you'd expect for a Monday."

"Did you get the contract you were hoping for?"

"The firm got it." Alex hoped his generic answer would appease her. Of course, it didn't.

"The firm? Does that mean you aren't getting credit again? Oh, Alex."

He could imagine her face, a mix of anger and disappointment, furrowed brow, pursed lips. Not at him, mind you, but at the company who made a habit of taking credit where credit wasn't due, and assigning contracts to people they wanted, rather than the people who brought them in.

"I wish you could find another job. They don't treat you very well."

"Yeah, I know."

"The benefits aren't even that great."

Alex appreciated the support, but he didn't need to be reminded of the many shortcomings of his employer. To be fair, maybe he shouldn't have shared them all with his mom if he didn't want her to bring it up.

"I keep checking the want ads to find something for you."

"Nobody reads the newspaper anymore."

"Obviously *somebody* does."

He heard an obnoxious crinkling sound as she rustled the newspaper against the phone. "You win this round."

"Of course I do. And you know, you can always come work for your dad and I. I know it's not exactly your dream job, but it's always an option."

"Thanks, Mom." He appreciated the offer, but working in his parents' insurance agency wasn't something he was the least bit interested in. His parents were semi-retired – which meant almost entirely retired, they worked when they felt like it – and his sister Holly ran the business. Working with her would be great. Selling insurance would not.

"We updated our wills. If anything happens to us, you and your sister will split the business down the middle. I'd suggest at least having a conversation about how that will go. We aren't going to live forever."

He shuddered at the thought of his parents not being immortal. "We already talked about it."

"You did? When?" She wasn't believing anything he said today, apparently.

"Last year. After Dad got out of the hospital and you guys told us about the wills."

"What's your plan?"

"Well, if Dad dies first, we're shoving you in a cheap nursing home and selling the business on Craigslist."

"Alex!"

He chuckled. "You already know this. Holly will keep running it day to day, and at some point, she'll buy out my half."

"If that's what you want…" She punctuated her words with a long-suffering sigh. "I do wish you'd think about looking into another job, though. Surely there are other security places you could work."

"I'm sure there are. I promise I'll keep my eye out and if anything comes up, I'll look into it." He hoped it was vague enough.

She screeched. "Oh shoot! My strawberries are boiling! *Loveyoubye.*"

Alex had to chuckle as he put his phone into his pocket. In spite of her not-so-subtle meddling, he knew how fortunate he was to have her as his mom. He thought briefly of his birth parents, like he did every so often, and wondered who they might be. Not that it mattered. Even if they were the Rockefellers, he'd gotten the far better deal being adopted by Dolly and Bert Myers.

Poof wound around his ankles and deposited a catnip mouse at his feet.

Alex reached down to scoop him up. "No more stealing stuff. Got it?"

Poof purred and rubbed his head on Alex's chin.

On the upside, and he'd never admit this to his meddling mom, he was kind of glad Poof introduced him and Avery. She was really tall – he guessed close to six feet – and she was gorgeous, smart, personable with his overzealous parents, and adorable when she blushed.

Too bad he had zero interest in dating anyone.

Chapter Three

Hannigan's Hardware was busier than the average Tuesday. Avery plucked a dusty box of nails from one of the upper storage shelves and came back down the ladder.

"Those are supposed to be two and a half inches."

She managed to control her face and not roll her eyes. Doug Fletcher had clearly said he needed three-inch nails. Which was the only reason she was up on the ladder in the first place. There were plenty of two and a half inch nails on the shelf.

"You said three."

He made a rude snorting noise. "That's why women shouldn't be working in a hardware store. Can't tell the difference between two and a half and three inches." He laughed at what he clearly thought was a witty comment, while the guy standing beside him in the aisle ignored him. Apparently, Doug assumed he hadn't heard. "Ain't that right, buddy?"

Avery put the nails back atop the shelf and climbed down the ladder. She reached the floor and rolled the ladder out of the way, pleased she had resisted the urge to make a comment about Doug and his two and a half inches. "Two and a half inch nails are right there, Doug."

He smirked. "I need the *three* inch nails."

"You know what, Doug?" Avery stood straight, using every bit of her five-foot-eleven-and-a-half inch height. She rarely did anything to call attention to her height, but towering over Doug, who couldn't clock in at more than five-two, and making him look up at her, was pretty satisfying. Especially since he pulled this crap almost every time he came in. "Go get your nails someplace else."

He at least looked shocked before he got angry. "What did you say to me?"

"Something wrong with your hearing, Doug? I said you need to leave."

He sneered. "You don't own this place—"

"But I do."

Avery felt a fair amount of glee that it was her mom, and not her dad, who'd come to back her up. Girl power.

"Ginny, you can't kick me out. I got a job I need to finish up. I don't have time to run to Lowe's." He honest to goodness whined.

"Then I'd suggest you head out now, because you were asked to leave."

Doug's eyes narrowed, then he spun toward the front of the store. "You'll regret this, bitches!"

"HEY!" Young Ernie Goyer, owner of the local junkyard, not young under even the most generous definition, and frequent flier at the hardware store, moved faster than he probably had in a decade. He stepped in front of Doug and poked a meaty finger into his chest. "You don't talk to ladies that way." He punctuated every word with another hard poke.

Doug pushed past him and shoved out the front door, his

shouted curses mixing with the cheerful jingle of the door chime.

Deputy Branson came in just as Doug stormed out. He raised an eyebrow and said to Ginny, "There a problem here?"

As Doug's truck peeled out of the parking lot, Ginny answered, "Not anymore."

"That guy's an idiot," another customer offered.

Ginny waved a hand as she walked back around the counter to the cash register. "Sorry to hold you up. Did you find everything okay?"

"Yes, ma'am."

She scrunched up her face and laughed. "You call me 'ma'am' again and I'll come over this counter."

Avery opened the second register and they got everyone checked out, Doug and his crappy attitude forgotten.

Or at least, she thought it was, until her dad came in to bring lunch for her and man the counter while she ate. She'd finished her sub in the back room when her parents both came back and sat down at the rickety table. Furious tension radiated from her mom.

"What's going on?" Immediately suspicious, she wrapped up her trash and took a sip of soda.

"Honey," her dad began. "Your mom told me about Doug."

"Okay?"

"That's the sort of thing you shouldn't have to worry about."

"Meaning what?" She already knew what he meant but she needed to hear it out loud. Her dad and grandfather thought the hardware business was just too hard for a poor little woman to handle. Let's ignore the fact that she came in and saved their asses, even without the guiding wisdom that came equipped in a penis.

"It's just that your granddad has some input and he thinks this might be too much for you."

Avery stood up and pushed her chair in. "The store's too busy to have this conversation right now."

Her parents exchanged a look. Her dad looked like he was pleading for help, while her mom had a raised eyebrow and straight face, her arms crossed. He'd find no assistance there.

She tossed her trash in the can and grabbed the doorknob.

"We're putting Jimmy in charge of the store."

Her idiot brother? Wow. Avery blinked a few times to keep the angry tears at bay. They would only serve to make her father think she was too emotional to handle the job, which he would promptly report to Grandpa. "Well. At least I didn't quit my job, move back here, and uproot my entire life for nothing."

"Avery…"

She heard her mom's voice, but didn't stop. Instead, she went back out on the floor, relieved their part-timer from the register, plastered a smile on her face, and waited on customers.

An hour before closing, Rick Lauder came in and leaned on the counter. "Hey, Avery."

He was one of her favorite customers. Funny, friendly, with a dash of harmless flirting thrown in for good measure. "What can I do for you, Rick?"

"I need to order six more cases of those fluorescent bulbs."

Avery typed into the computer to pull up his account and scanned down over the orders. "Forty-eight or ninety-six inch? Looks like you've ordered both in the last few months."

"Shoot, hang on." Rick poked at his cell phone and moved to the side while Avery waited on another customer.

A few minutes later, he came back to the counter. "Ninety-six."

Avery gave him a big smile. "You got it. Six cases. They

should be here..." she tapped on the screen, "... first thing Friday morning. Truck'll get here around seven. You want those invoiced to the account?"

"Yup. You're the best, Avery."

"Of course I am." She winked at him and typed a note into the computer.

The last of the customers finally left and Avery turned the lock with her right hand while she switched off the electronic "Open" sign with her left. She wanted nothing more than to flee to her car and avoid her parents. While she'd been busy, she hadn't had time to be angry and frustrated at their announcement. Unfortunately, she had paperwork to do.

Or did she? If they were letting Jimmy run the store, he should do it. Jimmy, who hadn't set foot in the store all day.

She finished counting the cash drawer, but had no idea how much money she'd just counted. Stifling a curse, she started over.

"Avery?"

"Counting."

From the corner of her eye, she watched her mother approach. She finished counting the money, added up the checks, filled out the deposit slip, and put it all in the cash bag to be dropped in the bank's night deposit. That done, she could no longer avoid her mother. "Yes?"

Ginny leaned on the counter across from Avery and looked her in the eye. "I know you're upset, and I don't blame you."

Avery slid the bank bag to her mom. "You and dad can drop the deposit. I have paperwork to do. Unless the new GM is going to get off his ass and do it?"

"Avery."

"Mom. You know this is bull. Jimmy can't manage his own checkbook, how is he going to run the store?"

"We'll help him." Ginny sighed. "You know this wasn't my decision."

"I'm going to the office." She was glad her voice didn't quiver.

Her mother's footsteps followed her. "We need to discuss this."

The urge to leave was overwhelming, but she knew that if she left, her parents would be stuck doing the work. She sat behind the desk in the office and shoved the mouse to wake the computer up. She began clicking and typing and updating while her mother dropped into the chair on the other side of the desk.

"Avery."

She stopped clicking and finally met her mom's eyes. "Please stop. There's nothing to discuss."

"Honey, we still want you here to help."

"You want me here to *help*? Help Jimmy? You asked me to come here. You asked me to leave my job, break my lease, walk away from everything I had and come back here so I could help you. I lost my security deposit. I lost my PTO. I just got out of my freaking gym membership last week! I work my ass off, get us back in the black, while Jimmy strolls in a couple of times a week, then you spit in my face and expect me to put on a smile. I'm here to help you and dad. I'm not here to help Jimmy." By the end of her speech, she was yelling. She felt bad for it, but she was yelling more *to* her mom than *at* her.

Ginny wore a tired, patient half-smile. "You know I don't agree with this."

"Wow, that makes me feel so much better." She didn't bother covering up the sarcasm. "I need to get this done." She felt bad snapping at her mom, because she was right – she didn't agree with the decision, but she only owned twenty-four percent of the store, not enough for her opinion to matter.

No, the decisions lay partly with her dad, twenty-five percent owner, and mostly with her grandfather, fifty-one percent owner and a firm believer in passing things from son to son to son like a bucket being passed along a penis brigade.

Ginny stood and hesitated as if she had something else to say, but in the end she simply sighed and left the office.

Avery heard her parents leaving, and bitterly called out, "You wouldn't trust Jimmy here alone. Think about that!"

Chapter Four

Tuesday after work, Alex held the fridge open with one hand– hoping something edible would manifest itself while he watched– and holding his phone with the other. "I have no idea." Alex rolled his eyes, glad his mother couldn't see him.

"I guess we'll head over and if she's home, I'll give them to her."

"Sure."

"Did you eat? I have leftovers if you want them."

That piqued his interest. "What is it?"

"It's that southwestern beef casserole with the jalapeños."

He closed the fridge. "Yum." Heck yeah, he'd take some southwestern casserole.

Her warm chuckle came across the line. "It's already packed up. Should I bring enough for Avery?" She didn't wait for an answer. "I'll make her a plate, too. Just in case she hasn't eaten yet."

"That's nice, Mom, but don't be offended if she doesn't want it." He quickly added, "Since a lot of people don't eat spicy stuff."

"Of course I won't be offended. Your dad's ready to leave.

We'll see you in a little bit." Which meant she already had a plate ready for Avery before she even asked. Typical.

Alex shook his head as he slipped his phone back into his pocket. Poof strolled into the kitchen and wound around his legs, then cast a meaningful look at his food dish.

"It's half full."

Poof was unimpressed.

"Fine." Alex filled the dish.

Poof rewarded him with a purr as he dropped a mouthful of vittles onto the floor beside the dish and daintily ate one piece at a time.

Alex left his apartment to knock on Avery's door and warn her about his mother's impending approach, but Avery was just stepping off the elevator. He closed his door behind him. "Hey."

"Hey." Her voice was flat.

"Rough day?"

She jammed the key into her lock and shook it, to no avail. Pulling it back out, the keyring fell to the floor and split open at the hinge, sending a handful of keys bouncing in every direction. Avery's shoulders slumped. "That. Right there. That sums up this whole lousy day." She bent to pick up keys.

Alex got on his hands and knees and gathered up the keys that had scattered in his direction. "That's a lot of keys."

"Half of them are junk," she grumbled.

"So why—" He knew the question was a mistake before he got any farther.

"I don't know! Okay? I don't know why I keep all these stupid keys! No need to interrogate me about my obsessive need to hang onto this old useless shit!" She shoved another key into the door and twisted it. The door opened and she pushed inside like she was trying to get away.

Alex paused in the doorway. "Avery?"

Her back was to him, her shoulders raising and lowering as she breathed hard. "Please go away."

"Okay." He set the handful of keys on the table beside the door. "This probably isn't the best time to tell you, but my mom's bringing those preserves."

She hadn't moved, one hand still clutching loose keys and the other holding her purse awkwardly against her body.

"I'll tell her you aren't home."

Avery finally turned. Her mouth was down-turned. She looked defeated. "Has your family ever done something really awful to you?"

Alex considered the question.

"I mean, like, something so awful you just want to walk away and never come back?"

"No. Sure, we've had our differences, but I've never wanted to walk away."

Avery came over and scooped the keys from the table into her hand. She poked through them. "This one goes to my grandparents' cabin." She laughed a little. "Well, it used to. They sold it more than fifteen years ago. This one is to my old apartment back in the city. I don't know why I keep them." She dropped her purse onto the table and fiddled with the key ring. "No wonder it broke, huh? Probably wasn't designed to hold seventeen keys."

"Probably not." He wasn't sure what to do.

"I'm so sorry I yelled at you. Again. Ever have one of those days where the entire universe is conspiring against you?"

"I take it today's your day?"

"It must be." She gave another little laugh. "I ran out of gas and had to walk home."

Whoa. She *was* having a crap day. "Where's your car?"

"I coasted into the McDonald's parking lot." Her eyes filled with tears. "I called my dad to bring me gas, but he was out to a celebratory dinner with Jimmy – my idiot brother."

Alex didn't miss the way the last words were bitten out. "I'll take you to get gas. It'll only take a few minutes."

"I hate asking people for favors."

"You didn't ask. I offered."

She looked uncertain.

"It's really not a big deal. Let's go before it gets dark. I just have to grab my keys." He pointed to the handful she was still holding. "Unless you happen to have one in there that'll start my car."

His dumb joke was rewarded with a smile. Just a small one, but it was genuine.

"Afraid not." She dropped the loose keys into her purse. "I really appreciate you helping me out."

"What are not-boyfriends for?"

That earned him a laugh. Progress.

Alex grabbed his keys and phone and met Avery at the elevator. Outside, he got a gas can from the maintenance shed and put it in the trunk of his car.

"You're putting a gas can in a brand new car?"

"That's what the mats are for." He pointed to the rubber liner in the trunk of his new Ford Fusion sedan. More than once he'd been glad he'd spent the money for upgraded custom liners.

On the way to the gas station, she repeated, "I really appreciate this."

"Remember that when my mom's plying you with strawberry preserves and refusing to accept that we're not dating."

"Your mom seems pretty awesome."

"She's the best." He was glad to see her smile.

He pulled up to a pump and Avery swiped her credit card while he got the gas can out of his trunk. Once it was full, he carefully set it back in the trunk and slowly drove the mile and a half to McDonald's.

They didn't say anything as Alex poured the gas into the tank of Avery's Rav4. When he'd secured the cap and closed the door, she slid into the driver's seat and pushed the ignition. The engine sputtered like it wanted to start, but couldn't quite get there. She tried the button again and the car roared to life. "Oh, thank goodness. I was afraid it would have gotten all messed up and not started."

Alex breathed his own small sigh of relief. "I'll follow you home, just in case you have any trouble." He got into his car and waited for her to pull out. The ride back to the apartment building was thankfully uneventful. Parking in his spot, three spaces down from hers, he glanced over. She held her cell phone up and shook her head. He saw her squeeze her eyes shut for a second, then run a hand down her face. The light blinked off and she

jumped out of her SUV and slammed the door.

Alex got out of his car and caught up to her on the sidewalk.

Before he could say anything, she whirled around and planted her fists on her hips. "I should have known since the car started that something else would happen, just to make sure I didn't get cocky and think this crap day was done being crap." Her purse vibrated and she yanked her phone out, then threw it back in. "You should take the gas can out of your trunk so it doesn't make your car stink."

He lifted his index finger in a "wait" gesture and got the gas can.

"I'm sorry. I don't need to contaminate your day with my crap."

"It's fine." He put the can back in the maintenance shed and pulled the door shut. "You want to talk about it?"

Chapter Five

"No. Yes. Maybe. I don't know where to even start." The entire day landed on her shoulders like a mountain. Taking deep breaths to calm herself, the last thing she wanted to do was cry in front of the nice new neighbor who probably thought she was always a hot mess. Just in case, she moved to root through her purse for a tissue. Surprising to no one, the flimsy handle chose that exact moment to break and dump her bag onto the sidewalk.

Oh, yeah, shit icing on this shit cake of a shit day.

All she could do was stare at the assortment of crap scattered across the concrete. Three Chapsticks, those freaking keys, her wallet, two tampons, cell phone, a lipstick that wasn't even a nice color, a screwdriver, a hopelessly tangled set of earphones, a pack of gum, and probably six dollars' worth of change. It would be the Mondayest Monday ever, except that it was Tuesday.

Alex practically dove to the ground to pick her things up and the sweet gesture pulled her out of her stupor. She bent down and started picking the coins off the sidewalk. She grabbed for a quarter and her fingernail hit the concrete at exactly the wrong angle and snapped. Below the skin line. A hysterical laugh bubbled up, and a split second later, she was sitting back on her knees, holding her bleeding finger and laughing like a deranged lunatic while Alex shoved everything back into her purse. Including the tampons.

A moment later, a bit of laughter caught in her throat and turned into a sob. She felt Alex's hands on her upper arms, helping her to her feet. Without meaning to, she leaned into him and his arms circled around her. He held her until the sobs finally died down.

A new voice materialized. "Oh, honey, what's wrong?"

Avery groaned into his chest and pulled back to wipe her face.

Alex said, "Mom…"

"Here, hold this," Dolly said to someone, and a second later she wiped Avery's cheeks with a fistful of tissues and wrapped a Band-Aid around the tip of her finger. "There, sweetie, it's okay." She turned her attention to Alex and demanded, "What happened? Are you two fighting?"

Avery was quick to defend him. "No, not at all. It's…" she trailed off before the words could turn back into tears.

"Let's get you inside," Dolly said kindly.

Alex held the traitorous purse with one arm, and had the handle of a large basket looped over his other. "Yeah. This is heavy."

Avery let herself be shuffled into the building, then the elevator. She didn't muster the energy to object to being pulled into Alex's apartment instead of her own.

Dolly steered her to the kitchen table. "Did you eat supper?"

"Not yet." She'd have sworn she wasn't even hungry, but her stomach rumbled just a little.

"Do you like jalapeños?"

"Yeah?" Jalapeños? How did the conversation turn to peppers?

"I brought a casserole but it has jalapeños in it. Alex, warm up the plates."

"That's not – you don't have to—" The objection was cursory at best. This probably wasn't helping to set the record straight about her relationship with Alex, but it was nice to be fussed over a little bit, to be taken care of for a few minutes, instead of always being the one holding everything together.

"Nonsense. There's plenty."

Alex set the basket on the counter and started taking plates out and removing the foil covering. He put one in the microwave and set the timer.

Dolly handed her another tissue. "Is there anything we can help with?"

"No." Avery blew her nose and was glad she couldn't see her own face. It was undoubtedly red and blotchy, complete with puffy eyes and smeared mascara.

Dolly tapped her finger against her bottom lip, and tilted her head, staring at Avery like she was about to say something. Then she dropped the bomb. "I bet you could use a vacation."

"What?" Avery and Alex said at the same time, with the same stunned disbelief.

"Mom, no."

"You hush," she said to Alex. "Avery, I know it's short notice, but we're taking a long weekend at the shore. We'll leave on Friday and come home Monday."

"Mom." Alex's eyes widened. "We. Are. Not. Dating."

"Yes, I know. You've said it enough," Dolly snapped. She turned back to Avery. "We rented a big house. There's an extra bedroom you can stay in." She eyed Alex and deliberately enunciated, "Since you're not dating."

Avery shook her head. "Thank you so much, but I don't

want to insert myself into your family vacation."

"It's very casual. The house is right on the beach, walking distance to the boardwalk. Everyone comes and goes as they want. And I *know* you aren't *dating*, but Alex is always on his own when we go to the beach. It might be nice to have a *friend* to do some things with."

"I appreciate the invitation." Her eyes flicked to Alex, who simply raised an eyebrow and shrugged.

"Might be fun," he offered. "It's up to you."

Before she could gauge his seriousness, her purse vibrated with an incoming call. Her chest instantly tightened. "Sorry, excuse me." She grabbed her phone and scurried into the bathroom.

"Hey, I got my car taken care of."

"Oh." Jimmy paused. "Oh, yeah. That."

She pulled in a deep breath. "I assumed you were calling to make sure I was okay." Clearly he hadn't given her predicament a single thought.

"Sure. Since everything's fine, I wanted to tell you that I need you to do a favor. Well," he chuckled, "I guess it's not really a *favor* since you work for me now, right?"

She was glad he couldn't see her expression through the phone, because there was no hiding her disgust. "What." She stared at the mirror over the sink and pointed to the phone and rolled her eyes like she was looking at a friend instead of her reflection.

"The Memorial Day sale. I'm really going to need you to help me out. Dad said I should be there, but I have some stuff I was already planning to do, and I can't let the guys down."

Guys. As in his online video game buddies. "Wow, that's unfortunate. I'm going to the shore. I'll be gone Friday through Monday. I'll be back to work on Tuesday."

There was a long pause. "No, seriously."

"Seriously."

"What if I won't approve the time off?"

Avery bit back the first words that sprang to mind. "I guess you can write me up, then. Or fire me." Not a chance he'd do either. If she wasn't there, the little weasel would have to do some actual work.

"Who are you going with? How come this is the first we're hearing of it?"

We? "It's actually not your business, but I'm going with Alex's family."

"Who's Alex?"

"My boyfriend." The word popped out, and only then did she think that she could have just said it was her neighbor. Oh, well. Let Jimmy stew on that a while.

"I'm calling Mom."

"Okay, Boss."

The line went dead. She stared at the bathroom door. His reaction didn't surprise her one bit. His entire life, he'd gone running to tattle to their parents for everything. Crap. Now she had to explain this to Alex.

She trudged back out to the kitchen. A warm plate of casserole with beef and beans and corn and jalapeños waited at her place, while Alex was just pulling his out of the microwave. He sat down across from her, but she avoided his gaze.

"Smells wonderful." It really did.

Dolly beamed. "I hope you like it. It's a bit on the spicy side."

"I love spicy food." She lifted a forkful. Strings of melted cheese stretched down to the plate. "What kind of cheese is this?"

"Monterey Jack. I'll give you the recipe." She looked at her watch. "I brought you four jars of strawberry preserves. They're on the table by the door."

Avery tried to smile around a full mouth. Swallowing, she pointed to her plate. "This is delicious."

"Glad you like it. Now how about that vacation?"

Avery's phone vibrated in her back pocket. It was undoubtedly her mother, calling in a frenzy. "Thanks for the invite. I'd love to go."

Dolly clapped in delight, then leaned over to hug Avery. "I'm so glad! This is wonderful."

Alex's eyebrows were raised, but he didn't say anything. Yet. Avery knew that as soon as his mother left, she'd have to come clean.

Her phone stopped vibrating, then started again. She pulled it out of her pocket and silenced it. "Sorry."

"I have to get going." Dolly stood and walked around the table to hug Alex. "Avery, I'm so glad you're coming with us. You and Holly will get along like sisters. I can't wait for you two to meet." She grinned, obviously genuinely happy.

Avery was touched. No grudging, half-hearted invitations here. "Thank you. For everything."

After Dolly left, Avery was hesitant to look at Alex. Her phone vibrated again.

"I'm guessing all those calls have something to do with your sudden change of heart?" He didn't seem particularly concerned about the situation.

"I'm really sorry about that. I panicked. I needed an out and it was the first thing I thought of. You can tell your mom I'm not going."

"Not a chance." Alex waved a forkful of casserole in her direction. "She'll think I told you that you shouldn't go."

He was right. What a mess. "I'm sorry."

"It'll be fun."

"How can you say that? I shouldn't even be going." Her phone vibrated again.

He looked at her for a long moment. "What's really going on, Ave?"

He'd been nothing but nice to her, even after she shoe-horned herself into his family vacation. She owed him the whole story. "Like I said the other day, I moved back home to help my parents. My dad had a stroke and thank God he's okay now, but it was really scary for a while. They told him he needed to start taking better care of himself, which means no more sixteen hour days, seven days a week."

"That's a lot of hours."

"Especially when it was completely unnecessary. He's a bit of a control freak, so for instance, he'd have someone do inventory, then after hours he'd redo it himself to make sure it was done right. Well, the stroke was a major wake up call for him, and he's done great at stepping back."

"That's good."

"It is."

"But?"

Avery set her fork down and pushed her empty plate away. "I knew things were bad when my mom actually asked me to come home to help them. I left my job, broke my lease, uprooted my entire life to come back here." She shrugged. "Full disclosure, the timing was good. I'd just broken up with my boyfriend and got passed over for a promotion, so moving on seemed to be a good idea."

Alex stood, picked up their dirty dishes and loaded them in the dishwasher.

"I've been back a little over a year. It's taken that long to get everything where it should be. My brother Jimmy was at the store part time, and never really stepped up to full time, not that I expected him to. I've reorganized and updated the entire office to make it more efficient, streamlined and regulated the part-timers' schedules, computerized everything, landed a few big accounts, and got us back into a comfortable place. I'm not bragging when I say *I* did all that. But they're making Jimmy the general manager instead of me."

Alex made a face. "What's he done?"

"He sails in twenty hours a week, sits in the office screwing around online, and questions everything I do." She sighed. "To be fair, he did take on a lot of shifts while Dad was in the hospital and I couldn't."

"You've done all the heavy lifting. So why—"

Avery laughed a humorless laugh. "Because he's a man. That's the real bottom line."

Alex sat back down, his brow furrowed. "You've got to be kidding."

"I wish." She took a drink.

"Are they aware it's not 1950?"

"My mom knows. My dad's on the fence. My grandfather, not so much. He's still half owner. Fifty-one percent, actually. His parents started the hardware store in the forties, then he eventually bought them out. He and my grandma sold half the business to my parents when they wanted to retire, and he got Grandma's shares when she passed away. He still believes it should pass from son to son to son."

"Even though…" Alex waved his hand questioningly.

"Yup. My mom is one hundred percent against Jimmy taking over because she knows he's incapable. My dad is way more wishy-washy. He wants to believe Jimmy'll do a good job, despite mountains of evidence to the contrary. They broke the news to me today."

"That sucks."

She huffed out a humorless laugh. "Of course I've been a complete basket case, which doesn't really lend itself to my argument that I'm level-headed enough to be in charge."

"You're handling it better than I would." He leaned back in

his chair and let out a long breath. "Wow. I think I need to have a talk with my parents."

"Why?"

"They want me to work for their insurance agency. Which my sister is running. I don't want her to feel like you feel right now, and my mom would be mortified if Holly thought they thought I'd do a better job than she does just because I'm a man. That's ridiculous."

Poof sprinted across the room like he was being chased by a demon, dashed up over the couch, then back into the kitchen, where he came to a dead stop and sat licking his front paw like nothing had happened.

"Your cat's weird."

"All cats are weird," he said affectionately.

"Why did your parents name your sister Holly? Dolly and Holly? Isn't that a little much?" She supposed it was a family thing. James was the traditional name in her family – Jamie for her grandfather, James for her dad, and Jimmy for her brother.

Alex nodded. "They didn't. My sister and I are adopted. Mom said everyone kept telling her to change Holly's name because it was confusing. But she said Holly had lost every-thing she ever had, she darn sure wasn't going to lose her name, too. That's pretty much a direct quote."

A new set of tears sprang to Avery's eyes. "Wow." She blinked them away.

"Yeah. She might not look like it, but when she makes her mind up, she's a pit bull. She's always been very protective of us."

"I can see that. Is Holly older or younger than you?"

"Older. She was three and I was only a few months old when we were adopted."

"Are you blood siblings then?"

"Yeah."

Curiosity made her want to ask more questions. Okay, she wanted to be nosy and pry. Somehow, she managed to keep her mouth shut.

Alex filled in a couple of blanks without prompting. "No, I don't know my birth parents, no, I don't want to, no, nothing is missing in my life, and just in case it ever comes up, don't refer to my birth parents as my 'real' parents because that's rude and dismissive of my really real parents."

Avery took in every word. "I guess you hear the same questions a lot, huh?"

"Ad nauseum."

"I can only imagine."

Poof strolled over and rubbed across Avery's legs. She leaned over to look at him. "Don't try buttering me up, you little thief."

He purred and rubbed his face on her knee.

Avery sat back up and shook her head.

Alex shrugged. "He's a brat. I think I managed to get a lock for the sliding door that he can't figure out. Hopefully that means your undergarments are safe from now on."

"Who'll watch him while you're at the beach?"

"My buddy Lincoln will come over twice a day. Poof has him trained to hand out extra treats." He studied her for a moment. "I'm glad you're going. Hopefully you'll go mini-golfing with me since nobody else ever wants to. It'll be fun."

Avery felt her face heat. It felt so awkward to accept the vacation invitation and have Alex be so okay with it. She stood and pushed her chair in. "I'm going to head home. Thanks for everything." She had three days to figure out how to get out of this mess.

Or not.

Chapter Six

Alex walked Avery to the door with her lifetime supply of strawberry preserves, then closed it behind her. He turned to Poof, who lounged on the back of the couch, surveying his kingdom. Good idea. Alex dropped onto the couch and grabbed the remote. "Let's see who's playing tonight, shall we?"

He propped his feet up on the coffee table and flipped through channels until he found a baseball game.

Poof turned his back to the screen.

"No, I'm not letting you watch any more crime television." He scratched Poof's head. "You get too many ideas."

The game was still tied at the bottom of the sixth when Poof jumped down and meowed loudly, which meant it was time for bed.

"Coming, your highness." Alex clicked the television off and followed Poof to bed.

———

Wednesday's workday was a slog.

By lunchtime, his jaw ached from clenching it. Two meetings with management, and a dozen more excuses about why he wasn't getting his commission for the two new accounts he'd just brought in.

Venting to Erin, his amazing assistant, didn't help take the edge off his growing stress headache.

By quitting time, he was ready to pack his desk and not come back. Unfortunately, his landlord probably wouldn't accept a good reason in lieu of rent. Nor would the electric company.

It was time for a change. But not to sell insurance. The thought made him shudder. He wasn't *that* desperate. Yet.

He stopped at the McDonald's drive through on his way home, too drained to even think about tossing something in the microwave, let alone actually cook something for real. As he pulled into his parking space just before six, he glanced over and saw Avery get out of her car. Her hair was pulled back in a high ponytail, her sunglasses perched on the top of her head. She was on the phone.

He met her on the sidewalk, where she gave him a wave and rolled her eyes at whoever was on the phone. It was a little awkward, but he waited while she finished.

"I don't care if you don't believe me. I won't be in. There's nothing to talk about. Well, you're wasting a trip. Yeah, sure you are." She pulled her phone away from her ear and frowned. "He hung up on me."

"Your dad?"

"Brother. He seems to think this trip is a farce."

"Ah." He nodded toward the Arby's bag in her hand. "I see we're both enjoying fine cuisine this evening."

"Their curly fries really are the finest."

"Now I'm even sadder about my fries." Alex opened the door to the lobby and let her pass through first.

She balked as they walked to the elevator. "Hang on."

"What?"

"Back up," she whispered.

Alex raised an eyebrow, but turned and walked back around the corner to the bank of mailboxes. A few seconds later, they heard the elevator ding. "We're missing our ride."

She poked her head around the corner. "Yeah, and that was Mr. Barrow from the fourth floor."

"So?"

"He creeps me out. Every time he sees me, he stares at my boobs."

"Oh. He never bothered me."

She rolled her eyes. "You don't have boobs."

They stood in front of the elevator and waited until the number four lit up, then Avery hit the button to bring it back down. The doors slid open and they stepped inside.

"Avery!" A voice from the lobby called out.

"Oh, no."

"Hey!" A man jumped into the elevator with them just before the doors slid shut.

Avery's face turned several shades of red.

Alex guessed from the man's eyes, which were the same shade of blue-green as Avery's, that this was the infamous brother. Alex made it a policy not to make snap judgments about people, but this guy was already getting on his last nerve. He supposed it could be from what he already knew about Avery's side of the current story, but probably not. The guy simply oozed jerk.

The man jabbed his hand in Alex's direction. "You the boyfriend?"

Alex blinked. He could practically feel Avery freaking out, so he simply nodded and shook his hand. "Yup."

"I'm Jimmy."

"Alex."

"So you're real."

"I like to think so."

Jimmy's eye roved up and down, stopping on the fast food bags. "Big spender. I guess nothing's too good for your woman, huh."

Alex said nothing, just held Jimmy's gaze until he got uncomfortable and shifted away. It didn't take long. What a little weasel.

The elevator opened and presented a conundrum. Should he go to his own apartment, or to hers?

"Can you please hold this while I get my key?"

"Sure." He took her drink while she unlocked the door. "Reorganized your keyring?"

"Yeah." She held it up and jingled it. "Down to four keys."

"Impressive."

"I only have two keys on my ring," Jimmy added.

She kept giving him looks, trying to convey something, but he wasn't quite understanding. She jerked her head toward her apartment, so he followed her inside. She gave him a little smile, so he guessed he'd done the right thing.

"I'd like to get to know my sister's significant other. Be friends." Jimmy leaned his hip against the kitchen table and crossed his arms. "How long have you two been dating?"

"Month, month and a half."

Jimmy's eyes narrowed. "You don't know?"

Great. This idiot was trying to play good cop/bad cop all by himself.

"Knock it off." Avery scowled and sat down.

Alex mirrored her movements on the other side of the table. He ate a fry. Which, of course, was stone cold. Yuck.

"What are your intentions with my sister?"

Alex really, *really* wanted to say something crude about

banging her silly right here on the table, but decided to take the high road.

"Why'd you come here instead of going to your place? Is your wife home?"

"Jimmy!"

Alex calmly dunked a chicken nugget into the container of honey mustard. "Avery's been to my place. Not married, no kids. Full time job, one cat. Had my appendix out when I was fourteen. If you wait until I finish eating, I can pull up my college transcripts and credit report."

Avery hid a smirk behind her soda cup while Jimmy looked rather irritated.

Then his expression turned smug. "This guy's a comedian. Well, sorry about your weekend plans, funny guy, but Avery has to work."

No wonder Avery was stressed out. And what were her parents thinking? Alex had known the guy five minutes and wouldn't put him in charge of Poof's litter box, let alone a business.

Avery took a long sip from her soda. "No, Avery *doesn't* have to work. Avery is going to the beach. Avery is not going to be available. Avery hasn't had time off for a few years."

"You just had time off before you moved back up here."

"You mean when I was packing and arranging to move and all that fun stuff?" She sounded incredulous.

"You weren't working."

"I also wasn't getting paid."

"Oh, please. Mom and Dad gave you money to move. They give you money all the time."

Avery set her sandwich down abruptly, lettuce and tzatziki-covered sliced turkey falling out of their cozy pita shell. "I haven't gotten one single red cent from them since I graduated from college, unless you want to be petty enough to count birthday and Christmas gifts."

Jimmy opened his mouth to say something, but Avery jumped to her feet and thrust her pointer finger in the direction of the door. "Leave. This conversation is over."

Jimmy glared as Avery ushered him to the door. "You have a bad attitude. That's why they're giving the store to me."

"Out!" She practically shoved Jimmy into the hallway and slammed the door, then locked it.

Alex ate another cold French fry while he waited for Avery to come back to the table.

When she finally did, she looked defeated. "Maybe I should just go in. I don't know."

Her phone vibrated with an incoming call. She swiped the screen and held it to her ear.

Alex couldn't make out all the words, but it was clear her mother was shouting. He could only imagine what Jimmy had told her about the exchange.

At some point, Avery set the phone down and reassembled her gyro. She ate it while the phone still yammered. When she'd finished her food, she picked the phone back up and said, "Are you done? I mean, it's not like *Jimmy's* taking a few days off, right?" The voice stopped. "Great. I'm hanging up now. I'll be in tomorrow, so I'll talk to you then. Bye."

Alex finished his chicken nuggets and the last of his soda. "Everything okay?"

She rubbed her eyes. "Obviously not. Sorry about Jimmy and the whole fake boyfriend bit. I didn't realize he was actually on his way over or I'd have given you a heads up."

"Might as well have both our families convinced we're dating, right?" Alex could think of worse ways to pass some time.

"Well, not-my-boyfriend, how was your day?"

Alex crumpled up his wrappers and stuffed them in the bag. "Only about two degrees better than yours."

"Good. Let's talk about your crap for a while instead of mine." She led him to the couch and settled at one end with her legs curled under her.

Alex sat at the other end of the couch and turned to face her, resting his arm across the back cushions. He summed it up as succinctly as he could. "The company I work for has been finding ways to screw me out of commissions."

"Oh, yikes. I feel like I should know this since I already met your family and all, but what do you do?"

He knew what she meant. They'd known each other for barely forty-eight hours, but it seemed longer. "I work for a security firm. We install alarm systems and monitor them, hire out security guards, et cetera. I'm on the sales side, so I go out and convince companies they need our service. When they sign up, I'm supposed to get a commission based on the size of the contract."

"Seems pretty straightforward."

"You'd think. But the last two companies I brought in are the biggest clients we've ever had, so the commissions are hefty. Instead of paying out like they're supposed to, they've been delaying and trying to find loopholes to not pay me. So far I've gotten zero."

She gasped a little. "Those assholes. What are you going to do?"

"Go on vacation and make some decisions when I have a little space." And when he was a lot less angry.

"Smart. Much smarter than running away on a whim, like some people, who shall remain nameless." She pointed at herself and made a funny face.

He laughed. "I'm not working for my family. Who knows what I'd do in that case."

"Sounds like our vacation goals are the same. Figure out what to do in our careers. I'll bring charts and we can brainstorm."

"Charts?"

"Sure. I'll bring my laptop and we can do spreadsheets with pros and cons."

"Spreadsheets."

"Of course. It's how I do my best decision-making."

"Did you make a spreadsheet for when you moved back from the city?"

Avery grinned and jumped up and grabbed her laptop from the end table beside her recliner. She popped the lid up and settled onto the couch beside him, cross-legged with the laptop in her lap. "Prepare to be impressed."

"I'm already impressed," he said as he watched her fingers fly over the keyboard, opening folders. Another click, and a spreadsheet opened and filled the screen. The top of the sheet had the bolded title: Atlanta vs. Hickory Hollow.

"Whoa, wait. You lived in Atlanta?" Alex couldn't believe what he was seeing.

"Yeah, why? I'm sure I mentioned it."

"I've only ever heard you say 'the city.' I would have remembered Atlanta because I used to live there."

"No way!" Avery's eyes rounded. "When?"

"A few years ago. After college."

"You're blowing my mind right now. What are the odds?"

"I know. We'll have to compare notes one of these days." He hoped today wasn't that day. His time in Atlanta was good, but leaving was painful. Literally. Thankfully, she turned her attention back to the laptop.

Color-coded columns spanned the page. Avery pointed. "Here are the pros for Atlanta, then this column ranks importance on a scale of one to five."

"More food delivery options. You only gave that a two?" He'd have given it a higher number. Then again, Hickory Hollow gave easy access to his mom's cooking, so maybe a two was the right ranking.

"It started as a four, but I'm a creature of habit, so even though there were more options, I really only got food from two or three places on a regular basis, so it wasn't as important as I first thought."

"Makes sense. What's this?" He touched the screen and the spreadsheet scrolled wildly. "Uh-oh, what did I just do?" He grimaced when the screen was full of empty spreadsheet cells.

"Touchscreen. It's fine." She tapped a few keys and the spreadsheet blinked back to the top like nothing had happened.

He breathed a sigh of relief. He would have hated to have deleted all her data with one touch. "Culture? You gave that one a five."

"Atlanta has the most amazing museums, art galleries, bookstores, sporting events, eateries, everything. I did something new pretty much every weekend. I do miss that."

He caught the wistful note in her voice. He missed the sporting events, too. More than anything. Back when he was in Atlanta, baseball was his life. "Yeah, there's not a lot of cultural variety around here."

Avery shrugged. "I mean, if I put in some effort, I could find things. I'm sure there are tons of local treasures I don't know about, and we can easily drive to Baltimore or Philly, or even be in New York City in a few hours by train."

"True." He couldn't remember the last time he'd made an effort to find something new to see or do. He saw the thing that tipped the scales. "Pro for Hickory Hollow. 'My family needs me.' You gave it a ten. On a scale of one to five."

"Yup." She looked over at him and muttered, "Kinda rethinking it now, though."

He'd bet anything she wasn't, and that if she had to do it over, she'd still come back home and help her family, even if Jimmy ended up with the store. He had a feeling that's just the kind of person she was. "Well, not-my-girlfriend, I need to go feed Poof before he figures out how to get the car started."

"Thanks. For everything."

"You got it." He was tempted to lean over and give her a quick kiss, but was sure she wouldn't appreciate the not-so-romantic gesture. Instead, he got to his feet and headed for the door.

"Good night, not-my-boyfriend."

He grinned and gave a little wave. "Night."

Chapter Seven

Avery watched the door close behind Alex. If nothing else, at least his easygoing attitude helped keep her calm while her family was trying its best to stress her out.

Speaking of which. She retrieved her phone from the kitchen. There were notifications for a dozen texts and one missed call. She called her mom back. Might as well get it over with.

As soon as her mom answered the phone, she said, "If you're going to yell again, I'm hanging up."

"No, I'm not going to yell." She sounded tired. "I'm sorry about earlier. When Jimmy told me you quit, I overreacted."

Avery gritted her teeth and took a long breath before she answered. Jimmy was such a lying jerk. "You believed him? Seriously? All I'm doing is taking a vacation. Do you not think I deserve to take a vacation?"

"Of course you deserve one. But it's really short notice, over a big sale weekend. How's Jimmy going to handle everything on his own?"

She set the phone on the arm of the couch and pushed the heels of her hands against her eyes. "Do you hear yourself?

When Jimmy disappears for weeks on end, you never ask, 'How's Avery going to handle everything on her own?' How can you possibly be concerned about Jimmy running the store over *one holiday weekend* when you're handing it over to him?" She wanted to scream.

"I know it doesn't seem fair."

"Seem?" It wasn't fair. Period. Nothing about this was fair.

"Jimmy's not getting everything. He's only getting your grandfather's shares."

"Ah. So he's only getting half. Fifty-one percent, actually, while Avery, who swooped in and worked her fingers to the bone and saved the store from going bankrupt, gets nothing." Bitterness colored every word.

"Not nothing. You'll get my shares."

"Who gets Dad's?"

The long pause gave Avery her answer. She was tempted to tell her mother to shove her shares, but she took a page from Alex's book and decided not to make any moves until after her vacation.

"Honey, I'm sorry. I know how this must feel."

"You actually don't. But it's late, I'm tired, and there's nothing more to discuss." She rubbed her temples. She didn't want to take her frustration out on her mom, because her hands were tied. There was nothing she could do to change the trajectory of a business that she'd married into.

"You're coming in tomorrow?"

"Of course."

"All right. I'll see you then."

Avery was not looking forward to it. Mom was trying to keep the peace, especially since what was done was done. In keeping the peace though, she was letting Avery get walked over. Again. While Golden Boy Jimmy could do no wrong.

Thursday dawned with no better disposition than Wednesday had ended with. Avery went through the motions, got to the store, and when she flipped the sign to open, she flipped the switch on her face that the customers would see. Smiling, helpful, competent, trustworthy, friendly. The customers would never guess there was turmoil brewing under the surface.

They would also never guess that Jimmy was supposed to be in charge, since he wasn't here. As usual.

Her dad came by and gave her a kiss on the cheek. "Good morning, pumpkin. Can you go through the invoices sometime this morning?"

Avery gave him the sweetest smile she could muster. "Sorry, Dad. That's Jimmy's job. I don't want to overstep." Not much he could argue with there.

"Avery, I know you're upset."

"I'm actually not." Irritated? Check. Slighted? Check. Upset? Not nearly as much.

"The invoices need done, and your mother is taking me to the doctor, so I can't do them. I'd appreciate it if—"

Avery gently cut him off. "Dad, do you remember when I got back home and we clearly defined the duties and responsibilities of each job? And do you remember being really happy with that because it made everything more organized?"

"Yes." His lips pressed together.

"It made things run a lot smoother when people knew what was expected of them, what they were responsible for, and what they're being paid to do. The manager needs to do the manager's

job. You can't possibly argue with that simple fact."

He sighed. "Avery. I just need you to do this one thing."

"It's not one thing, Dad. This week alone, I've put up the

schedule for the next two weeks. Which is the manager's job." She held up a hand, lifting a finger for each item she listed. "I've taken care of getting every single bill paid up. Scheduled the HVAC guy to come service the air conditioner. Verified all the ads for the Memorial Day sale, double checked they were being played on the radio, posted to all our social media accounts, and running in the newspapers. The Fourth of July sale information has been proofed and is ready to go to all the media outlets, and is already scheduled for our social media. I also talked to Bill Spencer about coming to take a look at the roof leak in the back storeroom. All of which is the manager's *responsibility*. Would you like me to go on?"

"You know we appreciate everything you do."

Avery's mouth snapped shut before she could educate her dad to the fact that no, she did not, in fact, know they appreciated everything she did. It was nice that he said it, but it would be even nicer to be shown.

Her dad changed the subject. "I don't know why you'd go away for a weekend with a guy we haven't even met."

The door chimed. "Sorry I'm late." Jimmy's breezy apology lacked even a hint of contriteness.

A customer came in the door behind him.

"Let us know if we can help you find anything," Jimmy mumbled to him, only because their dad was watching.

"Vice grips?"

Avery waited while Jimmy looked up at the aisle signs, trying to decide where the vice grips might be. After a full minute of tortured silence, broken only by Jimmy's "Uhhhh...", she couldn't stand it any longer. She cheerfully said to the customer, "Aisle twelve, all the way to the back, left hand side. They'll be just above eye-level."

"Thanks." He disappeared down aisle twelve.

Her dad's jaw twitched. "Good morning, Jimmy. First priority for today is getting the invoices done."

"I don't know how to print them in that crap software Avery set up. She can do it." Jimmy waved a dismissive hand in her general direction.

James shook his head. "No. Avery has other things she needs to take care of."

She was a little surprised her dad didn't immediately back Jimmy up. The customer with the vice grips came to the counter, so she moved to the cash register. "Did you find everything you needed?"

He shook his head. "It's kind of a long shot, but my wife needs some tiny screws with hooks on the top for a craft project."

"Does she need a hook or a loop? Let me show you what I've got." She came around the counter and led the customer to the aisle with the screws and nails. Bypassing the loose screws, she stopped in front of the pegboard where packaged screws hung, organized by shape and size. She scanned the rows, then found what she was looking for. "Screw eyes. Is this what she needs?" The package contained little screws with loops at the top.

"Yeah, that looks like it, but hers are smaller."

Avery pulled another package off the wall to show him. "These are the smallest ones I have."

"That looks about right. Thanks a lot, I didn't think anyone would have them."

"You'd be surprised." Avery smiled. "We sell a ton of the mini screw eyes in the fall when church groups are working on Christmas ornaments for the bazaars."

He took the package, then pulled another one off the wall and carried them to the front counter. "Glad I asked."

"I'm happy we could help. Anything else?" She rang his

purchase into the register.

"No, but I'm sure she'll give me a list since you had these."

Avery laughed and handed him his change. "Lists are good. Have a great day."

Her dad and brother had gone back to the office. She wondered if Jimmy had started the invoices, but curiosity wasn't enough to propel her in that direction. Instead, she straightened displays and stayed at the front of the store.

A few minutes before nine, her mother came in. "Is your dad ready?"

"I don't know. He's in the office with Jimmy."

Ginny raised an eyebrow. "Is he doing the invoices?"

"I think so."

"Good." She leaned on the counter and looked Avery in the eye. "I hope you're not still upset. This whole situation is a mess, and I'm sorry for that."

"I'll be fine." Wasn't that always the case? Avery was always fine. Nobody had to worry about Avery, she could handle everything.

"So you're not going away?" She sounded hopeful.

"I'm not going away because I'm mad." Okay, maybe that wasn't quite the truth. She wasn't *only* going away because she was mad. "It's a vacation. A short one." And right now, more than anything, she needed some space away from her family and the store.

"I can't believe you'd go away for a weekend with some guy we've never even met." Ginny echoed James's words.

"You hadn't met Keith, and he moved in with me," Avery reminded her.

"I wasn't thrilled about that, either."

"Alex is great."

"I want to meet him before your trip."

Avery was thankful when the door chimed and interrupted

them. She knew her mother had good intentions, but it sure felt like she thought Avery wasn't competent to vet a man, just like she wasn't competent to run the store.

"Bert! Hey." She was surprised to see Alex's dad come in.

"Hi, Avery. I need to get a new chain for my chainsaw."

"Aisle nine, right hand side."

"Dolly wants me to finish trimming the trees before we leave."

"Is this the right time of year?"

Bert chuckled. "Dolly wants it done now. That's the right time, don't you suppose?"

Avery laughed with him. "I better not hold you up with chit chat, then."

He walked away and returned a few minutes later with a chain.

Avery rung up his purchase and took his money. "By the way, Bert, this is my mom, Ginny. Mom, this is Alex's dad, Bert."

Ginny smiled. "So my daughter's going away with your family."

"Looks that way."

"Where will you be going?"

"Mom," Avery broke in, "I already told you. We're not sixteen, you don't need to confer with Alex's parents about our plans." She felt ridiculous, like a teenager and not a grown woman well into her thirties.

Bert shrugged and gave Avery a wink. "I can't help anyway. I just drive the car and carry the bags."

Avery handed him the bag with his chain. "Thanks, Bert. See you tomorrow."

"Yup." He nodded at Ginny. "Nice to meet you."

After he left, Ginny crossed her arms. "You didn't introduce him to your father."

"He was in a hurry. And aren't you and Dad supposed to be on your way to his appointment?"

Ginny looked at her watch. "Crap." She hurried toward the office.

Soon thereafter, Ginny and James came back through the store, waving their goodbyes as they hustled out the door.

A steady stream of customers kept Avery busy until lunchtime, when Jimmy finally emerged from the office. "I'm ordering subs. You want one?"

"Sure."

Half an hour later, their subs magically appeared. Okay, so the magic was in the form of a delivery driver, but still. Avery paid him out of the petty cash and buzzed the office. "Food's here."

Jimmy joined her at the counter. He pulled the subs out of the bag, handing one to Avery.

"Did you figure out the invoices?" she asked, half expecting him to say he'd left them for her to do.

"Psht, I thought it was going to be hard. I guess spending four hundred bucks for that folding machine wasn't so stupid after all."

High praise, coming from Jimmy. "It's already paid for itself in labor hours. Too bad it doesn't stuff envelopes, too."

"No kidding."

They ate their subs at the counter. By some miracle, no one came in while they were eating.

Jimmy crumpled his sub wrapper and tossed it in the trash can. "You're really not coming in for a week?"

"Four days, and no, I'm not coming in. I haven't been to the beach in years, so I'm looking forward to it."

"Alex seems like a real douche."

There it was. Jimmy couldn't be reasonable for long. "You didn't exactly try to make a good impression, either."

"Why should I?"

"Because Alex is great and I like him." Simple but true.

"Then why are we just now hearing about him?"

She'd prefer they hadn't heard of him at all, but she didn't want to confuse Jimmy with that complicated sentence. "I don't tell you guys everything."

"You should."

"Like you do?" She rolled her eyes. Jimmy didn't tell their parents anything.

"That's different."

"Why?"

"I'm a man."

Avery nearly choked on her sub. She swallowed and laughed. "You're such a chauvinist. Just like Dad and Grandpa. Someday it's going to bite you in the ass."

Chapter Eight

"That's the best we can do."

Alex stared at the check in his hand. "Decimal's in the wrong place, Dean."

His boss shrugged, his expression unconcerned. "Sorry, man, I don't know what to tell you." Dean's office was three times the size of Alex's and done in expensive mahogany finishes.

Not that Alex wanted a fancy office, but standing here surrounded by this excess made it hard to swallow excuses about the company not having the money to pay him the commissions he'd earned.

"'Complete commission payment'? What's that supposed to mean?" He showed the memo line to Dean. It meant if he cashed it, he was agreeing not to pursue the rest of the money he was owed.

Dean shrugged again and cast a pointed glance toward the door. "I didn't write it, I just signed it."

"I brought in that hospital contract, and I know they paid."

"And we're glad. But on a contract that size, we can't afford the ten percent commission. Things are tight right now. Times are tough."

"I get *one* percent instead? How is that fair?"

"I really wish I could do more." His tone was flat.

Alex knew any more discussion was pointless. He got up and left Dean's office without another word. The excuses and delays had been insulting enough, but this check was a slap in the face.

He walked past Erin's desk to get to his office, then turned abruptly and stood in front of her desk. "What do I have this afternoon?"

"Follow up with the nightclub venue. Just a call, I believe." She clicked onto her digital calendar to confirm. "Looks like that's it."

"Good. Please reschedule it for next week. I'm taking the rest of the afternoon off."

Erin looked at him over the rim of her glasses. "You okay?" Her brows creased, concerned.

"Good as gold." Ugh, when did his dad start coming out of his mouth?

"Oookayyy?"

"I think I might head out a little early. I want to get packed. Without rushing."

She wasn't buying his excuse any more than he was. Her eyes flicked toward Dean's office and Alex knew she made the connection. Of course she did. If anyone knew what was going on in the office at any given time, it was Erin.

Alex closed his office door and sat at his desk, staring at the pathetic check in his hand. He put it face down on the desk and slid it away. He got on his laptop and not for the first time, he was grateful he used his own computer instead of having his work on the company's. He always backed his finalized files up to the company intranet, but something had always held him back from keeping his leads and notes on the company drive.

Turned out it was a good idea to keep those to himself.

Alex ended up leaving at his normal time, but without accomplishing much of anything beyond staring out the window. Being screwed out of a lot of money was an effective demotivator, but his own work ethic wouldn't let him slack too much for too long.

He pulled in to the apartment parking lot the same time as Avery again.

She waved at him as she got out of her car. "Have we always gotten home at the same time and I just never noticed?" she asked when they reached the sidewalk.

"I'm wondering that myself. No fast food tonight?"

"Nah, I have some chicken in the crock pot." She leaned forward and pointed at his obviously empty hands. "No takeout for you, either?"

"I was going to order pizza. I'm not really in the mood to talk to anyone." A tired half-smile curved his lips. "Present company excluded."

Avery held the door open for him and they walked to the elevator. "Rough day?"

"Yeah."

"Do you want to come over and have dinner? Chicken and gravy. I'm going to put it over French fries. No talking necessary."

Alex's stomach rumbled a little. "It does sound a lot better than pizza."

"It is." They stepped out of the elevator and walked down the hall. "Go change and do whatever you need to do. Dinner's in thirty if you want to join me. No pressure, though."

Alex unlocked his door. He should make some excuse. He

didn't want to talk to anyone. That's why he didn't even go through the drive-thru. "I'll be over."

"Great." She gave him a megawatt smile and let herself into her own apartment.

Alex took a shower and tried to think of an excuse to not go over. But the bottom line was that he wanted to. Crap day aside, he wanted to spend some time with her.

Well, that complicated things, didn't it?

He threw on a pair of jeans and an old T-shirt, then filled Poof's food dish and washed out his water bowl, all under Poof's supervision.

When he set the water bowl back down, Poof immediately leaned over and sniffed the surface of the water. Then, of course, he turned and flounced away.

"Sorry, I'm all out of Perrier."

The cat steadfastly ignored him as he put his shoes on. And ignored him still as he got up and walked to the door. "I'm leaving now."

Poof stood and swished his tail, his behind letting Alex know exactly how much he cared.

He crossed the hallway and knocked on Avery's door.

"It's open," she called from inside.

He stepped inside and noticed several things at once. One, the loud whirr of the air fryer. Two, the tantalizing smell of the chicken and gravy. Three, Avery looked amazing in a tank top and jean shorts.

He indulged in watching her for a minute. "Can I help with anything?"

With oven mitts on her hands, she lifted the basket out of the air fryer and gave it a shake and a sprinkle of salt. "You can grab plates if you want." She inclined her head toward one of the upper cupboards. "In there. Silverware's in the drawer beside the dishwasher."

Alex got two plates and silverware. "Anything else?"

"Nope, almost done." She dumped the fries into a bowl she'd lined with a paper towel, sprinkled a little more salt over them, and gave the bowl a good shake. "Dinner is served." She filled a plate with fries, then spooned chicken and gravy out of the crock pot and smothered the fries.

Alex followed her lead. "I can't say I've ever had this before. Over mashed potatoes, yes, but not fries."

"You've been missing out."

He nodded as he chewed, swallowed, and said, "I have been. This is great."

"Super simple, too."

"Simple is good. I'll have to suggest this to Mom. I bet they'd like it."

They ate in silence for a few minutes.

"Do you want to tell me about your day, not-my-boyfriend?"

Not wanting to talk to anyone apparently meant anyone except Avery, because he did want to confide in her. "It sucked." He poked at his food. "I've been fighting for weeks – I was due a commission check that I should have had over a month ago. They kept giving me the runaround and all these excuses. Well, I got the check today."

"Wasn't what you expected?" She put her fork down and took a sip of water.

"Not even close." He leaned back in his chair. "We're supposed to get ten percent of whatever contracts we bring in. I brought in the two biggest clients we've ever had, and now that we're talking about a lot of money, they don't want to pay me."

She scowled and waved her fork. "But they wouldn't have the other ninety percent if you hadn't brought the clients in."

"Exactly."

"And screwing you isn't exactly the way to ensure you keep bringing in big clients. They're shooting themselves in the foot." She sounded disgusted. It felt nice to have her in his corner.

"I signed them both in the same month. If I'd known this was going to happen, I probably wouldn't have brought the second one in."

"Do you have a contract?"

"Yup."

"Then how do they expect to get away with it?" She scrunched up her face like she'd never heard something so stupid.

"They probably think I'll bend over and take it. They're claiming the company doesn't have the money to pay out, and I should be satisfied with what I got." It didn't feel good to realize that if the contracts were small ones, he probably would just roll over and not put up a fight.

"What *did* you get?"

"One percent."

Her eyes widened. "Instead of *ten*? That's quite a jump."

He finished his meal and pushed the plate away.

"Have you thought about suing?"

"It was my second thought. The first was to burn down the building."

She grinned. "Let's put that aside for now. We can circle back to it if we need to."

He returned her smile with something more like a grimace. "It's so frustrating. I was counting on that first commission check to pay off my car, and the second check was going into my savings for a down payment on a house."

"Wow, so we're talking about significant chunks of money."

Alex ran a hand through his hair. "Yeah."

Avery sat back and crossed her arms, shaking her head in angry disbelief. "You can't let them get away with this."

"I know, but it won't do me any good to go in with guns blazing and get myself fired."

"I bet you'd have a good case for wrongful termination."

"Hiring a lawyer would probably cost more than what they owe me, and small claims has a cap, so either way, I get screwed."

"I'm just trying to help." She sounded defensive.

Alex cringed, realizing he'd been snapping at her. Not really *at* her, but his tone had definitely taken a hard edge. "Sorry. I should have stayed home and microwaved something." He took his plate to the sink and rinsed it off. "Should I put this in the dishwasher?"

"No, the stuff in there's clean." She got up and popped it open and started taking out glasses and putting them in the cupboard.

She didn't sound bothered, so he relaxed just a fraction. "Can I help?"

"Sure."

He helped put the rest of the clean dishes away, then leaned his hip against the counter. "I'm sorry for being lousy company tonight, so I'll just head home. Thanks for dinner. It was great."

"I'm glad you liked it."

He wasn't sure what else to say, so he walked toward the door. "Um, I'll see you later?"

"Sure." She rested her hand on the door.

He stepped into the hallway and gave her a nod. "Thanks."

Avery tilted her head, setting her long ponytail into motion. "You're not going to spend all evening wallowing, are you?"

"Maybe." Definitely.

One graceful shoulder lifted in a shrug. "Suit yourself."

Curiosity got the better of him. "Why? What are you going to do?"

"I'm walking to General Custard's."

Alex hesitated. Why was she telling him this? Unless... "Are you inviting me to go with you?"

"If you want. Some fresh air and a long walk might do you some good."

Once again, she was right. "Let me change. I'll be back in a minute." He went into his apartment, where Poof was busy mauling a catnip mouse.

While he laced his sneakers, he watched Poof fling the toy across the floor, then dash over and pounce on it. A minute later, he pranced over and dropped it at Alex's feet with a proud meow.

"Good job, mighty hunter." Alex scratched the cat's head.

Poof purred loudly, then abruptly stopped when Alex dared to stop petting him.

"Sorry, buddy, I have to go."

Poof whipped his tail around and flounced out of the room.

Alex shook his head as he joined Avery in the hallway.

"Your demon cat not approve of you leaving again?"

"Hey now. I don't think he qualifies as a demon cat."

"Really? He broke into my apartment *twice*, stole my bra, then stole my thong, and dropped it on the kitchen table in front of your parents."

Alex grimaced. Poof definitely qualified as a demon cat. "Oh, yeah. I sort of forgot about that."

"I'm glad *one* of us could."

Chapter Nine

They rode the elevator to the main floor and walked through the lobby and out into the heat. The sun was hinting at setting, but the day hadn't cooled. Avery took the hair tie from her wrist and twisted her ponytail up into a messy bun to get her hair off her neck.

"You sure you don't want to drive?" Alex offered.

"Tempting, but I need some form of exercise. I've been stuck in the store and my attitude has been so bad lately that I just come home and do nothing." Avery stepped over an ant hauling a dead beetle across the sidewalk.

"Same. I haven't made it to the gym in over a week."

Avery reached over and patted his flat stomach. "Better get in gear, mister. I can't be showing off a flabby not-boyfriend at the beach."

He laughed and said, "Fine. After the ice cream, I'll go to the gym."

"Selfie or it didn't happen." As soon as the words were out, she imagined Alex lifting weights, sweaty, with muscles straining…

"—ber?"

"Huh?" Avery jerked her head over. She hadn't heard a single thing he'd said. Too busy fantasizing about him working out.

"I said I don't have your number to send you a selfie. I should probably get it anyway, since we'll probably need each other's numbers while we're at the beach."

"Oh. Yeah. Yes." She was sweating, and it had nothing to do with the heat and humidity. And now she couldn't get the image out of her head. "We'll do that when we get to Custard's. If I try it while I'm walking, I'll fall and break my face."

They stopped at an intersection and checked for traffic before crossing, then walked up the hill to the bridge over the railroad tracks. At the top, Alex pointed. "Train."

Avery stopped walking and leaned on the railing, watching the train approach slowly from around the bend. "When I was little, my dad used to take us over there," she pointed to a tiny gravel parking lot next to the tracks below them, "and we'd park and count the train cars."

"We would, too." Alex leaned beside her, their arms not quite touching.

The train's whistle blew and they both waved. "I wonder if that was for us."

"I bet it was." He pointed to the first car. "One, two, three…"

"Count in your head. See if we get the same number."

The train rumbled under them, hauling open cars of coal and closed cars of who-knows-what. Graffiti decorated most of the cars.

The last car passed under them. Avery looked up. "One hundred and twelve."

"I got one eleven."

"I might have counted one twice."

Alex shrugged and pushed back from the wall. "More likely I missed one."

Avery appreciated his willingness to concede. It was the opposite of dealing with Jimmy, who'd insist he was right if he said the grass was blue and the sky was green. Or even dealing with Keith, her ex-boyfriend, who had a habit of agreeing with Avery but then taking credit because he hated to be the slightest bit wrong about anything, but he wasn't a *total* jackass like her brother. "Let's call it one-eleven and a half."

They crossed the bridge and turned the corner toward General Custard's.

"Oh, my. They're packed."

The parking lot was full, and then some. Cars were parked in the grass and barely off the road. There was a hum of excitement as they entered the small white building, with a dull roar of chattering boys underscoring the atmosphere.

They waited in line and finally got to the window to order ice cream.

"What's going on?" Avery asked.

The young woman behind the counter grinned. "The 11- and 12-year-olds just won their first regional championship game."

"Little League?"

"Yup. We have a real shot at heading to Williamsport this year."

"That's incredible." Avery looked up at Alex, who was also impressed. A local team making it close to the Little League World Series was definitely something to get excited about. She made a mental note to get in touch with the team and see if they needed more sponsorship money. Supporting local youth activities – sports, scouts, arts – was one area her dad had refused to cut back even a dollar in the budget, and she'd had to admit more than once that he'd been completely right.

"What can I get you?"

She jerked, startled from her thoughts. "Oh, sorry. I'd like a small cone of vanilla, please."

Alex glanced over the menu. "Medium cone of teaberry."

The woman took Avery's money while a teenaged employee held a cone under a stream of ice cream, then expertly held it while filling the second cone. She handed their cones through the window. "Thanks!"

Alex put a couple of dollars in the tip cup and they walked outside. A group got up from one of the picnic tables, so they hurried over to claim the vacant seats.

"Oh, darn."

Avery looked up to see a mom with three little kids and a paper tray with cups of ice cream turning away.

"Did you want to sit here? We can squish on the same side."

The woman turned back with a tired smile. "Would you mind? I really, *really* don't want to give the kids their ice cream in the car."

Alex stood and gestured to the seat he'd vacated. "Can't blame you there. I have nieces and a nephew that I wouldn't let anywhere near upholstery with ice cream."

The kids – a boy and two girls – filled up the one side of the table, and the mom had them scoot closer together so she could sit, too. Alex and Avery sat on the other side.

"Are you part of the baseball crew?" Alex asked.

"Yes. My oldest is the one in green over there." The mom pointed to a group of rambunctious kids roughhousing in the grass.

"Congratulations. I'm sure these kids will remember being on a championship team forever."

Avery perched on the edge of the bench beside him and focused on her ice cream, which was getting meltier by the second. The boy had nearly all his ice cream lifted up in a ball on his plastic spoon. A heartbeat later, an earsplitting scream accompanied the ice cream's rapid tumble down the kid's shirt and onto his lap.

His quick-thinking older sister simply grabbed the wad of ice cream and plopped it back in his bowl, then wiped her hand down her shirt.

Avery and Alex exchanged a look while the mom sighed and handed out a stack of napkins.

"I take it you don't have kids," she said drily.

"Nope," they answered in unison.

"Are you planning to have any?"

Avery felt her eyes bug out. She couldn't immediately comprehend the invasive question – from a woman who'd probably gotten more than her fair share of nosy questions, since most women have. Definitely a girl code violation here. "Not anytime soon," she deflected.

"What's holding you back?" The woman sopped up melted ice cream from the closest toddler, then lasered in on Avery's face. "Your clock's gotta be ticking."

Unable to think of a suitable comeback, Avery simply said, "What a rude thing to say," and popped the last bite of cone into her mouth.

The woman abruptly sat straight, her glare clearly indicating that Avery was rude to suggest her comment had been rude.

The little girl piped up in a sing-song voice, "It isn't nice to be wude."

"No," her mother snapped, "it isn't."

Avery smiled sweetly at the child. "That's right. It isn't."

Alex's hand pressed into the middle of her back. He cleared his throat and said, "All done. We should let someone else have these seats." He nearly tripped over the bench in his haste to pull his leg out from under the table. "Nice to meet you guys."

"Nice to meet you," the little boy parroted with a grubby-handed wave.

Avery stood and brushed crumbs from her shorts. "Congratulations on the championship, hopefully we'll see your brother in the Little League World Series."

The mother managed a smile at that.

As they walked across the parking lot, back to the sidewalk, Alex said, "Is it just me, or was her comment really obnoxious?"

"Not just you. I felt a little blindsided. Totally did not expect her to blurt out questions about my reproductive choices over ice cream." She was glad he'd seen it as off-putting, too.

"No kidding." He shook his head. His fingers trailed across her back as he moved around her. "Switch sides with me."

"Huh? Why?"

Alex stepped around behind her, so he was walking closest to the road. "Because my mother would have my hide if I let a lady walk next to the road."

"Ah, you're being a gentleman." She appreciated the gesture. It was nice to spend time with a guy who opened doors and walked on the road-side of the sidewalk and let her go first in line. And it was clearly because he was polite, not because he thought she was fragile and incapable of opening her own doors.

"I try," he mumbled.

"You're succeeding. That's very chivalrous."

"Why thank you, milady." He leaned forward in a slight bow.

Avery chuckled at the theatrics. "Don't expect me to call you milord."

"Master will do."

She laughed, loud. "I wouldn't hold my breath for that one, either."

"Your Highness?"

"Not a chance."

"Hmm. I'm not sure this vacation is going to work out if you refuse to address me properly."

"And to think I was wondering why you're single. Mystery solved."

"Ouch." He clutched his chest. "Bullseye."

On the railroad bridge. Avery grabbed Alex's arm to stop him. "Train."

They leaned on the railing to count cars, and once the train rumbled past, Avery said, "Ninety-four."

"Ninety-four," he agreed.

They resumed walking. A nice breeze had kicked up. Avery asked, "Are you packed for tomorrow?"

"Not yet."

"Nothing like waiting 'til the last minute." She hated rushing, so she liked to get things done ahead of time, even though she still had a few last minute items to pack.

"All I have to do is throw some clothes in a bag and call it done."

"And a toothbrush. And deodorant." She ticked items off on her fingers.

"Come on, we're going to be at the beach. I'll rinse off in the ocean," he teased.

"As long as you have a plan."

Alex grinned at her. "You might have to roll the windows down for the ride home, though."

She shoved his arm. "Gross."

Chapter Ten

Alex opened the door to the apartment building and let Avery walk through. She peered suspiciously at the elevator before getting in.

He suggested, "You know you could talk to management about Mr. Barrow."

"And say what, exactly? He's never said or done anything inappropriate, aside from his roving eyeballs and the creepy feeling he gives me. What are they going to do, ask him to wear blinders?"

Alex wasn't sure what to think. It didn't seem right that a man could walk around leering and making people uncomfortable, but she was probably correct that nothing could be done. He pushed the button for the fifth floor and checked to make sure the car was Mr. Barrow-less before stepping aside to let Avery go in ahead of him.

The elevator slowly ascended.

"About tomorrow. What time are we leaving?" Avery asked.

"I figured we'd head out around six. That okay?"

"Perfect." Avery gave him a big smile. "I can't wait to put my feet in the ocean."

Alex agreed. It'd been too long since he'd been on the beach. "I have my boogie board in the trunk."

Her face fell. "Darn it, I don't have one."

He had to laugh at her crushed expression. Who knew boogie boarding would be such a priority. "Don't worry. There's a ton of water toys at the beach house, so there will definitely be extra boogie boards. There's also a pool."

"How many people are going to be there?"

The elevator dinged and opened on their floor. They slowly walked toward their apartments, stopping in front of Alex's door.

Alex ticked people off on his fingers. "My parents, obviously. Holly and her husband and three kids. My aunt Steph and uncle Frankie and their clan – my cousin Jack and his girlfriend du jour, and my cousin Sydney and her wife Analise, and their daughter, Hazel."

"I should probably know your sister's husband's name." Avery's tone was lighthearted.

"Michael. And their kids are Sophie – she's the one that named Poof. She's nine. And there's Braydon who's seven, and Kallie, who's six."

"Good job, Uncle, remembering how old the kids are. When are their birthdays?"

Alex held up a hand and shook his head. "Half the time I can't remember my *own* birthday. That's what the calendar in my phone is for. I'm even smart enough to have reminders set up a few weeks ahead of time so I can buy gifts."

"Genius."

He tapped his temple with his forefinger. "You know it."

"Who's driving?"

"I already told Mom we'd come down separately. I didn't figure you'd want to spend four hours in an ancient minivan with my parents. You can ride with them if you want, but I promise that four hours of I Spy and the license plate game get really old." He spoke from experience. His mom was crazy about travel games.

"I love the license plate game."

"Do you also love singing the states? Because that's what you have to do when you spot a new license plate."

"No way."

"Yup." He sang, "'Alabama and Alaska. Arizona, Arkansas. California, Colorado, and Connecticut and more.' Shall I go on?"

"I kind of want to say yes." Avery laughed. "Let's save the whole song for tomorrow. Something to look forward to."

"The rule is to sing it every time we spot a plate from a different state."

"That seems a bit much."

Alex agreed. "It started when we were little and Mom was teaching us the states. She just never stopped." Fond memories clicked through his mind of road trips they'd taken. "At least she didn't make us sing the one with the capitals. But between you and me, I think that's only because she didn't know it herself."

"That's sweet, though."

Alex pulled out his phone. "I'm making a note to ask you about your childhood vacations tomorrow."

She peered at his phone. "You have a list? Of travel conversation topics?"

He felt his face heat as he mumbled, "Sort of." Yes. He had a list of things for them to talk about. A list of things he wanted to know about her.

"What else is on it?"

He clicked the phone dark and slid it into his pocket. "I

guess you'll find out tomorrow." He felt kind of stupid for having the list in the first place, and now that she'd seen it, it was about ten times worse.

She took a step backward and jingled her pared down keyring. "I'm going to finish packing. And make my own list."

"I'm kind of worried." He was actually kind of relieved she seemed to think it was a fun idea, and not completely weird.

"You should be." Avery opened her door and stepped inside. She turned and grinned. "See you at six," she said over her shoulder as she shut the door.

Chapter Eleven

Avery finished packing her suitcase and double checked she had everything she needed. She showered and changed into her favorite yoga pants and tank top. Sitting cross-legged on her recliner, she pulled a spiral-bound notebook out of the stack of miscellany on the side table.

She turned the television on, finding a baseball game to serve as background noise. The Braves were leading, and the batter hit a double. She pumped her fist in the air. If there was one thing she'd brought back with her from her time in Atlanta, it was love for the Braves. She'd spent countless hours at The Battery Atlanta with forty-some thousand of her closest friends.

She made a note on her pad. *Baseball.* Perfect topic
of conversation for a long car ride. Unless he was a Mets fan. That would be an issue. She tapped the pen to her lip, watching the game but not really.

Work. Hobbies. Family.

She sighed. What did she want to know about Alex? Well, for starters, why the heck was he taking the next door neighbor he didn't know along on his family vacation? It seemed like something a desperate, lonely person would do. But in the short time she'd known him, she hadn't gotten a single vibe that he was either of those things.

Not that she was complaining. He was rescuing her from the nonsense that was her brother, and she was going to see the ocean for the first time in ages. And let's be real – it didn't hurt that Alex was ridiculously hot.

She jumped up and went back to her bedroom and into the closet, yanking open the bottom drawer of her dresser, where her bathing suits lived. She'd packed her sporty blue suit already, a nondescript suit meant for water sports and beach volleyball. Debating, she picked her cute red bikini that was definitely not meant for water sports. Standing, she held it in front of herself, scowling at the mirror. Too much. Or rather, not enough.

Five minutes later, the closet floor was littered with bathing suits. "Yes!" She grabbed the last bathing suit in the drawer, a pink two-piece that was modest enough to wear comfortably in front of Alex's parents, but still cute enough to get Alex's attention.

She shoved it into her suitcase. Wait, what? Did she *want* Alex's attention? She side-eyed herself in the mirror. Um, yes. Yes, she did.

Well *that* was a revelation. Okay, maybe it wasn't. Alex was nice, he was hot, and he was single. She stood abruptly and wheeled the suitcase to the living room and set it beside the front door. Back in her bedroom, she put her favorite quilted tote bag on the bathroom counter. She'd grab her toiletries and phone charger in the morning.

She settled back onto the chair and checked the score of the game. 7-1, Braves. Heck, yeah.

The notebook on her lap, she tried to think of other things she wanted to know about Alex.

Career.

She knew he was in sales for the security firm, but did he want to be in sales in general, or was it the security aspect he was drawn to?

Travel.

Other than the annual trip to Ocean City, did he travel? Did he want to?

She sighed and closed the notebook. This was silly. Conversation would flow organically. And they had a whole weekend to fill. And a return trip. Best not use up all the topics on the way down the road.

Not that she thought that their conversation would actually be an issue, because it certainly hadn't been so far.

She finally got up and got ready for bed. Setting her alarm, she had a pang of guilt about missing work. She scoffed at herself. It was the first she'd been off in a year. Literally. The only day she'd taken off was when she had some mild food poisoning after last Thanksgiving. Originally, she was supposed to rotate Saturdays with her idiot brother, but she ended up working at least three Saturdays a month. Feeling guilty over taking four days off was beyond ridiculous. If she kept up this pace, she'd end up having a stroke like her father had.

Her eyes popped open wide at the sobering revelation. Nope, she was done with that. She'd work her scheduled Saturdays and that was it. No more covering for Jimmy and his stupid lame excuses. He wants to be a manager, he can manage.

Making that decision, simple as it was, made her feel a little better. A little more in control.

Morning came, bright and warm. Avery turned her alarm off and checked the final score of the game. 11-3. Perfect start to the day. She unplugged her charger before rolling out of bed and carried it to the bathroom. She shoved it in the tote bag. Score one for remembering the charger.

She showered and dressed in her favorite gray and red Braves T-shirt and a pair of white shorts. She packed her toiletries and tied her long blonde hair back in a ponytail. A zipper hoodie and her sneakers, and she was ready to go.

At five before six, she double checked to make sure she had her phone, then wheeled her suitcase to the hallway in front of Alex's door. As she raised her hand to knock, the door popped open.

"Oh!" Alex's eyes widened. "I didn't know you were out here. I was going to come over and see if you were ready."

"Yep. Are you?"

"Almost. Lincoln will be here any min—" A gray streak bolted for the hallway. Alex's arm swooped down and thwarted Poof's impressive effort. "Oh, no, you don't."

Poof's ears flattened against his head, his pupils wide and angry. His fluffy tail swished back and forth as he fumed against Alex's chest.

The elevator dinged and a man stepped out.

"Hey, Lincoln," Alex said.

His friend was average height, on the lanky side, with light brown hair and black-framed glasses. Avery smiled as he shuffled past her into Alex's apartment, without a word or eye contact. *Okay, weirdo.*

She followed him inside and closed the door.

"He tries to escape," Alex said as he put Poof on the floor. "You have to watch the door super close and make sure he doesn't get out."

"Okay." Lincoln's back was to Avery. "Where's his food?"

"Kitchen."

They all walked into the kitchen. Avery was still baffled about why Lincoln hadn't even acknowledged her. Rude.

Alex opened a cupboard and pointed to a plastic container. "Food's in here. One scoop a day. He'll act like he's starving to death, but he's not. He'll also drop food into his water dish and then refuse to drink from the tainted water, so make sure you don't set them too close together."

Avery snickered. "Sounds like a kid."

Lincoln glanced at her and his pale face blushed bright red, all the way to the tips of his ears. He barked a completely awkward laugh.

Avery smiled and glanced at Alex. She quirked an eyebrow in question. He gave a slight shake of his head while Lincoln busied himself filling Poof's bowl.

She had no idea why he seemed to be uncomfortable around her, but no sense in dragging it out. "Uh, shoot. I forgot something, so I'm going to run back to my apartment. Nice to meet you, Lincoln."

He bolted straight upright and held the cat food scoop tight with both hands. "Yuh."

Avery waited in the hallway with her suitcase until Alex came out with his. He pulled the door shut behind him and they wheeled to the elevator. Once they were inside and the doors slid shut, he said, "Lincoln has some pretty intense social anxieties around new people, but especially women."

"Ah. I wasn't sure if I'd done something."

"No, I think he was surprised and just kind of short circuited. The next time he sees you it'll be better, and after he's been around you a few times he'll be totally fine."

Was Alex assuming she was going to be around his friends on a regular basis? The elevator stopped on the next floor and opened, so she didn't have time to consider any deeper meaning behind his words. Mr. Barrow stepped into the car, leered at her chest–her completely-covered-by-a-hoodie chest–and said to her boobs, "Good morning, Avery."

The way he said her name made her skin crawl. She instinctively rounded her shoulders forward, trying to shrink back from his gaze.

Alex answered, "Good morning, Mr. Barrow."

The creepy man's eyes flicked to Alex for a split second, then slid back to Avery's chest. "Hello, Alex," he said coolly as he turned to face the reflective doors.

Avery shifted closer to Alex, away from him. Little prickles ran up and down the back of her neck. So gross.

"Spending the weekend together? How nice." Mr. Barrow not-so-subtly licked his lips while staring at Avery in their reflection.

It took a hundred years for the elevator to sink to the lobby. When the doors slid open, Avery nearly ran over Alex to get out. She hustled to the parking lot and waited beside Alex's car. She held her tote bag in front of her, a sort of buffer between her chest and Barrow's creepy gaze as he walked down the sidewalk and finally turned away.

Alex popped the trunk and set Avery's suitcase inside. She nestled her tote bag safely in the back seat and slipped her phone into her pocket. Alex opened her door and she slid into her seat.

When he got in the driver's seat, he hesitated before starting the car. "That wasn't okay."

"I know. But there aren't any laws against being gross."

"I wasn't sure if you wanted me to say something."

"Like what? 'Hey, creep, quit staring at Avery's boobs?'" She shook her head. "No, I didn't want you to say anything."

"But—"

"Alex, this may come as a shock to you, but there's nothing

particularly unusual about what he's doing. Pretty much every woman you know has learned how to deal with assholes like that because they're everywhere. Mr. Barrow just happens to be a little more obvious than most."

He started the car and backed out of the parking space. "I don't even know what to say to that."

"Let's not say anything about it." The words came out sharper than she intended. She softened her tone. "I don't want to waste any more time thinking about Mr. Barrow. He's not worth the head space."

Alex glanced over at her. "Okay. But if I see that again, with you or anyone else, I'm not ignoring it."

"Deal."

He put on his turn signal at the Sheetz. "I have to get gas."

"Good. I'm going in to grab a giant Pepsi for the ride. You want anything?" She rested her hand on the door handle, waiting for his response.

He fished in his wallet for his card. "Yeah, just a bottle of water."

While Alex pumped his gas, Avery went inside and got herself the biggest fountain soda they had, then got Alex's water. She got back to the car just as he was tearing his receipt from the machine.

She pulled off her hoodie while he started the car and set the GPS on the center console with their destination. The day was already warming up. She couldn't wait to get to the beach.

He glanced over with a smile. "Ready, not-my-girlfriend?"

Avery tapped her giant Pepsi to Alex's water bottle. "Ready, not-my-boyfriend." As they turned onto the highway, she felt another pang of guilt about leaving for the weekend. Was making a point really worth having her entire family upset with her? Then again, it seemed like ticking everyone off was the only way to be heard.

Chapter Twelve

The sun peeked up over the mountainous horizon, while a few puffy white clouds floated in a brilliant blue sky. Alex took his eyes off the road for a second to glance over at Avery. She stared out the window, lost in her thoughts. "What's up?"

She turned her head toward him. "Sorry, just feeling conflicted about this trip."

"We can still go back," he offered.

"I'm not *that* conflicted. I need some sand and salt water therapy to clear my head." She smiled. "I can't wait to smell the ocean air."

Alex was on board with that. He was eager to change the scenery and clear his head. "Looks like it's going to be a good day for sand and salt water. I'm thinking once we get to the house, we'll do a quick lunch, grab you one of the extra boogie boards, then get in the water."

"That sounds amazing. Is the house right on the beach?"

Alex nodded. "Yeah. You literally walk off the back porch onto the beach."

She sighed. "I'm dying to get my feet in the sand. Nature's pedicure."

He chuckled. "There's usually a volleyball game at some point, too."

Avery sat up straight. Her gaze lasered on his face. "No way."

"What? You don't like volleyball?" He couldn't tell if her dramatic reaction was good or bad.

"I *love* volleyball. In fact, I went to Penn State on a volleyball scholarship." She clapped her hands together. "I'm so excited."

"Figures." He groaned.

"What?" she demanded.

"I was hoping you were at least bad at it. See, in our games, partners have to play on opposite teams."

"Oh. Sorry about your luck." She didn't sound sorry at all.

Alex teased, "Maybe everyone else on your team will stink."

A devilish grin crossed Avery's face. "It won't matter. I'm *that* good."

He didn't doubt it. In the short time he'd known her, it was clear Avery was someone who got things done. And if she wanted to beat him at volleyball, he was probably going to lose. "What got you into volleyball?"

She settled back into her seat. "It was either that or basketball. I'm sure you noticed that I'm practically an Amazon."

He glanced over. "How tall are you?" As soon as the question was out, he mentally kicked himself for asking it. It was obvious she was tall, and maybe she was self-conscious about it. "That was nosy, sorry."

She shrugged. "Not as bad as the woman at General Custard's."

He grimaced. "I hope not."

"Alex, it's fine. It was a reasonable question in the context of our conversation. And for the record, I'm five eleven and a half. I hit a growth spurt in middle school and I hated it. I always felt like I was towering over everyone like a freak. I actually enjoyed basketball until I started getting pushed into it. Then one summer I went to a sports camp and discovered that smashing a ball was a great outlet for a lot of frustration."

"Agreed."

"It did so much for my self-esteem, being really good at a sport where my height was an advantage. It kind of sucked with softball, though, because they tended to widen the strike zone too much."

"You didn't stick with basketball?"

Her long ponytail danced on her shoulder as she shook her head. "I quit after two years. Probably for spite because my family kept trying to push me into it. I did volleyball and soft-ball all through high school and college, though. How about you? You look like a baseball player."

He nearly choked. "Really?"

"Definitely."

"Perceptive. I use to play."

Avery took a long sip of her soda. "In college?"

His thumbs tapped the steering wheel. "Yeah. And after."

"Pro?"

He heard the interest in her voice. "Technically." He knew it would come up sooner or later, but it was a sad can of worms he wasn't particularly happy to open. Might as well rip the bandaid off. "After college I played for the Gwinnett Stripers—"

"What!" Avery's excited shriek could have shattered glass. "I've been to Coolray Field a million times. That's just crazy. Small world, huh? Sorry, I didn't mean to interrupt, I just was not expecting you to say that. I'm a huge Braves fan, so it's completely blowing my mind that you played for their feeder team." She pressed her fingers to her temples and pushed them out, miming an explosion.

Sure, he'd noticed the Braves T-shirt she was wearing, but most people didn't know what minor league teams fed into which major league teams. "You know your baseball."

She shrugged one shoulder. "I know a bit."

"I have to admit, I assumed you just had the shirt because you lived in Atlanta. I didn't know you were an actual baseball fan."

"You know what they say about assumptions. I take it the baseball thing didn't work out. Didn't you want to keep playing?"

He changed lanes to pass a slow-moving tractor trailer. She'd been open with him, so he took a breath and did the same. "I would have loved to keep playing. The Braves were calling me up when I got injured."

"Oh, no. Alex." There was real sympathy in her voice.

He blurted out the short version. "Runner came in way too hot on a pop fly and we got tangled. I ended up with a concussion and a torn ACL." He managed a little laugh. "I got the out, though."

Avery winced. "I'm so sorry. How's the ACL now?"

"Healed, thankfully. And no lasting damage from the concussion, thank God." He could guess she was still curious, so he filled in the blanks. "I would have gone back in a heartbeat, but it was my second tear on my lead leg so I was out for more than half a season. The next year I came back and struggled the whole season. So I got cut."

"I'm sorry."

He shot her a grin. "I guess my parents weren't so stupid for making me major in something practical so I'd have a fallback option."

"Mine, too. What was your fallback major?"

"Finance and marketing." It wasn't anything that rocked his world, but they'd been right–it was practical, and that background meant he had a lot of career options available to him.

"Me, too, sort of. I majored in business management with minors in marketing and finance."

One more thing they had in common. Nice. "No kidding. I'm sure it all comes in handy now that you're running the store." He adjusted his visor against the blinding sun.

"Pfft, obviously I bring nothing valuable to the table. Except for that whole saving their asses thing I can't seem to stop harping on."

"Sorry, didn't mean to bring that up."

She pushed her sunglasses to the top of her head. "Nah, I'm in my head. I keep ticking through the things I should be doing, and I'm getting frustrated. With myself, mostly, because I can't just relax."

He was glad she'd agreed to come along. Nothing better than sun and sand and surf to clear the head. "It's hard when you don't trust the people running things while you're gone."

"You hit the nail on the head there. I don't trust Jimmy to… well, to do anything right, and I don't trust my parents to make him do his job." Avery shifted in her seat and turned her head to look out the window. "I'm sure you understand, since your parents own a small business, too."

Alex could see some parallels, but the way his parents and her parents handled the family end of the family business was night and day. "Sort of. It's different for us since Holly was eager to take over and I'm happy to let her. I can't imagine treating my sister the way Jimmy is treating you, and I think if I tried, my parents would put a stop to it real fast."

She wiped at a spot on her shirt. "I think that's what's bothering me the most. My parents don't have my back. Well, my mom tries, but she's not in a great position." She pulled her sunglasses back down and pointed at the car in front of them. "There's a license plate from Louisiana."

The next few miles passed in silence, until Alex put his turn signal on to exit the highway. "I need another bottle of water."

"Excellent, because I have to pee."

He glanced at her almost-empty giant cup of soda and tried not to laugh. "No wonder."

They took a quick pit stop at a convenience store, where Alex topped off the gas tank while Avery went inside to find the restroom. When she came back, she had a bottle of water for him and another giant soda for herself.

Alex's excitement bubbled when they were back on the highway and got close to the state line. "Five miles to Delaware."

Avery grinned over at him. "Last chance to commit a crime before it's automatically a felony."

"Are you sure that's how it works?" He drummed his fingers on the steering wheel, now curious about crime.

"No, but it sounds like it should be right. Crossing state lines and all that." She got her phone out of her pocket and flipped the camera on. "Here we go."

She snapped a picture of the "Welcome to Delaware" sign.

"Were you planning to commit a crime? Is there something I should be aware of?"

Avery pulled her sunglasses down her nose and looked at him with a serious expression.

Laughing, he said, "Say no more. Plausible deniability."

When he glanced over again, she winked. "If we get pulled over, act natural. And keep the car running."

They both laughed, then fell into an easy silence. Alex couldn't wait to get to the shore. He was glad to put miles between him and Dean before he did something he'd regret. Like quitting without having another job lined up. He knew that was what he ultimately needed to do. Find another job. He ran through some possibilities in his mind.

"Earth to Alex. Where'd you go?" Her voice was soft, with a hint of concern.

He hadn't realized how long he'd been in his own head. Or that he'd been scowling. He relaxed his clenched jaw. "Just thinking about work stuff."

"Do you want to talk about it now?"

Glancing over, he gave her a smile. "Without a spreadsheet?"

Avery reached into the back seat and pulled a notebook and pen out of her bag. "Old school spreadsheet." She scrawled a line down the center of the page. "Pros and cons."

"Of?"

"Let's start with the pros of staying at your current job."

He tapped his thumbs on the steering wheel. "Pros. Okay, I already know the system. Erin, my assistant, is fantastic. I like what I do."

From the corner of his eye, he saw Avery make a sort of face.

"What?"

"I'm not sure that's job-specific." She waved her hand. "Never mind. I'm writing it down. We're brainstorming here. Sorry, go on."

"The money's good. Current situation excluded," he added. "Benefits are good. The corporate culture is mostly good. Coworkers are great. Potential for advancement is good. The commute is good." He thought for a minute. "I'm running out of things."

Avery nodded and wrote the word "Cons" at the top of the second column. She suddenly reached over and grabbed his arm as she pointed out her passenger window. "There's Miles!" She bounced excitedly in her seat.

"Miles?" What the heck was she talking about?

Her index finger tapped the glass. "The statue in front of the Dover speedway. His name is Miles."

Alex looked over at the giant gray rock monster holding a life-size racecar aloft in front of the NASCAR stadium. "I never knew he had a name."

"He's really cool up close. Even bigger than you think. My dad used to be really into NASCAR. When I was a kid, we'd either come here or Pocono every year for a race."

"Never been to a NASCAR race. I've gone to dirt track races and drag races, though."

Avery laughed, then pressed her fingers to her mouth.

"What?"

"I just remembered my friend who used to date a guy who drag raced. She warned me not to go out with any guy who thought fourteen seconds was a long time."

Laughing, her comment caught him a little off guard. "Ouch. That's brutal."

"But not bad advice. I did end up going on one date with a guy who raced, and it was bad enough for me to cross the entire sport off my list."

He decided to see if he could push her buttons. "Isn't that kind of stereotyping?"

She lifted a shoulder. "Meh. It's served me well. I also won't date guys who don't have jobs and/or never lived outside of their parents' house. I also won't date guys who are allegedly separated but are 'in the process' of getting a divorce. That goes double for the ones who still live with their wives 'for the kids' or 'to save money,'" she air quoted.

"Sounds like the voice of experience."

"Ugh. There are a lot of losers out there. It's not easy being a single woman these days." She took a long sip of her soda.

"Don't tell me you don't have any dealbreakers that could be considered stereotyping."

He cleared his throat. "Fair. Let's get back to the spreadsheet."

Avery smirked at him. "I'm sensing we've touched a nerve. You're pickier than I am, aren't you? You probably have a hundred dealbreakers."

"At least." He reached over and tapped the notepad. "Cons." She wasn't wrong. A hundred dealbreakers was probably a conservative estimate. He blamed it on his stint in professional sports, which brought the gold diggers out in droves.

"Okay, but just know that we'll circle back to this discussion at some point. Now. Cons of staying at your job."

"They stole my commissions."

"That's a big fat number one."

"I've felt like things were off for a while. Like I wasn't getting the truth, or at least the whole story, when Dean–my boss–would talk to me about anything. Even stupid petty stuff like whether he'd had a chance to look over reports or if a canceled meeting was being rescheduled."

Avery took another long sip of soda. "It's none of my business, being not-your-girlfriend and all, but are you really torn about leaving, or are you actually just working up the energy to bite the bullet and go?"

"Good question." He changed lanes to pass a minivan. "Up until the commission check thing, I hadn't been thinking about leaving, because it was all little stuff that wasn't a big deal." He signaled and moved back into the right lane. "And now the commission check situation is like putting a magnifying glass on everything."

"I'm really sorry. That sucks."

He glanced over and smiled at her. "Thanks."

She rapped the end of her pen against the notepad. "Okay. Pros of finding another job."

Alex grimaced. "There are no pros to job hunting." He hated the entire process. Updating his resume, finding companies who were hiring, applying, waiting, scheduling interviews, waiting, then even worse, interviewing. And waiting some more. "Let's finish this later. It's depressing."

"Okay." Avery turned in her seat and put the pad and paper back into her bag in the backseat. "What should we talk about?"

Might as well jump into a big topic, right? "How about, why'd you break up with your last boyfriend? You said it was one of the reasons coming back to Hickory Hollow was good timing."

"Ugh, I thought you didn't want to talk about depressing things?" She leaned her head back against the headrest and said, "I didn't break up with him. He broke up with me after I didn't accept his proposal."

His head jerked to look at her. "He proposed? So it was serious." He definitely hadn't seen that coming.

"I didn't know how serious it was. We were living together, and we'd had exactly one discussion about marriage, where I said it was something I'd consider way down the line, and he was adamant that he wasn't planning to ever get married. Which was fine at that point in my life."

"Wait. He explicitly told you he wasn't interested in marriage, and then proposed?" Why couldn't people just be honest about their intentions?

"Exactly. He took me to this super fancy restaurant. This was on my birthday, by the way. We had a lovely meal, except it was February and Keith complained about being freezing cold the whole way there, and I'm like, it's fifty-five degrees, it's not even cold. But anyhow, the waiter brought the ring in a dessert and he goes down on one knee–Keith, not the waiter–and the place was so crowded and everyone was watching. I tried to stop him but he just kept going. I seriously thought I was going to throw up. I couldn't even get up and walk away. All I could do was shake my head no."

"Not so romantic, huh?" He'd always thought those sorts of surprise proposals were a bad idea. Even now, retelling the story more than a year later, Avery looked half nauseated.

"The worst part was that he presented me with this two carat monstrosity a week after not having his half of the rent."

"Wow."

She held up a hand. "Believe me, I know I sound ungrateful and rude and blah blah blah, poor Keith, I've heard it all about how horrible I was and I should have said yes and then talked to him later."

"But then you'd be horrible for saying yes and then taking it back."

She smacked the dash. "Thank you! It was lose-lose for me no matter what."

Alex chuckled. "Monstrosity, huh?"

She ran her hand down over her face. "Okay, that's an awful word, and you'll probably jump ship here and agree with everyone who thinks I'm a terrible person, but I hated that ring. The diamond was like the size of a walnut and it was in this wide gold band with rubies on the side that were almost as big. It was gaudy and awful and it was like he didn't know me at all."

"That sounds pretty bad." He'd only known Avery for a few days, and couldn't imagine her wearing something so flashy. Unless she was dressed up for a special occasion.

"The worst part was when the head chef came out to congratulate us–like an actual celebrity chef–and he was embarrassed he didn't know there wasn't a happy ending, and then the entire dining room could hear him screaming at the staff in the kitchen for not warning him that I hadn't said yes. Everyone in the entire place was trying to act like they weren't watching, but come on. You could have heard a pin drop."

"No offense, but I would have been hanging on every word."

"Me, too. Keith was humiliated and grabbed the ring and ran out, at which point the waiter brought the bill. So I had to sit there staring at the tablecloth with everyone staring holes through me until he came back with my credit card."

"He stuck you with the bill." Alex could feel the second-hand embarrassment she must have been feeling with all those eyes on her.

"Not even done."

He glanced over at her, wondering what more there could possibly be.

"Keith cried the whole way home and I felt like a heartless monster. We got back to the apartment and he starts packing his stuff. I asked him if we could talk about it. Nope. I was feeling so guilty and miserable, and then I find out that he only proposed because his ex-girlfriend had just gotten married so he was feeling some kind of way about it."

"He told you that?"

"*He* didn't. I haven't spoken to him since. We exchanged a few text messages about the apartment and that was it. I found out from the mutual friend who came to pick up the last of his stuff and drop off his key."

He wasn't sure what to say. "Not the best birthday, huh?"

"Not even close."

"So not-my-girlfriend, I guess I should return this three-carat monstrosity I was planning to propose with on the beach. Should I also cancel the banner plane flyover?"

She put her index finger on her chin. "Depends. What's the banner say?"

"I didn't get that far."

"Make it short. I think they charge by the letter."

Alex shrugged. "It's okay, I have my rent money to use." For a second, he thought he might have gone too far and offended her, but she burst out laughing.

"That's awful. I shouldn't laugh. I know he must have been so embarrassed, but I wish he would have talked to me instead of… that."

"Sorry, I shouldn't have made a joke. I hope I didn't offend you."

She slurped the last of her soda. "Not at all."

They both retreated into their own thoughts. For the next several miles, the road and the radio were the only noise.

Chapter Thirteen

Avery stared out the window at the passing scenery.

The GPS instructed Alex to exit onto 13, but he either ignored it or didn't hear it.

"I think that's our exit."

"It'll recalculate in a minute. The traffic's better that way, but you'll get to see the ocean sooner this way."

"Oh, yay. I can't wait to see the water." She pulled in a deep breath as if she could smell the ocean from here. It felt like forever since she'd been to the beach and put her feet in the sand. Now that they were only about an hour away, she was getting more excited.

The sun blasted the landscape, coating everything in an orange glow.

A few minutes passed, then Alex excitedly said, "Look." He pointed at a spot on the horizon.

Avery leaned up in her seat and craned her neck. "I see it!"

A dip in the earth gave a glimpse of the ocean that lay just beyond the shore, and then it was gone again. The trees blurred as Avery kept watching for the next sight of ocean.

She settled back in her seat. "What about your last relationship? How did it end? No botched public proposals, I hope." She recalled his mother making some sort of snide comment about the ex when they met.

He grinned and shook her head. "Nothing so dramatic as that. She moved for her career."

She couldn't quite place the emotion in his voice. Regret? Disbelief? "You couldn't go with her?"

"It's not that I couldn't, or didn't want to. It's that she didn't ask me to."

"Oh." Soooo many questions. Since he'd probably already figured out she was nosey, she asked, "Would you have gone?"

"Yes."

Not even a moment of hesitation. "I'm sorry."

He shrugged a shoulder. "It was a while ago."

A while as in a month? Six months? Two days? "How long?"

"About a year." His reply was brusque, then he took a breath. "Sorry. I hadn't thought about it for a while."

"Did you ever talk to her? Find out why she didn't ask you to go along? Get some kind of closure?"

"Yup. She said I was getting too serious and she wasn't ready for a major commitment, so she thought the time apart would be best."

"Oh, ugh. That sounds like the flip side of my situation." Except that they'd had a private conversation to wrap things up, not a public spectacle with no resolution.

"Well, I *did* buy the ring, but it wasn't a two-carat monstrosity, and I wasn't stupid enough to propose without knowing if it was something she wanted."

Avery was glad her sunglasses hid her eyes, which were currently bugging out of her head. He bought a ring?? "Oh, look, there's the ocean again." Was Alex was still carrying a torch for his ex? Awesome.

He jumped on her subject change. "We're only about half an hour away. I can't wait to get in the water, even though it's probably freezing cold."

The radio blinked with an incoming call. Alex hit a button on his steering wheel. "Hey, Mom."

Dolly's melodic voice filled the car. "Hi. Just wanted to let you know everyone's here except Jack. Frankie says he'll be here this afternoon. Holly and Michael took the kids to the beach."

"Okay."

"There's lunch ready. I made sandwiches and have stuff for salads. It's all in the fridge, so you don't need to stop for lunch on the way if you don't want to. When will you be here?"

Avery automatically looked at the GPS's estimated arrival. She could easily imagine Dolly pacing the kitchen, making sure everything was in place and fussing over every detail.

Alex said, "About a half hour."

"Okay, well, be careful. The traffic was really heavy once we got into Ocean City."

"Gotcha."

"Alrighty, see you soon. Love you."

"Love you, too." He tapped the button again and the call disconnected.

"That's so sweet." Her own mom would be the same way on vacation, making sure everything was going according to plan.

"Yeah, she's pretty great."

Avery couldn't help but notice the way Alex's face radiated warmth when he talked about his family. "I'm looking forward to meeting your sister."

"You'll get along great. And I should warn you that Sophie will probably tag along with me–us–most of the weekend."

"She's the niece who named Poof."

"Yup."

Avery chuckled. "I wonder if Lincoln made it out of the apartment unscathed."

"Poof likes Lincoln, so he's probably fine."

"Probably? Not a confident answer."

"I mean, he's a cat. Nothing's ever certain with a cat."

A bubble of excitement fluttered through Avery as they passed the Ocean City welcome sign. "America's finest family resort," she read.

The GPS warned them of an upcoming left turn. Alex put his signal on and moved into the turning lane. "Almost there."

He turned onto the side road and immediately turned into a driveway. A cheerful two-story yellow house was already host to several cars. Alex pulled close to a minivan and turned the car off. He hit a button to pop the trunk.

Avery got out and stretched, then got their smaller bags out of the back seat while Alex got the suitcases out of the trunk. She could hear the ocean, but they were in the front of the house, so she couldn't see it yet.

Alex led her up a staircase to a small white porch. The door opened before they reached it. "You're here!" Dolly held the door and beamed as she ushered them into the living room. It was a nice sized room with three sofas arranged in a U-shape around a coffee table, with a big-screen tv as the focal point of the room.

"You'll both be upstairs. There are three open bedrooms up there, so take your pick. Jack will get what's left."

She followed Alex down a hallway, past three bedrooms, to a staircase that led to the second level. The upstairs had four bedrooms, each with its own private bathroom. The first room with a large bed and a set of bunk beds had suitcases already inside.

Avery peeked in the next bedroom while Alex checked out

the farthest one. "This one looks nice." Two twin beds and a dresser fit in the small room nicely.

"You'll want this one," Alex said, coming back into the hallway with his bag. He'd left hers inside the bedroom.

"Why?"

She shuffled down the hall and gasped. "Oh, Alex, are you sure?"

A huge window overlooked a tiny balcony, and beyond that, sand and sea. It was a view dreams are made of.

He leaned against the doorframe. "Nothing but the best for my not-girlfriend."

"Really, are you sure?"

"Ave, I'm sure." He shook his head and wheeled his suitcase next door.

The nickname he'd used yanked her attention from the view. He'd said it so casually, with such familiarity that her heart skipped a little. It was a complicated thing. She hated it when certain people shortened her name, but with Alex, it felt nice. Comfortable. Like they'd known each other a lot longer than a few days.

A second later, he called out, "No changing rooms!"

"What?" There was no way his view was better than hers. And even if it was, there was no way she'd change rooms. She dashed over to join him at the window.

He pointed. "I've got the dumpster view."

She opened her mouth, but he held up a hand. "Nope, no matter how much you beg, I'm not trading rooms."

"Dang." She crossed her arms. "I should have looked at all my options first."

"Sorry about your luck."

"Nothing I can do, huh?"

Alex shook his head. "I'm pulling rank."

"Wow. You're really not playing."

"I am not."

She knew he was joking, but she did feel bad about having the best view. "Seriously, Alex, I'm happy to take this room. I'm just tagging along, I shouldn't have the room with the best view."

"No. This one has a bigger bed, and we'll only be in our rooms to sleep. You keep that room."

She studied his face to gauge his words. He reached over and unhooked his messenger bag from her shoulder. "Go unpack and we'll grab a light lunch and hit the water."

As much as she wanted to argue and make him take the room with the better view, she wanted to get on the beach more, so she went back to her room and closed the door. She changed into her blue swimsuit and pulled a simple T-shirt dress over it. A pair of flip flops, a beach towel, and she was ready.

Alex met her in the hallway, wearing swim trunks and a tank top that showed off his muscular arms. His towel was slung over his shoulder. She wondered if he'd been a pitcher, because his arms were really defined. And tan.

Downstairs, Dolly and Bert were the only ones inside.

"I guess you'll meet everyone later," Dolly said as she pushed a plate toward Avery. "Get something to eat."

Avery took a sandwich and a pickle and ate them standing up. Alex leaned against the counter and did the same.

Dolly said, "We'll be going out for the buffet tonight, so be ready to go by five."

Avery put her plate in the dishwasher. "Oooh, seafood buffet is my favorite thing ever."

Alex added his plate to the dishwasher, wiped his mouth, and gave Dolly a kiss on the cheek. "Sounds great, but right now the ocean is calling."

Dolly shooed them toward the sliding glass doors. "Go, go. I'm anxious to get my feet in the sand, too."

Alex put a hand on Avery's back as they crossed the huge wooden deck. The stairs led directly into the sand. A handful of people were on the beach.

"Are those your people?"

"Yup." He pointed to a family digging and building a sand castle nearby. "Holly's clan." He then pointed to a group laying in the sand under an umbrella a fair distance away. "Steph, Frankie, Sydney, and Analise. I'm guessing Hazel is there somewhere."

Holly looked up and waved, so Alex steered her over.

"Nice castle," Avery said as they approached.

A young girl, she assumed it was Sophie, leaped to her feet and screamed, "Uncle Alex!" as she flew over to him, sand kicking up from her heels. She leaped at him and he caught her in midair and swung her around. The little boy and girl weren't far behind, each wanting their turn to be hugged and swung around by Uncle Alex.

Laughing, he set the youngest girl down and tugged on her pigtails. "Avery, this is Kallie, Brayden, and Sophie. My sister, Holly, and brother-in-law, Michael. Everybody, this is Avery."

"Are you his girlfriend?" Kallie asked.

"Nope, we're just friends," Avery answered. "I live next door to your uncle Alex."

Holly brushed sand off her legs. "Nice to meet you, Avery. We've heard a lot about you."

"Uh oh." She side-eyed Alex.

"From Mom," Holly was quick to clarify, "so you know it's all good. Sorry about all the strawberry preserves."

Avery laughed. "I'll never run out."

"You'll quickly find out that food is Mom's love language."

Michael gave her a wave/salute. "Nice to meet you."

"Nice to meet all of you, too," Avery said.

Alex cleared his throat. "Yeah, this is great, but I'm dying to get in the water, so we'll catch you later."

He tugged his tank top over his head and dropped it onto a picnic table near the deck. "Almost forgot the boogie boards." He opened a small shed at the corner of the house.

While he got the boogie boards, Avery kicked off her flip flops and pulled the dress over her head. She tossed it beside Alex's shirt.

Alex came around the deck and handed her a board. "Race you."

Avery watched him as she secured the tether to her wrist, then she took off, sprinting through the sand with Alex running right beside her. The sand was hot and rough and wonderful against the soles of her feet as she ran, her calf muscles working overtime through the loose grit, then her feet slapped against the wet sand at the edge of the water, then splashed into the surf and into knee-deep water that was freezing cold. She gasped at the sensation.

The momentum propelled her forward, even as Alex laughed beside her, "Holy crap it's cold!"

Cold or not, Avery bounced with the water, now waist-deep, and took a deep breath. She dove under the rolling water and came up on the other side. Another wave built, rolling toward them. Alex bobbed next to her. "Looks like a good one."

"It's perfect!" She dove under it and came up on the other side, twisting her torso onto her board and riding the top of the wave back to the shore.

Alex slid in a moment later and reached out for a high five.

She clapped his hand and they headed back into the deeper water.

Avery felt like a mermaid, diving and swooping under the water, then popping up into the warm air. The salt water clung to her skin, little crystals and grit sticking to her as they dried in the breeze, only to be wet again a moment later.

Diving under wave after wave, Avery felt like she could do this forever.

She swooped under another rolling wave and turned to ride it in. The bright late-afternoon sun caught the water at exactly the wrong angle, and suddenly both the sky and the sea blinded and disoriented her. She lost her balance and the wave knocked her under the water. She fought her instincts to flail against it and a moment later her feet found the sandy ground. She stood, coughing and sputtering.

Alex was by her side, his arm protectively around her waist. "You okay? That was a nasty wipeout."

She caught her breath and nodded. "Sun got me and I lost my balance. I'm okay."

Her board's tether tugged at the strap on her wrist. She pulled the board to her and picked it up.

Alex held up his wrist. "It's four thirty, should we call it a day and get ready for dinner?"

Avery coughed again and spit a mouthful of salty yuck into the ocean. "Yeah. Tomorrow's another day."

"You sure you're okay?" Alex stacked her board on top of his and waited while she pulled the strap off her wrist, then took off his own.

"I'm good. You want me to take that?" She reached for the board.

"Nah, I got it."

"Thanks." She pulled the elastic band from her ponytail and worked her fingers through the tangles. They trudged through the sand, back to the deck.

Alex stowed the boards back in the shed while she grabbed their clothes and shoes from the picnic table. At the corner of the house, they used the outside spigot to rinse the sand from their feet, then Alex pulled the sliding door open and put his hand on her back as they walked through.

"Hurry up," Dolly admonished them. "We're leaving in fifteen minutes."

"Plenty of time," Alex told her.

Avery hurried up the stairs, pausing in the doorway of Alex's room. "Here's your shirt and shoes."

"Thanks." He tossed the shoes on the floor beside the bed and took the shirt from her. "Better hurry."

"Bet I'm done before you," Avery challenged.

"You're on." He took a running step and rolled over the bed, popping up on the other side.

Avery laughed. "You're ridiculous."

"And you're losing." He winked and disappeared into the bathroom.

She took her shower and toweled her long hair as much as she could, then hurried to pull her clothes on. She smoothed her bright yellow sundress, then allowed herself two minutes with the hair dryer. Her hair was still damp, but she kept it loose around her shoulders and slipped on a pair of sandals. Grabbing her purse, she was ready to go.

Alex was in the hallway. When he saw her, he tapped his wrist. "Tick tock."

"We have three minutes to spare."

"You look amazing."

She couldn't help the flush of pleasure his words gave her. "Thanks, not-my-boyfriend. You don't look so bad yourself." His plain khakis and blue button-down shirt looked pretty darn fine. Especially with short sleeves that showed off his muscular forearms. Not bad at all.

Chapter Fourteen

Alex let Avery lead the way back to the living room, where about half the family was congregated. "See, Mom, plenty of time." Before she could respond, he said, "Hey, everybody."

The room quieted as everyone looked at him expectantly.

He put an arm around Avery. "This is my friend Avery. Avery, this is Aunt Steph–my mom's sister–and Uncle Frankie. Over here we have their daughter, my cousin Sydney, and her wife, Analise. The gorgeous little one with them is their daughter Hazel." Each person waved as he named them.

Avery gave a little wave. "Hi. Please don't quiz me on names for a day or two."

Analise laughed. "Nope, sorry, pop quiz will come at dinner. Say hello, Hazel."

Hazel, a cherubic curly-haired toddler, buried her face in Sydney's chest, then peeked out.

"Hello, Hazel," Avery said.

Hazel whispered, "Hi."

Steph came over and hugged Avery. "Dolly's told us all about you. We're so glad you could come along so we can get to know you."

"Aww, thank you."

Holly's crew came into the living room. "Okay, we're ready to roll."

Frankie said, "Jack's meeting us at the restaurant."

"Oh, good," Dolly said. "I was hoping he'd make it in time for dinner." She motioned to Alex. "You and Avery can ride with us," she said, then scurried off to fuss over everyone else's travel arrangements.

"You okay riding with my parents?"

It hadn't occurred to her to mind. "Sure, assuming I don't need to sign a waiver or something."

He laughed. "No, my dad retired from stunt driving. We'll be fine."

The crowd spilled out of the house and into their assigned vehicles. Alex pulled the sliding door of his parents' minivan open to let Avery climb in. A short ten minutes later, their group reconvened in the restaurant's parking lot.

"There's Jack." He waved to his cousin, who was leaning against his brand new Camaro. Red, of course. Convertible, of course.

Jack waved and came over. They shook hands and gave each other a one-armed hug. "Good to see you, cuz."

Alex saw Jack do a double take at Avery. A grin spread across his cousin's face. "Avery. What are you doing here with this joker?" He reached over to give Avery a hug, which she easily accepted.

"You two know each other?" He wasn't quite sure how he felt about this development.

"Sure." Jack slung an arm around Avery's shoulders as they started walking toward the restaurant. "She's the best hardware manager I've ever met. Best-looking, too."

She laughed and shoved at his arm. "Flattery won't get you any discounts."

The little pang of what might have been jealousy vanished. He'd half-expected to hear that they'd dated, and that might have made things a tad uncomfortable.

Inside, Jack greeted his parents and his sister's family while Dolly and Bert talked to the hostess. A moment later, their party of fifteen was led to a small room off the main dining area. A massive long table that could seat twenty dominated the room.

Alex noticed Jack was quick to take the seat on the other side of Avery. Not that he blamed him. The other options were limited to their parents or restless children.

Once everyone had staked their seat, Bert asked everyone to join hands while he said grace.

Alex ran his thumb over Avery's knuckles, rather liking the way her hand felt in his.

After the last "Amen," he leaned over and said, "We should get in line."

No hesitation. "Let's go. I'm starving."

Three long buffet tables held every seafood-related dish imaginable. A fourth held a salad bar and a hot non-seafood feast.

"Salad?"

Avery made a face. "Hard pass. I'm not filling up on salad with all this seafood."

"Same." He followed her down the first row, where they piled their plates with steamed shrimp, mussels, lobster macaroni and cheese, chunks of deep-fried fish, and a variety of seafood casserole concoctions. He balanced his plate in one hand and filled a second plate with sauces for them to share.

"I'll grab the silverware," Avery offered.

They made their way through the crowded room, back to their table.

Alex set his plate down. "What would you like to drink? I'll get it."

"Pepsi's good, thanks."

He went back out to get their drinks. Jack stood beside him, filling up his cup. "You and Avery, huh?"

"We're just friends."

Jack winked. "Good to know."

Foam overflowed from the cup and streamed down Alex's hand. "Gah!" He dumped the soda out and got a clean cup. By the time he got back to the table, his hand was sticky.

Jack was saying something to Avery, which made her laugh.

"I'm going to wash my hands," Alex said to no one. He made his way to the restroom. He caught his scowling reflection in the mirror. Well. This was interesting, wasn't it? On the way back to the table, he decided he was only bothered, and only a tiny bit, because Jack was a player. Avery was his friend, and he didn't want her to end up with a guy like Jack and get hurt. Yeah. That was it.

He settled onto his chair.

"All good now?" she asked.

"Yeah. I spilled soda on my hand and it was sticky."

"Eww, that's the worst. I stole some of your cocktail sauce." She pointed to the plate.

"It's for both of us."

She smiled at him. "Good, because I think I took half of it."

He laughed. "We'll get more when we go back for round two."

"You better catch up, I'm almost done with round one."

From across the table, Analise asked, "Avery, how did you and Alex meet?"

Avery set her fork down and gave a theatrical sigh. "His cat broke into my apartment and stole my bra."

That caught everyone's attention.

Alex clarified. "I did *not* have anything to do with it. He jimmied the balcony door open and got into her apartment."

"So I marched over and beat on his door until he let me in and I got my unmentionables back from the little thief."

Laughter filled the room.

"Oh, not even finished. So I'm standing there, holding it in my hand, and that's when I met his mom. She didn't quite believe that we'd just met five minutes ago, and then in comes his dad. While we're explaining that we're not together and I'm already going to die from embarrassment, the rotten little beast sneaks *back* over to my place and comes back with another undergarment."

Alex chimed in, "Yeah, I had to put extra security on the balcony door."

Steph's eyes widened. "Oh, my, if a cat could get in… that's dangerous. You could get robbed."

Avery shook her head. "We're up on the fifth floor. I suppose someone could rappel up the side of the building, but there's really no access. Alex and I share a kind of cement slab, but there's a railing divider that goes all the way up to the awning. Poof shimmied under the railing, but there's not really any way for a person to go from one apartment to the next." She picked her fork back up. "I wasn't worried about being robbed until I ended up with a literal cat burglar."

Sydney said, "Now let's address the elephant in the room. How come you're here by yourself, Jack? I was looking forward to meeting your most current airhead." She snickered behind her hand.

Jack cleared his throat dramatically and pushed his chair back. "Gosh, look at that, I think it's time to get my second plate."

Alex said, "I was wondering about that myself."

"I'm not seeing anyone right now. Taking a break from the whole scene." Jack shrugged, putting a period on the end of the story.

Alex said to Avery, "It's the first time he hasn't brought a new girl along in like ten years."

"Wow."

"He's jealous," Jack said. "He's only brought one girl along in like ten years. Well, two, counting you."

Alex felt his face warm. He and Jack were similar in many ways, but they were polar opposites when it came to women. Jack was all about fun and casualness, where Alex had never been about playing the field unless he was on an actual field.

Avery's eyebrow arched. She said, "Sounds like a matter of quality over quantity."

"Oooh," Sydney cheered. "Avery nailed it."

"Hey, now," Jack laughed. "No need to cast aspersions at my character."

"Not your character," Avery answered immediately. "Your taste."

Around the raucous laughter, Jack argued, "Hey, it's not easy to find a woman like you. If I could—"

"BZZZZT!!" Michael called out. "My BS meter just pegged. Probably not a lot of women like Avery swiping for randos on Tinder."

"What's a Tinder?" Steph asked.

Dolly shrugged, while everyone else had a good laugh.

"You guys suck," Jack said mildly. "I'm going back for more food."

"What's 'suck?'" Kallie asked. Loudly.

Holly sighed at Jack, who made a hasty exit.

Michael saved the situation by explaining, "It's what Hazel does to her binky, and what you used to do to your thumb."

"Oh." Kallie promptly lost interest.

"I'm heading back to the buffet. You coming?" Avery asked Alex.

He was glad for the escape from the chaos for a few minutes. "Right behind you."

When they got back to the table with their third plate of food and fresh drinks, there was an entirely new scene. A blood-curdling scream came from the far end of the table. Alex expected to see blood, but no.

Brayden screamed, "She touched my fish!"

Kallie screamed back, "He took my shrimp!" She grabbed a fistful of food off her brother's plate and flung it at his face.

Hazel sat, wide-eyed, watching the entire scene, then decided to screech in solidarity. Sophie kept eating, completely ignoring her siblings.

Seconds later, Brayden and Kallie were bawling. Holly and Michael looked mortified as they hauled their wailing children out of the room. Their cries echoed the whole way through the lobby, until they were cut off when they presumably got outside.

Dolly and Bert bent to pick the worst of the food off the floor.

Jack leaned over to Avery. "So. You want kids?"

Chapter Fifteen

Avery crawled into the back seat of the minivan, her hand over her belly, wondering how she'd managed to walk out of the restaurant. "I ate too much," she said.

Alex groaned beside her. "You and me both."

She held up her fist. "Worth it."

He bumped her fist with his. "Totally."

Dolly chatted happily, mostly to herself, about how wonderful it was to have everyone together. Bert just drove.

By a few minutes after seven, everyone was accounted for back at the house. The kids were changed and settled on the couch with a movie.

Jack carried his bags in from his car. "Where's my room?"

"Upstairs. You've got the twins."

A devilish grin spread across Jack's face as he wiggled his eyebrows.

"Twin *beds*, creep," Alex laughed.

"Ah, well, the weekend is young." Jack headed to the stairs.

Avery rolled her eyes and followed Alex upstairs. "I think I'm going to change and go sit on the beach," she told him.

"Want company?"

She smiled up at him. "Of course."

A few minutes later, she'd changed into shorts and a T-shirt. She carried a zipper hoodie. Alex met her in the hallway similarly dressed, carrying a rolled up blanket. "Didn't figure we'd be walking much."

"Good thinking. I feel like a slug."

Jack poked his head out of his room. "Best looking slug I've ever seen."

Avery rolled her eyes at him. "Too much, Jack."

He laughed and went back inside the bedroom.

Alex followed her down the stairs. He tapped her arm and motioned to the second hallway that led to the kitchen, so she made a left instead of walking down the hallway that led to the living room. In the kitchen, he pointed to the living room and whispered, "Didn't want the kids to think about going outside and get them all riled up again."

She gave him a thumbs up and tiptoed out the side door. Outside, they snuck across the deck, staying out of view of the living room windows. The sand was cool on her feet. They walked toward the ocean until they found a spot that was dry and away from the house. Alex spread the blanket out on the sand.

Avery sat cross-legged on the blanket and waited for Alex to get situated beside her.

"So, not-my-girlfriend, are you having a good time?"

"Aside from my gut being ready to burst, yes." She pressed a hand to her belly.

The clear blue sky was several shades darker than when they'd left for dinner. The moon was a small, pale circle, patiently waiting its turn to shine.

"Same. Mom's always happy when we get her money's worth, though."

Avery felt a small pang of guilt. "I wish she would have let me pay. I felt bad letting her buy my dinner." She hated feeling indebted to anyone.

"Please don't. She loves taking care of this big family dinner. And if you ask her, she'll tell you it's less work and cheaper than cooking a big meal for everyone. Which is what she used to do. Trust me, this is better, and it really makes her happy. Please don't offer her money. It'll offend her or hurt her feelings or something."

She knew he was right. Offering to pay would be seen, or felt, as a rejection of the gesture. The last thing she wanted to do was hurt Dolly's feelings. "Can I send her flowers when we get back? Would she like that?"

"She'd love it." He laid down, letting his arms fall open wide. "What's your plan for the hardware store when we get back?"

She laid down beside him, using his bicep as a pillow. "I have no idea. I dread checking my phone and seeing if I've missed any emergencies. It's actually been nice to not think about the store at all."

"Same. It's hard to think about short commission checks and updating my résumé with the sound of rolling waves in the background." He rolled onto his side so they faced each other. "I'm going to have to find another job. No matter how much I try to dress it up, what they're doing is theft. I can't live with that."

"Unless it's your cat," she teased.

He groaned. "I should have known you'd bring that up."

"He's more into petty thievery, I guess." She chuckled, thinking about Poof's antics. At least he was cute and mostly innocent. There was nothing cute or innocent about the kind of theft Alex's company was committing.

"I know we're supposed to be using this trip to consider

our options, but I don't want to think about work at all," Alex said.

"Me, either. I'm too stuffed and content." The hypnotic sound of the ocean, the cool breeze, and the slowly darkening sky worked together to make her sleepy. "And it's been a long day."

Alex yawned. "Tomorrow. We'll do the spreadsheet and pro-con lists tomorrow."

"Sounds good." Her eyes felt heavy.

"Think we should go inside before we end up falling asleep?"

She groaned. "That sounds like it requires moving."

"I'm afraid it does."

"Pass."

Alex reached over to brush an escaped lock of hair from her cheek. He tucked it behind her ear.

Avery held her breath, waiting to see what he might do next. She could easily imagine him leaning toward her until their lips met. She would definitely welcome a kiss, if that's where this was headed.

He didn't lean, but his voice was soft. "I'm really glad you decided to come along."

"Me, too," she managed to whisper.

Her hand rested on the blanket between them. Alex brushed another errant piece of hair from her forehead, then put his hand on top of hers. Not quite holding her hand, not quite not.

A seagull squawked loudly and swooped down near them, breaking whatever spell had been weaving around them.

Alex cleared his throat. "The volleyball game will be tomorrow after lunch. I was thinking we could go down to the boardwalk for breakfast."

"How are you talking about food right now?" Avery couldn't imagine a less appealing topic at the moment.

He smirked. "I could probably eat right now."

"You're insane."

Alex laughed as he pulled his arm out from under her head and sat up. Groaning, he got to his knees, then to his feet. "C'mon, let's head in."

"Noooooooo." Avery rolled onto her back and held her hands up in the air.

Alex grabbed them and pulled her up to sitting.

"Ugh."

"You can do it." He was a little too chipper at the prospect of being up and moving.

"Don't blame me if you throw your back out."

"Ready?"

"No," she grumbled.

"One. Two."

"Wait. Are we going *on* three, or after three?"

"Three." He tugged her hands until she got to her feet. "See? I knew you could do it."

"Meh." She watched as he bent down to pick up the blanket.

He shook the loose sand and folded the blanket, then tucked it under his arm. He offered his other elbow to Avery. "Okay, not-my-girlfriend, let's get inside."

She slipped her hand around his elbow. "I don't wanna." It wasn't totally true. After the sun set, the air got chillier by the minute.

They snuck in the same side kitchen door they'd exited through, and tiptoed toward the hallway. They needn't have bothered. All the kids were fast asleep across the couches. As were the adults.

Avery hurried past the doorway and up the stairs. Standing

between their bedroom doors, she said, "I'm going to get up early to hunt for seashells."

"I think high tide is around six, so I'm not sure we'll get too much."

"Really? Dang." She hadn't given the tide any thought.

"We could try around seven, see if anything washed up."

"You're coming with me?" She liked the idea a lot.

"Of course."

On a whim, she wrapped her arms around his middle and squeezed. "You're such a good not-boyfriend."

She had a split second of wondering if she'd made a mistake before he hugged her back and softly chuckled against her hair. "I try my best. Good night."

"Night."

They both hesitated for a moment, and again, Avery wondered if he was going to kiss her. A thump in the stairwell made her pull away from him.

"Hey, guys. You going to bed already?" Jack came up the stairs. "I was going to have a drink if you want to join me?"

The moment evaporated. Avery shook her head. "I'm pretty well frozen and tired. Maybe tomorrow night."

He winked. "It's a date. Alex?"

Alex looked at her, then back to Jack. "Yeah, sure."

Avery stepped into her room and gave them a finger-wiggle wave. "You boys have fun. I'll see you in the morning."

"Night," Alex said.

She gave him a smile and closed the door. A few minutes later, she was in her pajamas, warming up under the covers. Her mind played the evening over and over. Twice she'd thought Alex might kiss her.

She couldn't wait to see what developments the next day might bring on that front.

Chapter Sixteen

Alex would have rather gone to bed, but it was barely nine o'clock and he hadn't spent time with Jack in months.

Jack bounded down the stairs.

Alex tossed the beach blanket on the floor next to his bed and followed his cousin to the kitchen, where Jack had already mixed a drink. He pushed the glass of dark, bubbly liquid to Alex.

Alex sat on a barstool at the island. "What is it?"

"My namesake, of course. Jack and Coke. What else?"

Alex held his glass up and clinked it with Jack's. "What have you been up to these days?"

Jack sat on the stool catty-cornered from Alex and pushed out a breath. "Work, work, and more work. We just finished a major remodel this morning, which is why I ended up not getting here until late. The homeowners were thrilled and took a stack of business cards. Said they have a bunch of friends who are looking to have work done. Rick's been hiring left and right to keep up with the demand."

"That's great." He meant it. Jack had always been able to

build anything, and now he was making a nice career for himself.

Jack made an abrupt subject change. "I didn't know you live next to Avery."

Alex knew he was fishing for information. "You know her pretty well?" He got the vibe they were friendly acquaintances, and probably nothing more, but with Jack, anything was possible. It seemed like he'd dated ninety percent of the single women in the tristate area.

"Nah. Just from the hardware store. You guys giving it a go?"

Alex had no idea how to answer that one. He couldn't very well jump the gun and say yes, even though they were having a great time together, but saying no didn't feel accurate either. "We're friends. I don't know if it'll ever go somewhere else or not."

Jack drained the last of his drink. "You should lock that down. The two of you are a great match. Unless you're still waiting on Chelsea."

He nearly choked on his drink. "No. That ship has sailed."

"Have you heard from her at all?"

"Nope." Something in Jack's voice made him curious. "Have you?"

Jack poured another drink. "She texts me every now and then but never really says anything. It's kind of weird."

Alex sat back and nearly slipped off the barstool. "Why would she text you?"

"Beats me." He shrugged. "If you ask me though, Avery's a major upgrade."

"Oooh, what are we having?" Sydney came through the doorway and sat down on the stool next to Alex. "Jack and Coke, I bet."

"We have a winner," Jack said, pouring a drink for his sister.

Alex wanted to know more about Chelsea texting Jack, but he decided to let it go. He didn't like the idea of them getting together–or hooking up–but it wasn't his business anymore. And now that he gave it some thought, he knew that was a line Jack wouldn't cross.

They spent the next hour talking about Hazel and the plans for Sydney and Analise's new house. Alex nodded in all the right places and asked the right questions, but he had trouble keeping his attention on the conversation. Just before eleven, he decided to tap out.

"I'm heading to bed. Avery wants to get up early and look for shells." He gave Sydney a kiss on the cheek and clapped Jack's shoulder. "Night."

He left his cousins and went upstairs to bed.

In the morning, he was awakened by the lilting melody of the trash truck under his window. He groaned and pulled the pillow over his head. It was barely light out. He rolled over and smacked his phone to light it up. Just after five. He debated going back to sleep or getting up. The drinks he'd had the night suddenly demanded to be released, so he got up to pee, trying to keep his eyes almost shut, but it didn't work. He woke up fully, against his will. Might as well get dressed and ready to go seashell hunting.

The mornings were chilly, so he pulled on a pair of jeans and tugged a hoodie over his T-shirt. He scrolled through social media for a few minutes, until a soft tap at the door got his attention. He hurried over to pull the door open.

"Good morning," he said quietly.

"Good morning," Avery whispered back. "I wasn't sure if you'd be up." She held up a mesh bag. "I'm heading out for shells if you want to come along."

Alex nodded. The other bedroom doors were still closed, so they tiptoed downstairs, past the closed bedroom doors on the first floor. He quietly unlocked the sliding door and tugged it open.

The sound of the ocean roared into the room. They hurried outside and Alex closed the door. The sky over the ocean was slowly turning from black to blue, the stars fading as the light inched higher up the horizon.

The sand was cold under his bare feet. "I figured Mom would be up already."

"Is she typically an early bird?" She tugged her hoodie tighter around her.

"She is on vacation, anyway. She likes to come out onto the beach and watch the sun rise."

Avery nudged his arm. "That might be her."

He looked to where she was pointing, along the water's edge, probably three hundred yards away from them, where a person walked. He squinted, not that it helped him see. "I bet it is."

"So much for being the first ones up, huh?"

They reached the wettest sand. Alex sucked a breath through his teeth as the white foamy edge of the water slid over his feet. "Hooooooooooly crap that's cold."

Avery picked up a tiny white shell. "Slim pickings. You were probably right about the tide being too high."

She sounded disappointed. Alex looked around, but didn't see any other shells. "Don't worry. This section of the beach is mostly private, so it doesn't get too picked over. I bet if we go get breakfast and come back, we'll have a lot better luck."

He took a step back. The odd sensation of the sand leaking out from under his feet took him a little off balance.

"At least we can still catch the sunrise," she said. She was standing calf-deep in the cold water.

"Aren't your feet freezing?"

She turned around, grinning. "I can't feel my toes, but it's totally worth it."

"I think you're right about being a mermaid."

A couple jogged past, and up ahead, Dolly had turned around and was heading back in their direction.

The sky grew lighter by tiny degrees. At the far edge of the ocean, the sky had turned a bright baby blue.

"You want to sit and watch the sun come up?" He had no intention of standing in the freezing water. He backed up until he was far enough from the rolling ocean that his feet would stay dry.

Avery bounded over to him, sand sticking to her feet. "This looks like a good spot."

They settled onto a mound of sand.

The first streak of pink touched the horizon as Dolly reached them. "Good morning," she called cheerily.

Avery patted the sand beside her. "Come watch the sun rise with us."

He appreciated that she made the gesture before he could.

"Are you sure?" his mom was a little out of breath.

"Absolutely," Avery answered.

Dolly settled onto the sand. "Whew, what a beautiful walk. I've already got my ten thousand steps in for the day." She tapped her FitBit watch.

"Wow."

"And I'm planning to walk the Boardwalk after the volley-ball game. My calves are going to be screaming tonight." She stopped abruptly. "Oh, would you look at that."

They lapsed into silence, simply watching the tiniest sliver of the sun slip up out of the ocean. The blue in the sky made way for spectacular splashes of orange and pink that seemed to pull the sun upward.

Over the next several minutes, the sun peeked over the horizon, then inched upward, its brightness chasing away the last of the stars. A bright orange path appeared over the water, pointing the way to the sun.

A sandpiper landed in front of them, running toward the water, poking its beak into the sand, then running away as the water rolled back toward the shore. A handful of squawking gulls broke the quiet sanctity of the moment.

Alex stretched. "We're heading to breakfast, Mom. You want to come along?"

"No, thanks. Your dad found a place he wants to try."

Alex nodded. That was his mom's code for "your dad and I are doing our own thing and don't want anyone else tagging along." When he was a kid, he'd never understood why his parents made such a fuss about spending time alone together, but as an adult, he couldn't be more grateful that his parents had made their marriage a priority.

"I hope it's good."

"The website looks like their pancakes are as big as your head."

Avery said, "Mmm, you can't go wrong with giant pancakes."

They all stood and brushed sand off their pants, then walked to the house.

Alex said, "I just have to grab my shoes and my wallet."

Avery said, "I need to use the bathroom quick, then I'm ready."

Five minutes later, Alex opened the car door for Avery to get in. Fifteen minutes after that, they found the one lone spot in one of the public lots and walked the block to the boardwalk.

Avery pulled in a deep breath. "There's nothing better than fresh ocean air."

"I can think of something better."

She looked at him, surprised. "What?"

He inclined his head toward a set of stairs leading to a huge deck with smiling hostess at a podium. "Breakfast in the fresh ocean air." Gesturing for her to walk ahead of him, they were soon seated at a table overlooking the boardwalk.

"You're right. Breakfast definitely adds something."

The boardwalk was still mostly sleeping. Only a handful of shops were open, and even fewer restaurants were operating and serving breakfast. The beach was peppered with people jogging, looking for shells, or just sitting in the sand.

The outdoor dining area they were in was nearly half-full. The heady scent of bacon and pancakes wafted over the deck, mingling with the ocean air.

"What are you having?" Alex asked.

Avery tapped her finger on the menu. "Strawberry stuffed French toast with a side of bacon."

His stomach rumbled. "That sounds good. Where'd you see that?"

She reached over and lightly touched his menu. "Flip it over."

He flipped his menu over and sighed when Avery tapped the French toast section. "Too many options."

"Better decide, our waitress is coming."

"Go ahead, I'll be ready."

They ordered their food and sat in comfortable silence, looking out over the beach. The waitress brought a carafe of orange juice and surprisingly, delivered their food just a few minutes later.

Alex popped a piece of bacon in his mouth. "How are you feeling about the hardware store today?"

She carefully spread the whipped topping over her French toast, considering her answer. "It's easy to say that if it wasn't my family, I'd quit in a heartbeat, because I would. But it *is* my family, and I just can't take that out of the equation. I think what I really need to do is set some boundaries, but don't ask me how I plan to do that."

"How do you plan to do that?" Alex joked, then grew serious. "No, I get it. My parents haven't really pushed, but they constantly remind me that the family insurance agency is always an option for me. I know they just want to make sure I know I have an option to fall back on, but sometimes it makes me feel guilty. I can only imagine how much pressure you've got on you."

She swallowed her food. "I texted Mom last night to see how things were going, but she ignored the question and asked how the trip was. I'm not sure if that means she's mad that I'm not there, or if things are fine, or what. And don't bother telling me not to read too much into it, because I can't help it."

Alex mimed zipping his lips and tossed the imaginary key over his shoulder. That's exactly the advice he would have given her, but then again, maybe she didn't want advice at all. "You'll figure it out, Avery."

They finished their breakfast. Alex paid the check and followed Avery down the restaurant stairs and onto the boardwalk.

She looked up at him. "Do you want to see what's open?"

"Sure."

They walked down the boardwalk, stopping in a handful of shops that were opening for the day. "I need to stop at the candy place and get some taffy and fudge for my parents."

"Get them all sugared up and then lay down the law. Good plan."

She laughed. "I hadn't thought of that, but yes, that's exactly what I'll do."

As they walked, Alex came to a sudden stop. "I have to buy you that T-shirt. You need it."

"What?" Avery squinted, trying to see which display he was referring to.

"Come on." He laughed and stepped into the shop. He stopped in front of a row of T-shirts. "This one."

"That. Is. Brilliant."

Avery's reaction to the bright red T-shirt emblazoned with the words THIS IS NOT A DRILL over a picture of a hammer was exactly what he'd hoped.

"You're right. I need that. I'll wear it to work. Oh! You need this one." She grabbed the hem of a bright green T-shirt.

"Yes!" He laughed and pulled it from the rack. The shirt had a drawing of a beer pitcher with the words "Relief Pitcher."

Alex paid for their shirts and they strolled next door to the candy place.

"What do you like?" Avery asked.

"All of it."

"I'll buy you some candy since you bought me a shirt."

"What are you getting?"

"Like fifty pounds of fudge and a box of taffy."

He studied the flavor board hanging behind the glass cases. "Yeah, I want in on the fudge. Peanut butter ripple."

"My favorite." She ordered four pounds of peanut butter ripple fudge, fudge with peanut butter cups, fudge with Snickers bar chunks, fudge with caramel, chocolate marshmallow fudge, something else… and a box of salt water taffy. "Should I get fudge for your parents? Do they like fudge?"

"They like the taffy." It impressed him that she considered his parents so often. It was so nice to be hanging out with someone who didn't stir up a bunch of unnecessary drama in his family.

She grabbed another box of taffy.

"I'll grab a box for Lincoln, too." Alex paid for his box after Avery checked out.

"Have you talked to him? How's the devil cat?"

"Har, har. I texted him this morning. Lincoln, not Poof, and they're doing fine. Mostly."

Avery looked at him, her eyebrow arched, suspicious. "Mostly?"

Alex held the door open for her to pass through with her heavy bag of sweets. "Lincoln might have mentioned that Poof snuck out into the hallway, but he wrangled him back inside before he could get too far."

She smirked, but said nothing.

"Yeah, I know. At least he didn't get into any trouble."

"This time. The weekend is young." She laughed and shifted her bag to her other hand.

"Need anything else?"

"We're coming back, aren't we?"

"Definitely."

"I'll need to get some sort of cheesy souvenir to take home."

"Of course. It's practically beach law."

The amount of people on the boardwalk seemed to increase in direct relation to the rising temperature. A police officer rode past on a bicycle, while a handful of shirtless teenage boys on skateboards whizzed by in the opposite direction. They crossed the hot blacktop road back to Alex's car, then inched with the slow-moving traffic headed back to the house.

Alex helped carry the fudge into the house, where, as he

expected, his mother was touched and excited to have a box of taffy. She gathered Avery into a hug. "You're so thoughtful."

"It's the least I could do."

Alex could have predicted Dolly's response, right down to the hand-waving dismissal and exact inflection of her "Don't be silly." He grinned as he leaned over and gave her a kiss on the cheek. "Just say thanks, Mom."

She shooed him away. "Thank you, Avery. Now both of you get out of the kitchen so I can make lunch."

Chapter Seventeen

After a light lunch of sandwiches and fruit, Avery changed into her blue sporty bathing suit and twisted her long hair into a tight braid so it wouldn't end up in her face, and hopefully wouldn't accumulate a ton of sand. The entire family congregated on the deck overlooking the beach. The kids were seated at the picnic table with popsicles.

Dolly hollered for everyone's attention. "All right, let's get the teams sorted. Couples can't play on the same team. Sydney, you're over here. Analise, there." She directed each person to a side, until the two teams were set. Avery, Sydney, Michael, and Frankie made up the first team, while the second team was Alex, Analise, Steph, and Holly. "Oh, dear. Jack, you're the odd man out."

"No," Steph said. "He can take my spot. Bert and I can sub as needed."

"Why can't we play?" Kallie asked, orange syrup dripping down her chin.

"You'll play soon. This game is for the grownups." Dolly leaned down and said, "but when they're done, we'll get some ice cream."

"Ice cream!" Kallie and Brayden bounced up and down, clapping their sticky hands.

Avery took her spot in the back row with Sydney.

Sydney grinned at her. "We play for blood, not for fun. Just so you know."

Avery tossed the ball up and caught it. "My favorite way to play."

They high fived and got into position.

Dolly blew a whistle and Avery served the ball, smacking it hard to the other team. Holly tapped the ball into the air and Jack smacked it back over the net, where Michael hit it right back. It flew through Alex's hands and landed in the sand.

"YEAH!" Avery high-fived her teammates. She hadn't realized how much she missed playing. The adrenaline rush, the high fives, the workout, the sweat, she missed all of it.

Despite the fast start, both teams were evenly matched, and the score stayed close. The sun was high in the sky, but the steady breeze from the water took the edge off the heat.

The ball sailed into the net off Michael's hand, giving the other team another point. Michael picked the ball up. "Argh, sorry guys."

"Alex!"

The unfamiliar woman's singsong voice made all their heads turn.

Avery noticed two things immediately. One, Dolly was frowning. It was the first time Avery had ever seen her without a smile on her face. Two, the newcomer was stunning.

Alex hesitated, but he left the game and hurried toward the woman. "Chelsea."

Oh, geez. This was the ex. Avery wanted to gag. Chelsea was five feet tall, tops, with perfectly curled ombre-blonde hair that fell to the middle of her back. Her figure was perfectly proportioned, expertly showcased in a low-cut white sundress that stopped mid-thigh, with stunning tanned legs set off by her sky-high wedge sandals. Her makeup was on point, highlighting her cheekbones, plumped lips, and emerald-green eyes, which were home to a set of eyelashes Avery couldn't even imagine blinking with.

Avery felt like a toad in comparison, standing there in her utilitarian swimsuit, sand caked to her sweaty skin. She felt her face heat as Alex bent to hug Chelsea. She didn't mean to stare but couldn't seem to help it.

Steph hopped up from her lounge chair and took Alex's place on the team.

"Avery, your serve," Jack called.

Grateful for the distraction, Avery took the ball from Michael and served it. Straight into the net. "Sorry, guys."

Jack clapped his hands. "Re-serve it. I'm granting you one do over."

Frankie tossed the ball back to her. She gave Jack a grateful nod, then served the ball high over the net. Analise batted it up into the air to Holly, who sent it sailing across the net. Michael hit the ball up. It arced over his head. Sydney tapped it toward Avery.

From the deck, Chelsea squealed and giggled Alex's name.

The ball smacked Avery in the face. It bounced off her cheek and landed in the sand at her feet. She pressed a hand to her face. The sand from the ball had scraped the sand on her face, stinging her skin. Great.

"You okay?" Sydney ran over and grabbed Avery's wrist to pull her hand off her face. She put her finger under Avery's chin to tilt her face and inspect the injury. "That sounded like it hurt."

Grains of sand had found their way into her eye, which watered uncomfortably. Now she felt ten times stupider, and she'd probably end up sporting a nice bruise on her cheek.

Dolly ran over with a clean towel and reached up to gently wipe the sand off her cheek. "Did it hit you in the eye?"

"No." Avery shook her head and submitted to Dolly's fussing. "I'm fine, thanks. It's just sand from the ball."

Bert came over and patted her shoulder. "You take five. I'll fill in."

Avery wanted to argue, but it looked like Bert actually wanted to play, so she took the towel from Dolly and nodded. "Good luck."

He held up his fist for her to bump with her own.

She bumped his fist, then trotted over to the deck. For a second, she wondered why Alex hadn't checked on her. Then she realized Alex and Chelsea were gone. She kept as much focus on the game as she could, half-heartedly cheering and clapping for her team. The kids had abandoned the deck in favor of playing in the sand under a shade canopy.

Avery sat alone, trying to focus on the sea air and the game and the fact that her eye had stopped watering, but it was no use. Her mind wanted to know where Alex and Chelsea disappeared to… and it didn't want to know. It conjured up all sorts of scenarios, none of them pleasant or reassuring.

"That's game," Frankie announced.

Jack walked over and held out his hand for her to shake. "Congrats. I'll buy you a beer."

"Thanks." She jerked her thumb over her shoulder. "I'm going to go grab a shower."

"You sure? I was going to boogie board for a little bit. Wanna come?"

She looked out at the ocean. Going into the water sounded infinitely better than walking inside and seeing something she didn't want to see. "Yeah."

They got the boards out of the shed, reapplied sunscreen, and walked across the hot sand.

"Full disclosure," Jack began. "Chelsea texted me a few weeks ago and asked if Alex was going to be here. I said I thought so, but I never asked her why, and she never told me she was planning to show up."

She didn't know what to say, so she just said, "Okay." What was Chelsea's game if she didn't even ask Alex himself?

"I mean it, Avery. If I had any idea she was going to show up, I would have told Alex. I had no idea, and I guarantee you *he* had no clue."

"I believe you." She reached the edge of the water and fastened the strap to her wrist. "But we're just friends, so it's not a big deal. Just super awkward."

He gave her a look, like he didn't quite believe her, but she ignored it and pushed into the water.

For a while, she swam and dove and reveled in the feel of the water on her skin, forgetting all about her sore face, the almost-kiss with Alex, and Chelsea's unexpected appearance. She dove under a wave and rode it to the shore, where Jack sat in the sand. She called to him, "Are you done already?"

"I'm getting hungry. But if you're not done, don't get out on my account."

She shook the water out of her ears. Her long braid slapped over her shoulder. She squeezed the dripping water out of it. "Nah, I'm starting to get hungry, too." The light lunch had been great to fuel up for the game, but she was definitely ready to eat again.

He jumped up and brushed sand off his legs. "What are you hungry for?"

"Anything. I could gorge myself again at the buffet, or I could go for pizza or a sub or wings or a burger."

He flashed a brilliant smile. "I know a place with great wings and loaded tater tots."

Avery laughed. "Do you mean Hooters? Really?"

"I know, I know, but the wings really are good."

"Let's see what Al- everyone else wants to do." A lump of dread settled in her belly as she walked up the deck stairs. She took more time than necessary spraying the sand from her legs and feet, but couldn't stall any longer when Jack opened the door for her.

She stepped into the living room and could immediately feel the tension in the room. Chelsea stood, arms crossed, looking up at Alex while Dolly scowled at her. Sydney and Analise hustled Hazel out of the room under the mumbled pretense of getting her changed. Michael and Holly and the kids were already absent. Bert stood next to Dolly, his hand on her back.

Dolly straightened her shoulders and put a smile on her face. "Avery, sweetheart, I don't think you met… Chelsea." The name sounded like it was being forced out of her mouth.

"I haven't." She managed a smile. "Hi."

Chelsea's tarantula eyelashes swept down and back up. She smirked and gave a snide, "My goodness aren't you… *tall.*"

Avery took half a step back as a tidal wave of old emotions and insecurities washed over her. *Oh, so that's how it's gonna be.* She fought the urge to slouch down, and instead stood straight. No way was this bitch getting under her skin. "Yeah. I was *invited* to get stuff off the high shelves."

"Ave," Alex began.

"I'm going to get a shower." She walked down the hall, forcing herself not to go too fast, but she couldn't help but run up the stairs to her room. She turned to close her door and saw straight into Alex's room. A floral suitcase mocked her from its place beside his bed. Great. Just great.

As she climbed into the shower, she caught her reflection.

Her cheek was still fiery red from the impact of the ball. With her luck, it would probably bruise. Perfect.

This was turning into the worst weekend ever. She should have just gone to work.

<h1 style="text-align:center">Chapter Eighteen</h1>

Alex turned to Chelsea. "Don't do that again." He was louder than he'd intended, but he was still flustered from her sudden appearance and now her rudeness to Avery.

"What?" She batted her eyes innocently.

"Knock it off. You're not going to be like that with Avery." Whatever happened, he valued Avery's friendship.

Dolly cleared her throat. "We're going to have to get ready for dinner, Chelsea. Where are you staying?"

Chelsea gave her a brilliant smile. "Here." She quickly added, "If that's okay."

Dolly's eyebrows climbed. "We don't have any extra rooms."

"I'll just stay with Alex. We have a lot to talk about. It'll be just like old times."

Alex saw the angry red streaks climbing up the skin above his mom's neckline. He shook his head. The message in her hard look was crystal clear: "Handle this. Now." She stalked into the kitchen without another word, closely followed by Bert, who didn't look any happier than his wife. Most likely because his wife wasn't happy. Alex knew his parents lived the old adage: *If mama ain't happy, ain't nobody happy.*

He gestured to the door. "Let's go outside and talk." Since she'd arrived, all she'd done was gush about how happy she was to see him. It was time to find out why.

On the deck, Chelsea sat on one of the chairs and lifted her hand to shield her eyes from the brightness. "Alex, you must know why I came."

"I assure you, I don't."

"I have a lot of regrets about how things ended." She crossed her legs, letting her skirt slide up on her leg. "I guess I should have let you know I was coming."

"Yeah. You should have." Wait, no, it was even simpler than that. She shouldn't have come at all.

"I thought you'd like the surprise. I certainly didn't expect you to have a friend tagging along." She waved her hand dismissively.

He hated surprises. And the way she referred to Avery made him bristle. He had no idea what she might be thinking, but it probably wasn't good. "How'd you know I was going to be here at all?"

"I texted Jack."

Would have been nice if he'd have mentioned that Chelsea was planning to drop in when he said they occasionally texted. "Why do you even have his number?" He shook his head. "Never mind."

"Don't be jealous, baby." Chelsea reached over and brushed her fingertips on his knee. "Who is she? I couldn't help but notice you're not sharing a room. Seems like that means something."

Alex pulled his leg away. "Yeah, well, I'm not sharing a room with you, either. You can't stay here." He heard voices inside the house.

"You can't be serious." She crossed her arms over her chest, making it a point to lift her boobs.

He looked away. "I am." Yes, she was beautiful. Yes, he missed her sometimes. But he thought of all the times he'd imagined this very scenario. Chelsea, back and admitting she'd been wrong, wanting to try again. In his imagination, he'd always taken her in his arms and they'd decide to live happily ever after. But sitting here, right now, he didn't want to. Whether it was Avery or the time that had passed, he didn't know.

The door slid open. Avery stepped out, wearing denim shorts and a pink sweatshirt. "Sorry to interrupt."

He hated the uncertainty behind those words. "You're not. What's up?"

"We were deciding on dinner. It looks like everyone else has plans, but Jack suggested we go to Hooters."

He raised an eyebrow. "You're okay with that?"

"They have good wings."

"It's fine with me." To be honest, he would have agreed to go anywhere Avery wanted.

Chelsea said, "Me, too."

"Oh." Alex wasn't sure what to say.

"Great." Avery's voice was flat. She turned and went back inside, sliding the door shut behind her.

"Ooohhh, was I not invited?" Chelsea smirked, but quickly forced her face into a neutral expression.

His nerves were beginning to wear. "You should figure out where you're staying."

"I'm hungry, Alex. I can do that after we eat, okay?"

With a sigh, he went inside to put shoes on and grab his wallet from his room.

Jack popped his head in Alex's bedroom and said, "For the

record, this is a horrible idea. I'll drive Avery, because I'm not putting the two of them in the same vehicle."

Alex glared. "It's a horrible idea because you invited Chelsea."

Jack pushed back from the doorframe and stood straight. Scowling, he pointed at Alex. "Whoa there, get your story straight. Chelsea texted me one question. If you were going to be here. I said yes. That was the entire conversation. I didn't invite her. Mom'd have my head on a platter if I did that."

True enough. Alex backed down. He'd known Jack forever. He had his faults, but he wasn't a liar. "You didn't invite her, and she never told you she was coming."

"Never. I'll show you the texts." He pulled out his phone, tapped it a few times, and handed it to Alex. "See?"

Alex looked at the texts. All two of them. "Sorry."

"You don't need to apologize to me. I just hope you know what you're doing."

Downstairs, Chelsea stood in the living room, while Avery was in the kitchen with Dolly and Steph.

Jack held up his keys. "Your chariot awaits, milady."

Avery smiled at him and Alex's jaw clenched. Jack was right. This was a terrible idea.

Chelsea grabbed his hand and he pulled it away. They all filed outside and Alex watched as Jack opened the car door for Avery. He let Chelsea open her own door. She shouldn't be here anyway.

On the way, Chelsea put her hand on his leg and he nearly drove into the median. "Stop it." He shoved her hand off.

"Alex. Look. I made a mistake leaving you like I did. I'm sorry, and I want to fix things between us."

"I'm not here alone."

She threw her head back and laughed. The sound was

musical, but in a scary way that reminded him of a fairy tale villainess.

"What's so funny?"

"You say that, but the fact is, you picked me, Alex."

Her words sent a chill down his spine. "What do you mean I picked you?"

"I'm here with you. She's not. You didn't even suggest that I go with Jack so she could go with you. It's pretty clear." She leaned over and put her hand on his arm. "I'm sorry. I guess I'm just a little jealous. I wasn't expecting you to be with someone, at least not seriously enough to bring them on your family vacation." She sighed and looked demurely down at the floor. "Your parents seem to like her."

"She's amazing, and they like her a lot."

Chelsea winced.

He hadn't meant it as any kind of dig at her, but it wasn't any secret that she'd never really connected with his parents–or wanted to. And Avery fit right in. Avery. Did *she* think he'd picked Chelsea just because he was driving her to the restaurant? Probably. *Crap.*

"I want to talk about us."

"There hasn't been an 'us' for a year."

"Yeah, but we were together for four years before that. Doesn't our history mean anything? Don't we owe it to ourselves to try again? Give me a chance, Alex, just one chance to show you we should be together."

The scent of her expensive Dior J'adore perfume brought back a flood of memories. They weren't all bad.

He pulled into the parking space beside Jack's car. The four of them walked the block to the restaurant without a word.

A hostess greeted them with a big smile. "Right this way." She led them to a bar-height table.

Chelsea pulled an innocent face and said, "It must be nice for you that these big tables are so popular now."

Avery shot back, "How inconsiderate of me. I'll ask the waitress to bring you a step stool and a booster seat."

Alex noticed Jack's arm go around Avery. He leaned close and said something in her ear.

She nodded, took a deep breath, and focused all her attention on her menu.

Alex felt awful. This situation was crap, and it was mostly his fault. He shouldn't have let Chelsea come along. In fact, he shouldn't have agreed to talk to her at all. He should have sent her packing the minute she showed up. And *he* should be the one backing Avery up and putting his arm around her, because if anyone was one hundred percent blameless here, it was Avery.

But he couldn't change anything, so now his goal was to get through this awful dinner and then get Chelsea gone.

It felt like a hundred years before the waitress set their appetizers on the table. Alex felt a pang as Jack and Avery shared an order of the loaded tater tots. He looked at his onion rings. "Want some?" He held the basket over to Avery.

She held his eyes for a moment, then reached to take one. "Sure."

He set the basket back down.

Chelsea reached over him to grab an onion ring from his basket. "I'd love one, thanks."

He kept his eyes on Avery, willing her to understand that he wasn't enjoying this.

Jack broke the silence. "So Chelsea. What are you doing these days?"

"Fashion design." She sat up straight and moved her shoulders. "I designed this dress." Her eyes swung to Avery. "What do *you* do?"

Avery took a long sip of her soda. "I manage a hardware store."

"How positively *fascinating*."

"Knock it off." Alex nudged Chelsea with his elbow.

"I'm surprised is all. I assumed you worked for… I don't know… Amazon." She giggled at her own joke, adding a hand gesture to indicate height. Hilarious.

Chapter Nineteen

The waitress chose that exact moment to bring their entrees to the table. Avery focused on adjusting the napkin in her lap, glad she'd been interrupted before the nasty comment on the tip of her tongue had slipped out. She didn't want to be the kind of person who made belittling jokes at someone else's expense. Even if that someone was Chelsea.

As soon as the waitress left, Alex leaned close to Chelsea and said something too low to overhear. It must have been good, though, because Chelsea's smile vanished. Her brow furrowed and her eyes flashed with anger.

Alex straightened.

Chelsea took a sip of her soda—diet, of course—and fixed her gaze on Avery. With the fakest of fake smiles, she said, "I am *so* sorry for teasing you about being freakishly tall."

"Chelsea!" Alex's tone was exasperation and anger.

Jack's arm came to rest on her back, a show of support.

"You know what, I'm sorry." Alex's hand came across the table to squeeze Avery's. "This was a huge mistake." He lifted his arm to get the waitress's attention. When she came over, he said, "Could we get some to go boxes, please?"

"Sure thing, is everything okay?"

"Yeah. Thanks."

Chelsea glared. "I'm not eating my dinner out of a Styrofoam container."

"Then don't eat." Alex met her glare with one of his own.

Her eyes widened in surprise, then narrowed. "What?"

The waitress came back with to go containers for everyone.

Jack leaned over to Avery's ear. "Let's stay here. Doesn't make sense for us to all go back to the house at the same time and continue this."

"Excellent point." Avery completely agreed with Jack's assessment. She watched Alex and Chelsea box up their meals and get up to leave.

Alex hesitated, looking at Avery. "We'll talk later, okay?"

"Sure." She didn't want to admit how much it stung that he was leaving, even though it was probably the best of the current options. At least he seemed reluctant.

She watched Alex walk out, following Chelsea's swinging hips. "Seriously? They were together four years? I can barely stand her for four minutes."

Jack said, "She's not usually this bad." He dipped a chicken wing in ranch dressing and gnawed the meat off the bone. Around the mouthful of chicken, he added, "Bet she expected to come in and have Alex fall all over her, and you're here, so she's crazy jealous. He's such a steady one-woman man that she probably figured he was still mooning over her. Never thought he'd move on."

Had he? He'd seemed a little wistful when they were talking about past relationships on their way down the road. She ate her wings and used the wet wipe to clean barbecue sauce off her fingers.

"Wings were pretty good," Jack said, washing them down with a swig of soda.

"Yeah. Would have been better hot, though." The drama had taken too long and the food cooled down.

"Agreed."

The waitress cleared their empty plates. "Dessert?"

Before Avery could answer, Jack said, "Yes. I want a set of shooters."

"What are they?" Avery assumed it was something alcoholic.

The waitress gave her a big smile. "They're amazing. It's four shot glass-sized desserts. There's a peanut butter pie with a cookie crumble, strawberry cheesecake with cookie crumbles, a key lime pie with graham cracker crumble, and my favorite, a chocolate mousse with chocolate ganache over a chocolate crumble."

"Sounds fantastic. I'll have that as well."

With another smile, the waitress left to get their desserts and drink refills.

"Can I ask you a personal question?" Jack asked.

"You can ask." With Jack, there was no telling what he might be thinking.

"Is being tall an issue? I mean, she was really going to town with the tall insults."

Definitely not what she thought he was going to ask. "Not so much anymore. I was really self-conscious about it when I was a teenager. Surrounded by mean girls like her, of course. Being a teenage girl sucks. Anything that makes you stand out is fuel for trifling petty people like Chelsea. Braces, glasses, being tall, being poor... all of it."

"I kind of get it. I was scrawny and had braces and bad acne all through high school. Didn't do my social life any favors."

She couldn't imagine Jack as anything other than confident and good looking. He might not be steady boyfriend material, but he was easy on the eyes. "You seem to have made up for it as an adult."

"Yeah, getting hot helped." He flexed an arm and winked at her.

Avery rolled her eyes. "Dessert's here."

Laughing, he put his arm down and thanked the waitress.

Avery looked at the four little desserts in front of her. "Oh, gosh, I'm not sure whether to start with the one that looks best, or save it for last."

"Let's rank them. My top choice would be the chocolate." He put the chocolate shot glass at the front of his line.

She wrinkled her nose. "That's my last choice."

"Really?"

"Yes. My top choice would be the strawberry cheesecake or the peanut butter." They both looked delicious.

"Hmm. My ranking goes: chocolate, key lime, peanut butter, with strawberry coming in a distant last."

She rearranged her shot glasses in order. "Mine is: strawberry, peanut butter, key lime, chocolate."

"Wanna trade?"

"Huh?" Trade rankings? What was he talking about?

Jack pointed to her chocolate mousse. "I'll give you my strawberry for your chocolate. Then we can start *and* finish with our favorite."

That was the best offer she could imagine. "Deal." She put her chocolate mousse cup on Jack's plate while he put his strawberry dessert on hers. She took a bite of the first cup of strawberry cheesecake. "Mmm, this is amazing."

"So's this." Jack clinked his chocolate shot glass against her strawberry one. "Teamwork."

She polished off her peanut butter and key lime desserts, then leaned back in her chair. "If we hadn't swapped, I'd tap out. But the strawberry was so good I can't let it go to waste."

Jack patted his flat belly. "Tell me about it."

Avery picked up her spoon.

"We can do this." He grabbed his chocolate dessert. "Last one done pays the check."

"What?"

"Ready?"

She looked at the strawberry dessert. Three bites. Two if she tried hard.

"Set."

She poised her spoon.

"Go." Jack shoveled a bite of chocolate dessert in his mouth, smearing a blob on his lip.

Avery tried not to laugh as she wolfed down her dessert, then slammed the shot glass on the table. "Done!"

Jack swallowed and set his cup down. "Dang. You beat me by this much." He held his thumb and forefinger a quarter of an inch apart.

"I'm gonna barf." Avery groaned and rubbed her stomach.

"Here. Have a little hair of the dog." He offered her a cold onion ring.

"Eww. I think that only works for alcohol. And I think it's for the morning after."

Jack grinned as he pulled out his wallet. "I've had that a time or two."

"Why am I not surprised?"

The waitress came back over. "How'd you like the dessert?"

"It was incredible," Avery said. "Loved it."

"Great, I'm glad. Can I get you guys anything else?"

"Just the check," Jack said.

She whisked a black folder out of her apron and set it on the table. "I'll take that whenever you're ready." She walked away.

Jack opened the folder. "Uh oh."

"What's wrong?"

"Alex is gonna owe me some money." He showed her the slip. "They left in such a hurry they didn't get their check."

"Here, I'll help." She reached for her purse.

He gently swatted at her hand. "No, I've got it. Let's get our story straight, though. Alex and Chelsea's part is eighty bucks." He laid a few bills in the folder to cover the bill and a generous tip.

Avery laughed. "That's what it looked like to me. Oh, plus tip."

"A hundred bucks, then."

"Don't forget tax."

"Oooh yeah, that's like thirty percent, isn't it?" he joked.

The waitress came back and took the folder.

Jack said, "No change, thanks."

"Thanks, you two have a great day."

Back in the parking lot, Jack opened the car door for Avery. He got in the driver's seat and said, "Want the top down?"

"Heck yeah. Just give me a second." Avery pulled a hair tie out of her purse and whipped her long hair into a ponytail while the top retracted to the back of the car. She used a second hair tie to secure her hair into a messy bun. "Ready."

Jack pulled out of the parking lot and made a right.

"You know we're going the wrong way, right?"

"Are we?" He laughed and turned the radio up.

They cruised up and down the strip for a while, until the sky darkened with angry clouds. Jack pulled into a parking space beside the beach house and put the top up just as the first fat drops of rain splattered against the windshield.

"Better run for it," he said.

They ran up the steps and into the house just as a large bolt of lightning split the sky and let loose a torrential downpour.

Laughing, they burst into the living room, straight into a wall of tension.

"Whoa, what did we walk into," Jack said to no one in particular.

Chelsea sat on one sofa, her arms crossed, looking affronted. Alex leaned in the doorway to the kitchen. Dolly and Bert looked at each other, exchanging some sort of silent telepathic communication that long-married couples seemed to master.

Analise and Sydney took advantage of the distraction to grab Hazel and disappear down the hall to their room. Holly sat on the same couch as Chelsea, at the other end. Michael and the kids took up the other couch.

"I don't know what to tell you," Dolly said. "We don't have any extra rooms."

Chelsea made her eyes wide and pitiful as she looked up at Bert. "I don't have anywhere to go, and now it's storming. What should I do?"

Bert was too smart to fall for that. He shrugged and deferred. "Don't ask me."

Alex sighed, weary, and added, "I checked every hotel and motel in a ten mile radius. Either no vacancies, or three-night minimum stay."

"I'm starting to think I never should have come," Chelsea pouted, turning her doe eyes on Alex.

"Ya think?" Jack said.

Avery bit her lips together to keep from smiling.

Then Chelsea turned it on full blast. Tears filled her tarantula-lined eyes.

Avery rolled her eyes and shook her head. "I'm heading upstairs to work on my spreadsheet." She shot one meaningful look at Alex, then turned and went back the hallway.

She was at the top of the stairs when a massive boom of

thunder drummed through the house and the power cut out. "Shit!" She tripped in the sudden blackness, but caught herself with her hands on the top stair. She stood carefully, rotating the wrist that took the brunt of her almost-fall. As if taking a ball to the face wasn't enough, now her wrist hurt. She'd probably end up in a full body cast before the weekend was over.

"Avery? You okay?" Jack's concerned voice called up the stairs.

"I'm fine, just stumbled a little." It annoyed her that Alex hadn't been the one to ask. Maybe that was a little unfair, since Jack was closer, but still.

"You sure?"

"Yeah, I'm good." She brushed the front of her shirt, mostly to give her shaky hands something to do after the shot of adrenaline ran its course. She tapped her phone and used the light to make her way to her bedroom.

She felt around in her suitcase to find her yoga pants and tank top for bed, then changed in the dark and slipped into bed. After tossing and turning for hours, she got up and looked out the window. The rain and clouds were gone, the moon bright and reflecting on the ocean.

The power had come back on at some point, and the small clock on the stand beside her bed blinked 12:00.

Unable to sleep, she scrolled on her phone, then decided to check the tides to see what time might be best to get seashells. According to what she found, low tide would be around 1:00 a.m. She checked the time. Half past midnight. Since she wasn't going to be sleeping anyway, she changed into jean capris and a T-shirt. She zipped her hoodie and grabbed her mesh bag to collect shells.

Tiptoeing out of her room, she didn't hear anyone else moving around in the silent house. She debated waking Alex, and crept across the hall. She lifted her hand to tap on the door when she heard the unmistakable sound of Chelsea quietly talking from inside the room.

An unexpected lump formed in her throat. It shouldn't bother her. They were just friends. They'd both been super clear about that fact. Still, it stung.

She once again turned on her phone's light and used it to make her way down the stairs as quietly as she possibly could. The downstairs was dark. She tiptoed across the living room and cringed as the sliding door let the loud ocean noise roar in. Hurrying, she slipped outside and slid the door shut behind her.

The air was chilly. The sand was still wet from the downpour, sticking to her feet as she crossed it to the ocean. A wide expanse of sand was flattened by the water. The nearly-full moon illuminated the beach with a milky glow. Dozens of seashells dotted the water's edge, their white feathers glowing in the moonlight.

Avery bent to pick up a shell. The surf rushed in, so she used it to rinse the shell before she put it in her bag. The second shell she picked up was occupied. "Sorry, mister hermit crab." She put the crab back down where she got it, and went on to the next. She made her way up the beach, picking up shells and making sure they were empty before putting them in her bag.

The sky was black as ink, dotted with bright stars and a handful of ghostly clouds. Tendrils of hair tickled her face as the breeze off the ocean tossed them. More shells glinted as the surf rolled back, exposing them. She dashed forward and grabbed one shell, then a second, before the cold water slid back toward her.

"Ooh, look at that," she said to no one.

A perfect sand dollar lay on the beach. She carefully picked it up and put the delicate piece in her bag. Not wanting to risk breaking it, she made her way back down the shoreline and across the beach to the house's deck. She looked up at the sky just in time to see a shooting star. Squeezing her eyes closed, she made a wish. *I wish this weekend would get better.*

Her hand rested on the door handle, but it was so peaceful and relaxing here in the dark that she changed her mind and settled onto one of the padded lounge chairs instead and just watched the ocean rolling in the bright moonlight.

She blinked, and when she opened her eyes, the sky was beginning to lighten. She shivered and pulled her hoodie tighter around her, then crept into the still-silent house. Upstairs, she reached the landing just as Alex's door clicked open. A faint light from inside illuminated Chelsea's shape slipping into the room. Wearing a towel.

Avery froze, waiting until the door closed, then scurried into her own room and closed the door. She winced at the loud click and hoped it didn't wake anyone up.

Fully dressed, she climbed into the bed, pulled the covers up, and willed herself not to cry.

Chapter Twenty

Alex rolled to his side and nearly fell out of the tiny twin bed. Jack's snoring from the twin on other side of the room was quiet, but loud enough that getting back to sleep wasn't going to happen.

He slipped out of bed and grabbed the pile of clothes he'd brought with him the night before. He changed in the bathroom and brushed his teeth, trying to be quiet, though he needn't have bothered. Jack was still sound asleep when he crept across the room and out the door.

The kitchen was already bustling with activity. Dolly and Bert were laying out food for Bert to make his famous annual vacation breakfast feast, while Michael and Holly washed dishes left over from the night before.

Sophie was the only kid up. She sat at the island, coloring.

"Whatcha doing, kiddo?" Alex asked as he got a bottle of water from the fridge.

"Getting peace and quiet," she grumbled.

"Wow, you sound like your mom."

"Do not. She snores like a bigfoot."

"Sophie! I do not." Holly turned from the sink to gape at her daughter.

Michael snorted, trying to choke back laughter.

Sophie waited until Holly turned back to the sink, then nodded her head and mouthed, "She does." Out loud, she said, "Kallie and Braydon kept kicking me all night."

Alex picked up a gray crayon and a coloring book. He flipped to a page with a cat. "Sounds like you need a vacation from your vacation."

She huffed. "You aren't kidding."

He had to laugh. She sounded so grown up. Sometimes it was hard to remember she was only nine.

She demanded, "Are you coloring that like Poof?"

"Of course."

She nodded, approving of his decision. "How did Poof steal Avery's bra?"

He nearly spit out a mouthful of water. Apparently she heard the whole story. "He snuck out on my balcony, over to her balcony, and her door was open. I'm not sure what else he did, but then he came home with her… things."

"Was she like super mad at him?"

He colored the cat's face. "She wasn't impressed with him, I can tell you."

Sophie snickered. "I bet she was really mad at him." She concentrated on coloring the next flower petal on the flower she was working on. "Was she mad at you?"

"Me? Why?"

"Because you let Poof get out."

"I didn't *let* him get out."

Sophie put her crayon down and crossed her arms. She looked him dead in the eye. "Well, you didn't keep him inside, did you? That was irresponsible."

Wow. Getting called out by a nine-year-old was not fun. "You're right."

Her shoulders relaxed and she turned her attention back to coloring.

Holly said, "They just had a discussion about responsible pet ownership in school."

"Ah."

"We now have a strict schedule for replacing the filters in the fish tank." She ran a hand over Sophie's hair and bent down to kiss her forehead.

"Sounds like you learned a lot," Alex said.

"Yeah, but everybody wanted to talk about dogs. Dogs, dogs, dogs, so we hardly had time for fish. And I told Mrs. Eicher that a lot of us have fish or hamsters. Jacie and Keefer and Minnie all have hamsters." She put her crayon back down with force. "So like why are we spending all the whole time on dogs? Petra even has a chinchilla. Like why aren't we talking about how to take care of it? So at lunch I made a list of all the different pets everyone in my class has and then gave it to Mrs. Eicher and then we talked about all of them and not just dogs and cats. I got an A plus plus."

Alex felt a swell of pride in his chest. "Wow. I'm really proud of you, Soph. You totally earned your plus plus."

"When I'm a teacher, I'll make a list first and make sure everyone is included. Not just the regular stuff like dogs and cats."

He exchanged a proud smile with Holly.

"You want to be a teacher?" Chelsea came in and sat at the island beside Alex.

"Yeah." Sophie eyed her and offered nothing more.

Alex focused on coloring his gray cat, then added a red collar with a silver bell. "What do you think?" he asked Sophie.

"Not bad." She slid her coloring book over to him. "How do you like mine?"

Alex studied the colorful superhero scene. "Love it. You're better at staying in the lines than I am."

"You should practice more." She closed the coloring books and put them in the basket.

Alex helped her pick up all the crayons and put them back in the plastic box.

Sophie snapped it shut and put it in the basket with the books. "This was fun. Can we play a game later?"

"Of course."

She hopped off the stool and carried her basket out of the kitchen.

Alex watched her go. He knew he wasn't supposed to have a favorite niece/nephew, but he couldn't help it. Sure, he loved Kallie and Brayden with all his heart, but Sophie was extra-special. A plus plus.

"I couldn't find another room anywhere. Probably since it's a holiday weekend," Chelsea said. "I guess that means I'll head home after breakfast?"

Alex knew she was hinting for him to tell her she didn't have to go. He looked over at her, the woman he'd bought a ring for, the woman he thought he'd spend the rest of his life with. The woman he really didn't know anymore, if he ever did. Once he couldn't wait to spend every minute with her. Now, he couldn't wait until she left.

"Alex?"

He couldn't give her what she wanted. Not today. Not anymore. "Yeah. Definitely have breakfast first. It's supposed to be nice weather today. Good day for a drive, at least." He knew it was lame, but there wasn't much else he could say.

She turned her head, pressed a hand to her mouth, then got

up and scurried from the kitchen. He felt like he should feel guilty, but all he felt was relief.

His parents were at the stove, cracking eggs and peeling thick slices of bacon apart. Michael and Holly stood shoulder to shoulder at the counter, chopping potatoes and onions for Bert's famous home fries. Alex was so glad Holly had found Michael. They belonged together like peanut butter and chocolate–wonderful on their own, but even better together.

"Here we go!" Bert lifted his spatula, gleefully tossing food onto the griddle. Steam and sizzling filled the kitchen. "Round up the troops, breakfast will be done in about ten minutes."

Alex hopped off his stool. "I'll go spread the word." He did his best town crier impression, making the kids laugh as he knocked on doors, shouting, "Hear ye, hear ye, breakfast is about to be served! Make haste to ye olde kitchen table!"

The family poured out of their rooms and headed toward the kitchen. Alex took the stairs two at a time. He opened the door to the room he'd shared with Jack.

Jack came out of the bathroom, brushing his teeth, and gave a thumbs up. The door to Alex's room was open. Chelsea sat on the edge of the bed, dabbing at her eyes.

"Hey, uh, breakfast is about ready."

"Yeah, I heard you shouting," she snapped.

He hesitated for a moment, then tapped on Avery's door. It opened a second later, but she only held it open a crack.

"Good morning. Breakfast is almost ready."

"Thanks."

She hadn't smiled at him. "Everything okay?"

"Sure." She moved to close the door.

"Ave?" He looked over her shoulder. Her open suitcase took up half the bed. "What's going on?"

Chelsea stepped into the hallway and put her hand on his arm. "Are we heading down for breakfast?"

The second he was distracted, Avery closed the door.

Alex shook his head, irritated, even though Chelsea hadn't really done anything wrong. Aside from being here in the first place. "No. Go ahead down."

She gave him a wide-eyed wounded look before walking down the stairs.

He tapped on the door, but Avery didn't answer. He debated for a long moment, then turned the knob and pushed the door open an arm's length. "Ave?"

She sat on the bed, her suitcase full of everything she'd brought along.

"Can we talk?"

"I can't imagine what there is to say."

"What are you doing?" He gestured to the suitcase.

"I'm trying to find a rental car." She looked down at her hands in her lap, clasped around her phone. "This was supposed to be a fun weekend. Well, I'm not having fun. So I'm going to head home and figure out why I've got nothing but radio silence from the store."

For a second, he dared to hope that was her only reason for wanting to go. "I don't want you to leave."

Her eyes narrowed, but it felt more like disbelief than anger. "You've got Chelsea. What do you need me for?"

At least he could clear that up. "Chelsea's leaving after breakfast. I told her I wasn't interested in getting back together."

"Was that before or after you slept together?"

He took a step back, confused and blindsided. "What?"

"She went into your room in a towel, Alex. I can put two and two together."

Now he *was* irritated. He stepped all the way into the room and closed the door behind him. "Seriously, Avery?"

She crossed her arms and lifted her chin. "What? Are you

going to deny it?"

"You know what? I shouldn't even entertain this at all because you're making some pretty crappy assumptions about me." He ran a hand down his face. How could she actually think he'd sleep with Chelsea while she was right across the hall? "Chelsea stayed in that room last night." He pointed through the door. "And I slept in a cramped twin bed in Jack's room."

She blinked half a dozen times, her mouth forming a surprised "O".

"All because I didn't want you to get the wrong idea about anything, but here we are." He spread his hands to encompass the situation.

Her gaze shifted to the floor. "Alex—"

"I'm going down to breakfast." He didn't want to hear any apology or explanation. Right now, all he wanted was to rewind this whole weekend and find some excuse to not go.

Chapter Twenty-One

Avery watched Alex leave. Her face burned with embarrassment that she'd accused him of sleeping with Chelsea. Something that really wasn't her business anyway, and she'd ended up offending him and hurting his feelings. *Way to kick off the day, genius.*

She took a minute to psych herself up, then went downstairs. There were no rental cars to be found in the entire city, apparently. The kitchen island was full of food and the air was full of laughter and conversations. Bert stood at the stove, spooning ladles of scrambled eggs into a bowl. She paused in the doorway.

Bert glanced over his shoulder and gave Avery a big smile. "You're just in time for the second round of fresh eggs. Grab a plate."

Despite the lump in her belly, she picked up a plate and filled it with food.

"What do we need more of?" Dolly asked.

One of the kids yelled, "Bacon!"

"Coming up." Bert put strips on the griddle and the loud sizzle joined the cacophony.

The only empty seat was beside Alex. "Can I sit here?" She half expected him to get up and move completely away from her. Or ignore her. Or something to punish her.

Instead, he said, "Of course," and took the plate from her hands and set it on the table so she could maneuver onto the barstool.

Alex put his arm around her waist and gave her a little squeeze.

"You're not mad?" she asked quietly.

"I'm not *not* mad, but we'll talk about it later."

She wasn't sure what to make of that. She tried to avoid looking over at Chelsea, who perched on a stool on the other side of the table, talking to Holly. She looked out of place in her fully done hair and makeup and her frilly blouse and wrap skirt, while everyone else wore T-shirts and some variation of shorts.

Her contemplation of Alex's ex was halted by fisticuffs from the far end of the table.

Brayden screamed, "She touched my eggs!" as he swung at his sister.

Kallie shoved him and screamed back, "He stole my bacon!"

Just as she had during the meltdown at the restaurant, Sophie offered an eye roll and kept eating.

Chelsea sat wide-eyed, looking traumatized by the display. Avery suddenly wondered if that wasn't one of the reasons for the split. Alex was very clear that he wanted a family. Did Chelsea not want kids? It would help explain a lot, like why she was nice enough and everyone seemed to like her well enough, but she just didn't quite fit in.

Jack burst into the kitchen, holding his phone up. "Avery. We've got problems."

She paused, fork in midair. "What?" She wasn't sure if he

was joking, but he looked serious.

He glanced around the room, where everyone waited to see what was going on. "Rick called me. He's pissed."

A hard knot formed in Avery's gut. Rick Lauder was one of their biggest customers. She hopped off the stool and grabbed Jack's arm, pulling him into the living room. "What happened? What's going on?"

"I hate to tell you, I really do. But he sent Steve in to pick up his order and they wouldn't give it to him."

Avery's brow furrowed, confused. "I don't understand. I placed the order myself before I left. Was it the wrong thing?" Her heart dropped. She hated making mistakes, especially when it affected her customers.

"No." Jack's gaze was intense. "They wouldn't let Steve pick it up without paying for it right then."

"That doesn't make sense. We always invoice Rick. I'm so sorry." She fumbled with her phone. "I bet it was one of the new kids who didn't understand how…" For the life of her, she couldn't imagine who didn't know how to invoice a customer.

"Avery, it was Jimmy."

Her head snapped up. "Jimmy?"

"Rick went back in himself, and Jimmy told him no more ordering on store credit."

Suddenly lightheaded, Avery reached out and grabbed Jack's arm to steady herself. Was Jimmy *trying* to destroy their business?

Jack continued, his tone sympathetic. "Rick told him he'd go elsewhere."

"Oh, no."

"Jimmy told him losing one customer wasn't much of a threat."

Her stomach clenched. Jimmy was so stupid. Rick may be one customer, but word of mouth traveled like wildfire, and

Rick's word was gold. He was a good, honest businessman, and had brought them more business than any amount of advertising they'd ever paid for. "Oh, this is bad." She pressed a hand to her roiling belly. "There aren't any rentals. I gotta get home."

"I'll take you. We can leave in like thirty minutes."

She couldn't even argue with his offer. "Yeah. I gotta get home and fix this."

"Everything okay?" Alex came alongside them.

"Just my brother single-handedly destroying our family business." She straightened and let go of Jack's arm. "I have to go home."

Alex nodded. "I can—"

"I'm heading home, too. No sense in all of us leaving," Jack said.

Avery didn't wait to hear any more conversation. She ran upstairs, glad she'd already been packing. She threw the last of her things in her suitcase and zipped it shut. She heard Jack and Alex tromping up the stairs. Alex appeared in her doorway.

"Hey."

She glanced up. "I'm sorry, I have to go."

"I know. I can take you home."

She shoved her feet in her sandals. "I'll be fine with Jack. No need for both of us to cut our vacation short." She managed a smile. "But you do need to do your pros and cons."

Alex pulled her into a hug. "So do you."

She tapped her temple. "It all just got real clear in here. If I manage to save this account and they still want Jimmy in charge, I'm gone." She gave him a squeeze and pulled away. "I think I got everything."

"If you forget anything, I'll bring it home, don't worry."

"Thanks." She picked up her tote bag with her laptop and

extended the handle on her suitcase.

"I'll get that." Alex took the suitcase from her and wheeled it to the stairs.

Jack was coming out of his room, his duffel bag slung over his shoulder. "I'm ready when you are."

"Ready," she said.

They lugged everything downstairs. Avery set her bag down and popped into the kitchen. "Sorry, guys, there's a problem at the store and I have to go."

Dolly came over and gave her a big hug. "You just be careful." She pointed at Jack. "No driving like a maniac."

He grinned and hugged her. "No worries, Aunt Dolly. My insurance would go through the roof if I got a ticket."

After a quick round of hugs and goodbyes, Avery adjusted her tote bag on her shoulder and waved. "It was so nice to meet you all."

She caught Chelsea staring hopefully at Alex, and pushed the image aside. She had bigger things to worry about.

Alex carried her suitcase to the car and put it in Jack's trunk. "Keep me posted, okay?" He leaned over and hugged her. "Everything's going to be okay, Ave."

"I hope so." Without thinking about it, she gave him a quick kiss.

Alex looked like he wanted to say something, but he simply opened her car door, waited for her to get situated, then shut the door. He waved as they pulled out.

"Do you mind if I turn this down?" She gestured to the radio.

"Got it." Jack touched a button on the steering wheel and the volume dropped to almost nothing.

She tapped her mother's number and waited.

"Avery." Ginny's voice was strained.

"Mom, what is going on?"

"We're handling it."

"Are you seriously shutting me out right now?"

Ginny snapped, "I'm sorry, Avery, but we've been dealing with this for three days while you've been on *vacation*. After all your talk about wanting what's best for the business… If you'd been here, this never wouldn't have happened."

Avery didn't bother moderating her voice. She yelled, "Do you even hear yourself? All *your* talk about wanting what's best for the business and it's being handed over to Jimmy? I know you're frustrated right now, but why are you lashing out at me? Have you bothered to go off on Jimmy? You know, the idiot who created this mess? Let's not hurt his precious feelings, right? Let's just unload on Avery because she's not going anywhere? Is that how it is?" She blinked back the tears that stung the backs of her eyes. "Whatever. Let me talk to Jimmy."

"He's not here." Ginny sounded tired.

"I thought you were at the store."

"We are. Your dad and I."

Avery's jaw clenched. "Where is he?"

"I don't know. He was talking to Rick and I guess Rick hung up on him. After that, he left."

Avery had the feeling there was a lot more to that than her mother was letting on.

"I can't be on the phone right now, your father and I need to figure out what to do next. Enjoy the rest of your trip."

"I'm on my way home. I'll see you in a few hours. Don't do anything without me."

"Avery…"

She shouted, "Don't do anything! I'm on my way to save the damn day again!" With that, she hung up the phone.

Jack reached over and patted her hand. "It'll be okay."

Avery leaned her head back against the seat and stared out the window. "I'm not so sure."

Chapter Twenty-Two

Alex watched Jack's car until it turned the corner. As much as he dreaded the questions waiting for him in the kitchen, that's where he went.

"I hope everything's alright," Dolly said, coming over to give him a half-hug.

"What was that all about, anyway?" Analise asked.

"I guess there was some kind of mix-up between Avery's store and Jack's boss. I'm sure the two of them will be able to get it sorted out." He hoped so anyway, and more than that, he selfishly hoped their spending time together didn't evolve into anything more.

Sydney made a sympathetic noise. "I hope it's resolved sooner than later."

"Me, too. Sounds like it's a mess." He didn't bother filling them in on his opinions of her family's handling of their business. Business—as in, none of his. He stood awkwardly for a minute, then cleaned up his and Avery's plates. He put the plates in the dishwasher and caught a glimpse of the box of taffy Avery had bought his parents.

"Hey, um, I'll be back in a bit."

"Where are you going?" Dolly asked.

"Boardwalk."

"Great." Chelsea jumped up from her chair. "There's something I need."

Alex bit his lower lip and waited until she followed him away from his family's prying eyes. "I thought you were leaving."

She touched his arm. "I thought that since Avery's gone, we might have a chance to really talk things over."

"There isn't anything to talk over."

"Really? Because it seems like Avery and Jack have lots in common. Half a day in the car together might make them realize it."

He pulled in a deep breath. He'd thought the same thing, but it irritated him that she'd said it out loud. It was none of her business. He was also sure that Jack wasn't Avery's type. Pretty sure. But one thing he *did* know for certain was that spending time with Chelsea wasn't the way to build anything with Avery.

"Alex, it's just a conversation."

"I'm going down the boardwalk to get souvenirs for Avery. We didn't get a chance to go back so she could buy some."

Chelsea's smile remained fixed. A beat later, she said, "Sounds good, let's go."

Well, that didn't work out the way he expected, but what could he do? "Fine."

They got in Alex's car and drove through the city to the public parking lot. Then to a second public parking lot. Then a third, where he finally found a space.

He couldn't think of anything to say, so he didn't say anything at all. He just got out of the car and waited for Chelsea to join him. She grabbed his arm as they crossed the street. He ignored it until they were on the sidewalk, then he pulled his arm away. They walked up the sloping sidewalk and he paused as they stepped onto the boardwalk to take in the view of the ocean.

"It never gets old."

"What?" She followed his gaze. "Oh."

"That view."

She tugged on his arm. "What were you thinking of getting her?"

Alex let her pull him toward the shops with their colorful shirts and beach dresses on rack after rack.

"What about this?" Chelsea pulled a T-shirt off the rack and held it up.

"Yeah, it's okay."

"Not for me, silly, for Avery."

"What? No." He bristled at the intrusion. He didn't want Chelsea to pick anything out for Avery, what was she doing? "I'll get something for her, you just worry about getting your own stuff."

"Wow, okay." She lifted an eyebrow and turned away, clearly offended.

Instead of following her, he let it go. Maybe she'd get the hint. If she wanted to insert herself into his business, she didn't need to get offended when he didn't let her. He wandered into the store, among racks of touristy tchotchkes, cheesy magnets and mugs and spoon rests. He found an hourglass with a seashell base and allegedly authentic Ocean City sand inside. It stood about five inches high. He flipped it over and watched the sand filter down from the top to the bottom. She'd love it.

He picked up the hourglass and then spied a frog made of seashells, wearing a straw hat. Perfect. He picked it up, too, and made his way to the counter. At the last second, he picked up a bright turquoise T-shirt with white letters shouting

OCEAN CITY, MARYLAND across it, and put it on the counter.

The clerk wrapped his items in paper, then bagged them. He swiped his card and walked back to the boardwalk, where Chelsea waited, arms folded across her chest. The breeze blew her dress tight to her legs before sending it billowing out behind her.

It wasn't lost on Alex that she was stunning, but he couldn't find any emotion inside himself. Whatever he had thought might be left, wasn't.

"Did you want to look around?"

"No, it's fine."

"We can head back to the house, then."

"Yeah, and then I guess I'll go."

"It's for the best." They left the boardwalk and waited to cross the busy street.

"You really don't even want to have this conversation?"

There was a break in the traffic, so he stepped into the crosswalk.

She latched onto his hand and they dashed across the street. In the parking lot, he tried to let go, but she held on. "Alex, please. There's so much I need to say."

He stifled his sigh of impatience. "Let's get in the car."

He hit the button to unlock the doors, then popped the trunk to put his bag in. As Chelsea slid past him to get to the passenger side of the car, she stopped and looked up at him. She grasped handfuls of his shirt and leaned up to kiss him.

Alex jerked to the side, trying to step backwards. As he did, his heel connected with the concrete barrier and he toppled painfully backwards onto his butt.

Chelsea gasped and clamped her hands over her mouth. "Alex!"

He cursed and stumbled awkwardly to his feet.

"I'm so sorry."

He said nothing, just walked around to his side of the car and got in. He closed the door and sat for a second. His tailbone hurt terribly, as did his shin, which must have hit the car as he fell. He brushed mulch and tiny stones off his arm.

Chelsea closed her door and slowly fastened her seatbelt. "I'm sorry."

"Don't." He started the car and buckled his seatbelt.

"I'm sorry I didn't ask you to move to Houston with me."

He pulled out of the parking space and waited until it was clear to pull into traffic. "Okay."

"I wanted to. But I also wanted to try being on my own. I'd never lived on my own."

"Okay."

"I thought I wanted different things out of life than what we were working toward."

"Okay." He stared out the windshield, focused entirely on the car in front of them.

"Can you say something else, please?"

"No." He did not want to have this conversation that was about twelve months overdue. He put on his turn signal as they approached the driveway.

"I want to have babies with you."

"What?!" Alex took his eyes off the road and gaped at her for a second.

"Yes, Alex, we can have kids. All the kids you want."

"Damn it!" He missed the turnoff and had to change lanes so he could make a U-turn and get back to the house. "Can you just stop for now? Please?"

She sniffled and looked out her window.

Alex turned into the parking lot of a convenience store and drove to the far side of the parking lot. He put the car in park and turned to look at her. "What are you doing, Chelsea?"

Tears rolled down her face. "I made the biggest mistake of my life, Alex."

He wasn't sure if she meant leaving him, or something that had happened in Houston. Either way, not his circus, not his monkeys. "Okay."

"Please stop saying, 'Okay,' I can't take it!"

"O—Alright."

"Alex, I'm so sorry. You were the best thing that ever happened to me. I never should have left the way I did. I want to make it right. Make it better. Please let me fix it. You said yourself that you and Avery are just friends, and I'm sure she's super nice, but she's not the right person for you, Alex, I am." She sobbed and more tears rolled down her face.

One of her strips of fake eyelashes worked its way off her eye. Alex tried looking away, but he couldn't. It was like a little clump of spiders sliding down her cheek, holding on for dear life.

She said something through thick tears, but he couldn't pull his attention from the scene playing out on her cheek.

"Alex, please," she sobbed again. The fresh wave of tears sent the eyelash off her face. It landed with a plop on her cleavage. "What was—" Chelsea screamed, slapping and swiping at her chest. "Kill it!"

The soggy eyelashes flew from her fingertip to the windshield, where they stuck.

"What is—oh, no," she wailed. She yanked the visor down and flipped the mirror shield. She inspected her face. "Oh, no. I look horrible."

He reached across her and popped the glovebox open. "Tissues."

She snatched a handful of tissues and wiped her face and blew her nose. "No wonder you don't want to get back together." She sniffled again.

"Don't act like it has anything to do with how you look."

She folded a tissue in her lap and took a deep breath. "I'll do whatever you want, Alex. Let's get married and have babies and live in your little town and get a dog. I can run an Etsy shop from a spare room in our little house with a picket fence and raise a litter of brats." She broke down again. "My life is over," she sobbed.

"I'm not in the same place I was when you left." He wasn't sure what was going on. Whatever she was talking about didn't feel like it had much to do with him.

"You don't want to marry me?"

"Chelsea."

She pressed her hand to her mouth and sobbed again. "Alex, I'm so scared."

"What? What are you afraid of? What's going on?" He reached over and put his hand on her arm.

"I'm pregnant."

He jerked his hand off her arm as if it had scalded him. That's why she was pushing this? Did she think she could just run back to him and get married and act like this kid was his or something? "Wait, what?"

"I mean, I *thought* I was pregnant. I wasn't, but it was super real for like *hours* until I could take a test and found out I wasn't." She cried for a few minutes, then mopped her tears with the wad of tissues. She sniffled and pulled herself together. "It was a mistake. All of it. I've made so many mistakes."

He reached over again, since pregnancy wasn't contagious, and awkwardly patted her arm. "Chelsea, it's going to be okay."

"It's not okay."

"Who's the… I mean, where's the father? Er, the guy who

would have been the father?" He wondered how one got booked on the Jerry Springer show.

Fresh tears rolled down her cheek. "I'm so stupid, Alex. I don't deserve you."

He didn't bother pointing out that she didn't *have* him anymore.

She started talking.

Alex let her clutch his hand in a death grip while she told her tale. She'd met someone online a few months before she and Alex had broken up. Someone who lived in Houston. She moved to be near him. Things were going great until her period was late and she called to tell him she might be pregnant. That was when he told her to pound sand because he had two very young children, one wife, and zero plans to deal with her. Chelsea panicked, and thought running to Alex would solve her problems.

He tried to be sympathetic, but the only thing running through his head was that Chelsea had cheated on him. Technically she hadn't cheated physically, but that didn't make it any better. The fresh betrayal made it hard to believe her tearful apologies. When he could no longer stand it, he pulled his hand away.

When she finished sniffling, he drove back to the house and helped her pack.

Dolly fed her some lunch, and then Alex walked her to her car. "Drive safe."

He watched until the taillights of her car were out of sight. He couldn't decide how he felt. Angry? Yes. Betrayed? Definitely. Hurt? Yup, that too. Relieved? For sure.

So what did he want?

He wanted to talk to Avery.

But she was with Jack.

Chapter Twenty-Three

"Why does it always seem to take so much longer to get home from vacation?" Avery itched to get out of the car, but they were still an hour from home.

Jack changed lanes to pass another string of slow-moving cars. "Beats me."

"Do you think he'll get back together with Chelsea?" she blurted out before she could filter herself.

"Nah." Jack didn't hesitate.

"Do you think she actually left, like she was planning to do before this?" She waved her hands to encompass the current situation.

He glanced over at her, then put his eyes back on the highway. "I don't know. But even if she didn't leave, I really don't think Alex would go down that road again. She hurt him pretty bad."

"I can't even imagine showing up to a family vacation uninvited. Unless I was really determined to win someone back, I guess." She flopped her head back against the headrest. "It's not like it's any of my business anyway. We're just friends."

Jack snort-laughed. "If you say so."

Avery ignored his comment as her mind churned in a dozen different directions. A few miles passed. She said, "What are you going to say to Rick?"

"I'm just going to tell him to take your call. He hates throwing his weight around, and I know it must have been pretty bad for him to get this mad. He likes you, Avery, but don't be shocked if you can't save the account. Once Rick makes up his mind…" Jack trailed off, shaking his head. "I'll do what I can."

"I know. Thanks. It'll suck if he takes his business, but I wouldn't blame him." She leaned her head back, trying to form their best offer to keep Rick's business. She knew Jack was right. Once Rick made up his mind, it wouldn't be easy to convince him to undecide to take his business elsewhere. She also knew Rick didn't like change, and if he left, he'd have to shop farther away, which wouldn't be as convenient. Hopefully that would work in her favor.

The miles stretched out, but finally Jack made the turn into the apartment's parking lot.

Avery jolted upright, taking in the two police cars with active lights and the four police officers standing on the sidewalk with a handful of building tenants. "What on earth?" She grabbed the door handle, anxious for the car to stop so she could get out.

Jack parked in Alex's vacant spot. "Whoa. Looks like something big's going down."

"Uh oh. Is that Lincoln?" An uneasy feeling settled in Avery's gut. She climbed out of the car and tried to make sense of the scene in front of her as Jack joined her. Esther Simmons, the third tenant on Avery's floor, was gesturing wildly at one of the police cars as she explained something to one of the officers. Another officer was speaking with Lincoln. A third was talking with Mr. Barrow. Ugh. The fourth was standing near Lincoln, writing in a notebook.

Another official-looking SUV pulled into the parking lot.

Avery's throat clenched as she realized it wasn't a police vehicle. The side of the SUV was emblazoned with the words, "ANIMAL CONTROL." She reached over and grabbed Jack's arm. "Oh, no. Poof."

As if summoned, a thump against the back window of the police car drew her attention. Poof rapped at the window as if he could break the glass with his paw. His eyes were wide and terrified. His mouth opened. Avery couldn't hear him, but she knew he was yowling. He leapt again, smacking his head on the glass.

She felt awful for the rotten beast. Mind made up, she started walking toward the officers. "Call Alex," she said to Jack.

"Why? I mean—"

"That's his cat!"

"Oh!" Jack's eyebrows rose with sudden understanding. He stepped away, pulling his phone out of his pocket.

Avery approached the officers who were talking with Lincoln. Or trying to.

Lincoln's face was tomato-red. Veins popped out along his forehead and up his neck.

"Sir, if you aren't going to tell us anything here, we'll take you in."

His entire body was shaking. His words wheezed out like he was having an asthma attack. "Cat... got... out..."

The female officer tapped the pad in her hand. "That doesn't explain how Mrs. Simmons's necklace and bracelet ended up in your possession."

He sucked in a breath.

At the risk of ticking off the police officers, Avery came alongside Lincoln. "I may be able to help."

Officer Pennick, according to the tag on her uniform, did not look amused. "And you are?"

"Avery Hannigan. I live in 5B. Lincoln—"

The officer cut her off and exchanged a look with the other officer, who grasped Lincoln's elbow and pulled him away. She took down Avery's contact information. "What can you tell me?"

"As I was saying, Lincoln–the man who was just here–has been cat sitting for 5C. Alex Myers, who lives in 5C, is away for the weekend. Unfortunately, Poof has a bad habit of breaking out of the apartment and taking things that don't belong to him. Lincoln has super bad anxiety that makes it hard for him to talk to strangers. What's going to happen to Poof?" She felt bad for Lincoln. She was practically buzzing with anxiety at the moment, herself.

"The cat's name is Poof?"

Avery felt ridiculous, but she nodded. "Yeah. Alex's niece named him."

The officer made another note. "When will Mr. Myers be returning?"

"He's in Maryland. He can be home in like 5 or 6 hours. What about Poof?"

Her tone was firm, but not unkind. "Animal Control will take him to a shelter. Tomorrow's a holiday, so he can probably claim the cat on Tuesday."

Probably? That sounded awful. "Isn't there some way we can avoid that?" She swallowed hard. "What if I took custody of him?"

Officer Pennick regarded her for a moment. "You'll have to check with Animal Control."

As much as the little brat drove Avery nuts, she wouldn't let Poof get sent to a shelter if she could avoid it at all.

The Animal Control officer ambled over, a large man who looked annoyed to be there. He stared at her boobs as she asked if she could take custody of Poof, made a joke about "skipping all that paperwork," and agreed to let Avery take the cat without asking her a single question.

Officer Pennick opened the car's back door. Poof offered no resistance as Avery scooped him into her arms. "Keep him inside," she warned.

"Yes, ma'am." Avery hurried toward the building's doors, praying she could get to the apartment without Poof escaping. Or stealing anything. Or murdering anyone.

Jack ran to catch up with her and opened the door. "I'll bring your stuff up."

"Thanks so much." She'd forgotten all about her suitcase. "My laptop bag is in the back seat."

"Got it," Jack answered as the door swung closed.

Avery pressed the button for the elevator and breathed a sigh of relief when it slid open, empty.

Poof clutched her arm, his claws digging into her skin. The poor little demon trembled against her.

"I should have let them put you in kitty prison to teach you a lesson." As soon as she said it, she felt bad.

He didn't argue.

"You better be taking this experience to heart and turning over a new leaf. Let's hope Lincoln isn't going to real prison for your shenanigans." She hoped Lincoln was faring okay. She fumbled to get her keys out of her purse, half afraid Poof would take advantage of the distraction and bolt, but he remained pressed against her chest, trembling.

The elevator doors slid open to an empty hallway. Avery carefully unlocked her door and quickly closed it behind them so he didn't have an opportunity to bolt. She took Poof straight through her bedroom and into the bathroom. No window that opened, only one door.

"You're going to have to stay at my place until we can get the key from Lincoln or until Alex gets home. He's going to strangle you, you know." She set Poof on the counter. "Don't shred the toilet paper, either."

He immediately curled his tail around his body and sank down onto his haunches. His wide eyes darted around the room.

Avery gently smoothed the fur on his head. "I know you're scared, but you're safe now." She closed the bathroom door behind her. She double checked that her balcony door was locked, then closed her bedroom door on her way out. After a moment's thought, she wedged a kitchen chair under the knob. Just in case.

Her apartment door popped open and Jack came in, pulling her suitcase and carrying her tote bag. She hurried over to relieve him. "Thank you so much."

"Lincoln's on his way up. Luckily, Poof stole something from Mrs. Simmons last summer, so she bought the story and declined to press charges since she got her jewelry back."

"Holy crap. I'm so glad we got back when we did. They probably would have arrested Lincoln *and* Poof."

A tentative knock caught her attention. She opened the door. Lincoln stood in the hallway, clutching the hem of his shirt in his fists. He avoided her eyes. "Thank you," he managed.

"No problem. Poof's in my bathroom. We'll just leave him there for now, if that's okay?"

Lincoln nodded rapidly.

She looked at Jack. "Did you get ahold of Alex?"

"I left him a voicemail."

"Lincoln, go stay in his apartment until he gets home."

He squeaked out an, "Okay," and hustled away from her door to Alex's.

Avery absently watched until he was inside Alex's apartment, then said to Jack, "Okay. One crisis averted. Now I need to get to the store."

Chapter Twenty-Four

Alex sat in the kitchen with the family when his phone vibrated for the millionth time. He had to suck it up and tell Chelsea to lose his number. She'd exhausted every ounce of patience he had, and now his phone was blowing up. "I'm going to take this," he muttered to no one in particular.

Only it wasn't Chelsea. There were four missed calls from her, but half a dozen from Jack, along with a handful of text messages telling him to pick up the phone. He startled. Had Jack and Avery been in an accident? Is that why Jack was trying to reach him?

He clutched his phone and ran outside, sliding the door shut behind him. He hurried across the deck and into the sand until he found a spot with no one around.

He swiped to access his voicemail. There were several.

Jack's voice was a little confused. And confusing. "Hey, uh, the police are talking to Lincoln? I don't know, man. Call me back."

The police? What was going on?

The second message said, "So, uh, I think it looks like your cat stole something? Animal Control's here now. Call me back ASAP."

Animal Control? His heart pounded.

Third. "Yeah, dude, where the heck are you? You need to call me back. ASAP. That means *now*."

Fourth. "Seriously, Alex, why do you even have a phone? Get home."

He checked the time. The last message was almost twenty minutes ago. Alex cursed and poked at his phone to call Jack. In an obnoxious example of karma, his call went straight to voicemail.

He dialed Avery.

She picked up. "Alex."

"What's going on? Is Poof okay? What about Lincoln? What's happening?"

"Poof is in my bathroom, Lincoln is in your apartment. Poof got out and robbed Mrs. Simmons again. Everything's under control now."

The tension ratcheted down about a dozen notches. "How did he get out?"

"Alex, I just got to the store, I can't talk now. Call Jack."

"But how did he—"

She snapped, "Thank you for getting my cat, Avery, I know you've got bigger things going on right now, Avery, but you handled my crap anyway, Avery."

Before he could say anything, the line went dead.

On the one hand, he could hear the strain in her voice, but on the other... what the heck did he do to deserve that? He raced back to the house and up the stairs. He grabbed his dirty clothes from Jack's room, then went into the room Chelsea had commandeered, where the rest of his things were. Footsteps echoed up the stairs while he threw his clothes in his suitcase.

"Alex? What's going on?" His mom appeared in the doorway, her voice full of concern.

"Something happened with Poof and Lincoln. I don't have the details, but there were police and Animal Control all over the apartment and it must have been a mess. I'm going home to sort it out."

She pressed a hand to her throat. "Goodness."

He took a step back and took a calming breath. No need to be racing around, frazzled, when he couldn't do anything more than head home. "Sounds like it's okay now, but I just need to get home. I'm sorry this trip hasn't gone the way you wanted it to."

"Oh, honey. It never does." She chuckled and gave him a big hug. "Drive carefully. Don't be an idiot just because you want to get home faster."

"I know." He pulled away and grabbed his phone charger from the nightstand. "I think I got everything."

"We'll double check before we leave."

Of course they would. His mom was the queen of the smallest detail. He zipped his suitcase shut and kissed her lightly on the cheek. "Gotta go. Love you."

"Love you, too."

In the living room, Bert looked up from a book he was reading, concerned. "You leaving?"

"Mom'll fill you in. Love you." All he wanted to do was get home and make sure Poof was okay. And Lincoln. And Avery.

"Love you, too. Drive safe."

The rest of the family was out on the beach, but he couldn't leave without saying goodbye, especially to Sophie. He hurried out the back and jogged across the beach to where the kids were building a sand castle.

"Hey, I have to leave."

Sophie's shoulders deflated. "I thought we were doing mini-golf."

"I know, pumpkin, I'm sorry. Poof got into some trouble and I have to go home and make sure he's okay."

She jumped up to her feet and pointed a finger up at his face. "Be more responsible." Then she threw her arms around his middle and hugged him tight.

"I'll do my best. And I promise I'll take you mini-golfing some weekend back home, okay?"

"Okay."

He gave her another hug, then hustled back to the house, grabbed his suitcase, and went out the front door. He shoved the suitcase in the trunk of his car and jumped in the driver's seat. He queued up the GPS and headed for home.

Every mile brought him relief from the Chelsea situation, and anxiety about what might be awaiting him at home. Two and a half hours into the trek, he crossed the state line from Delaware into Pennsylvania. His console lit up with an incoming call. Jack. Finally.

He hit the button on the steering wheel to connect. "What's going on?"

"Ah, man, you wouldn't believe the shitshow we came home to. We pulled in the parking lot and there were cops all over the place. Avery jumped out and was talking to one of the cops who was talking to Lincoln and your cat was in the back of a cop car raising a holy ruckus. Then Animal Control showed up to take the cat."

Alex's fingers clutched the steering wheel. At least he already knew this part of the story had a happy ending.

"Avery talked to the cops and the dude from Animal Control for quite a while and they eventually let her take the cat, so he's locked in her bathroom for the time being."

He hoped her bathroom was more secure than his apartment. "Do you know how he got out in the first place?"

"Didn't ask. Lincoln was pretty shook up, so I didn't ask for details. Avery told him to stay in your apartment until you get home. She scared him, so I'm pretty sure he's not moving an inch until you show up."

"Yeah, she seemed pretty mad when I talked to her a couple hours ago."

"Dude. She was *not* happy about cleaning up this mess in the middle of her own stuff, but she got it done like a champ. You wanna hang onto this one."

"We're just friends." He kept saying it, but that didn't make it true.

"So you're good with it if I ask her out?"

He immediately bristled. Jack? And Avery? Not a pleasant thought. "You? No."

"I'm serious."

Alex shoved the notion away. "Back to Poof. What did he do, exactly?"

"He got out of the apartment and broke into Mrs. Simpson's."

"Simmons."

"Yeah. He got into her place and stole a diamond bracelet and necklace. Your cat's got expensive taste."

Normally, Alex appreciated Jack's sarcasm. Today, not so much. "She got them back?"

"Yeah. Lincoln found a stash under a dresser and gave it back to her."

"A stash?" Crap. How many times had he gotten out–and back in–without getting caught?

"Oh, yeah. There were also a couple of earrings, a bunch of pens, and a pair of ladies underwear."

"You've got to be kidding." Were cat therapists a thing? Because it seemed like Poof had some recurring issues.

"It's all good now, though. You can relax."

"Relax? Not likely."

"It'll be fine. Oh, hey, I gotta go, Rick's calling me." The call disconnected.

Alex let out a sigh and flexed his cramping fingers. He couldn't wait to get home and see everything with his own eyes.

The miles seemed to drag, but he finally pulled into the parking lot and into his space. He left his suitcase in the trunk and ran inside. The elevator had just closed and was heading up, so he took the stairs, two at a time, until he got to the fifth floor. There was no one in the hallway.

He unlocked the door to his apartment and went inside.

Lincoln sat on the couch, scrolling through his phone and not really watching television. He jumped to his feet. "Hey. Alex. I'm so sorry."

Alex held up a hand. "Everything's okay, right?"

Lincoln nodded.

"Start at the beginning." He took a step. "No, wait, I better get a drink first."

They sat across from each other at the kitchen table.

Lincoln ran a hand down his face. "Okay, so Poof got out last evening. I didn't think much of it because I got here to feed him and he was sitting in the hallway. So I brought him in and everything seemed to be okay. I got him fed and I double checked all the doors and windows and I have no idea how he got out. So when I left, I put his food and water in the spare room and closed him in there. I figured he might be mad, but he'd be fine since his litter box is in there, too."

"Okay." Alex's brow crunched as he tried to figure out how Poof had gotten out of the bedroom *and* the apartment.

"When I got here this morning, the police were here in the hallway talking to Mrs. Simmons. While she was talking, Poof ran out of her apartment with a bracelet. She said she had other missing jewelry, so I checked the whole apartment and he had a stash under the dresser in the spare room. I gave them everything, and they took him down to put him in the cop car until Animal Control showed up. I went down to make sure he was okay and they started questioning me." His face turned red. "I... it was hard to answer her questions, so they said I was suspicious and they were going to arrest me."

"Are you okay?" Alex knew all about Lincoln's struggles with anxiety. As annoyed as he was that Poof got out on Lincoln's watch, he was sorry his friend had to go through this ordeal.

"Yeah, I'm okay." He took a sip of water. "They were ready to handcuff me when Avery and Jack got here. She came over and talked to the cops. She told them about my anxiety."

Alex tensed, ready to defend his friend. "I'm sorry she said anything about it. That's private."

"No." Lincoln held up a hand. "I'm glad she did because I couldn't get it out. By that time, I was so scared I could hardly say anything at all."

"Oh."

"Then the Animal Control guy got there and Avery managed to get them to release Poof to her custody. She took him and the cops let me go with a warning." He took another long sip of water. "I tried to thank her, but she ordered me to stay in your apartment until you got home and she'd keep Poof over there. So here I am."

"Is Jack still at her place?"

"No idea."

"She didn't need to be rude to you."

Lincoln waved his concern away. "Nah, it's fine. She just saved both our asses, so I'm not going to complain about a little snippiness."

Alex wasn't so sure he was going to let it go. Yes, she'd helped them out, but she knew about Lincoln's anxiety and didn't need to add to it. "Still."

"Seriously, man, it's all good. If she hadn't come home right then, I'd be in jail and Poof'd be in a shelter. Don't give her a hard time on my account."

"I'll see what she says about it. I don't want her being mean to you."

Lincoln managed a laugh. "In spite of evidence to the contrary, I don't need you to fight any battles for me, okay? Especially after she stuck her neck out for me. And for Poof. She didn't have to do either."

Okay, that was true. "Fine. I'll let it go."

"Good. And now I'm going to go home and never, ever cat sit for anyone again. Ever."

Alex groaned. "I'm sorry about all this."

"It's not your fault. I have no idea how Houdini got out, though, so good luck."

"Thanks."

Lincoln put his glass in the sink and paused. "I'm really sorry I let him get out. I'm just glad nothing happened to him."

Alex stood and put a hand on his shoulder. "It's not your fault. Like you said, he's Houdini."

After Lincoln left, Alex walked through the apartment, trying to figure out how the little jerk had escaped. The balcony door was closed, the security bar undisturbed. All of the windows were closed and locked. He checked the spare room—technically it was a second bedroom, but in reality it was Poof's litter box room and storage. He closed the door and jiggled the knob. Nope, no clue how Poof jimmied it open.

And no clue what to say when he saw Avery again. Sure, he was glad she'd swooped in and saved the day, but he wasn't loving the attitude.

Chapter Twenty-Five

Avery sat at her desk. Correction, the *manager's* desk, scrolling through Rick's canceled order on the computer and running numbers in her adding machine.

"What are you thinking?" Ginny asked.

"Thirty-five percent off this order, assuming he hasn't already gotten everything elsewhere, and –"

"Thirty-five percent?" Jimmy appeared in the doorway. "This is why you can't be in charge," he sneered. "You'd give everything away."

"Jimmy!" their mother snapped.

Avery wanted to throw the stapler and hit him in the face.

"Mom," he whined, "we don't need business like Rick's. These people who charge everything and then never pay are just going to run us out of business."

Ginny squeezed her eyes shut and rubbed her temples. "Rick always pays. Always. What were you thinking?"

He crossed his arms. "You put me in charge, didn't you? Well, I'm taking charge and making some changes. We can't keep extending credit."

Avery watched, knowing from the twitch in her jaw that her mother was trying her best to keep her temper under control.

James came back into the office, looking haggard. "What have we decided?"

Jimmy slid closer, no doubt assuming James would be on his side. "Avery wants to give Rick his order practically free."

"Fine." James sounded tired.

"Dad," Jimmy's eyes were wide.

"No. Enough. Avery, what's your idea?"

She cleared her throat, shocked that her parents seemed to be taking her side and not Jimmy's. "I was thinking we offer him a thirty-five percent discount on this order. This was a big deal, and we need to make a significant gesture to keep his business."

"Thirty-five is too much. Then we're only making ten percent." Jimmy held up his hands and wiggled his fingers. "Can't stay in business only making ten percent, genius."

She bit her tongue. Literally. And mentally counted to ten, then twenty before saying, "As opposed to zero, not to mention losing his future business, not to mention losing a lot of other business."

Jimmy snorted. "Oh, come on. It's one guy."

Avery itched to smack him. How could they have come from the same gene pool?? "It's not one guy. It's *Rick Lauder*, who not only gives us all of his business, but he's brought in at least two dozen other good accounts over the past three years, and who knows how many more that just come in and buy stuff over the counter."

"You're giving him too much credit."

"And you're not giving him enough." She pounded her fist on the desk. It was time to make a stand. An ultimatum. If

Jimmy was still the manager when they left this office, she was done. "Look. We need –"

The doorway darkened. A man with a cane walked in, scowling.

Avery's mouth dropped open. "Grandpa."

He was stern, his presence filling the small room. "Don't mind me, I'm just here to see how you're all going to fix this." He sat in a chair in the corner.

"Avery wants to give everything away," Jimmy tattled.

She sat up straight. No way was she shrinking back from her own grandfather, even though he thought Jimmy was more deserving of his shares simply because he had a penis. "As I was saying. We give Rick a thirty-five percent–or even forty–discount on this order, assuming he hasn't already gone elsewhere. Then we offer twenty percent on his next order as well."

Jimmy scoffed. "Forty! That leaves us with no profit on these orders. And you think you can run this business? You don't make money by giving merchandise away."

Avery leaned back in her chair. "You don't make money by driving good customers away, either."

Their grandfather's shrewd eyes flitted back and forth between them.

She threw up her hands and leaned back. "Well. I guess the final decision is the manger's, eh?"

James sighed. "Rick won't take my call. I think we figure out what we want to do going forward because it's too late to save this account."

Avery pinched the bridge of her nose. "No, it's not. He'll talk to me, but I'm not going in without something solid to offer. Why did you try calling him? What were you even going to say?" Seriously? Her father had run this business for years, and he was screwing the pooch just as bad as Jimmy. You didn't approach people like Rick with some wishy-washy half-assed apology and no solid plan. "Never mind. What are we doing? Am I reaching out to him or not?"

Ginny crossed her arms and glared at James. "Well?"

Jimmy stood straight. "We're doing what Dad said. We'll figure out our policy on invoicing and move forward from here."

"So, avoid conflict, basically." Avery shook her head in disgust. "Just so you don't have to man up and apologize."

"I have nothing to apologize for."

"ENOUGH." Ginny rose and glared at James. "This? This is how we're running this business?"

James sighed and sounded tired. "Look. I don't think Dad would appreciate us basically giving away this order. Right, Dad?" He swiveled in his chair to look at his father.

Jamie Hannigan rested his large hands atop his cane and slowly shook his head, locking eyes with each one of them in turn, Avery last. He pushed himself up from the chair and made his way to the door, ignoring James. There, he paused and nodded once at Avery. "Make the call. Forty percent. And whatever future discount you think is fair." No one dared to move.

Stunned, Avery wasn't sure at first if she'd heard him correctly.

The only noise in the silence was the sound of Grandpa's footsteps and his clunking cane against the tile floor, growing fainter with each step. The front doorbells jangled, marking his exit.

Avery's breath whooshed out of her lungs.

Ginny still stood, her face frozen in surprise.

James's elbows were on his knees, his head in his hands. He let out a long sigh of relief.

Jimmy gaped at the empty doorway. His mouth opened

and closed like a fish out of water. "What... How... That's... No." He shook his head and pointed at Avery. "I am the manager, and I say we are not reaching out. If he wants to act like a spoiled baby and pull his business, good riddance."

"No, we have to do what he says," James said.

We? Avery wanted to scream. We. What a joke. She stared at the top of her father's bowed head, at the growing bald spot, and was a little overwhelmed by the anger she felt. Surely he hadn't always been this wishy-washy and... dare she say it? Weak?

Ouch. That was never a word she would have used to describe her dad, but right now, the shoe seemed to fit a little too well.

Her phone vibrated in her back pocket, thankfully pulling her out of her thoughts. She read the message from Jack.

Rick ok 2 talk 2 u

"Rick'll talk to me."

Jimmy crossed his arms and huffed. "What, you're texting him now? What else are you doing to get business?"

Ginny reached over and smacked the back of his head. Hard. "Out!" She pointed to the door. "And so help me, if you talk to your sister like that again..." Her jaw clenched.

James sighed heavily. "That was uncalled for, Jimmy."

"Wow, don't go too hard on him, Dad." Avery had had enough. "I'd like to have the office, please."

"Wow, secret phone call. What are you offering good ole' Rick that you don't want Mom and Dad to overhear?"

Avery gave him the finger.

Ginny grabbed both men by the arm and ushered them out the door.

When the door closed behind them, Avery pulled in a shaky breath. So much was riding on this phone call.

And the person they'd made manager didn't even understand that.

Chapter Twenty-Six

Alex busied himself setting up cameras on the front door, the balcony door, and the door to the spare room, from the inside. His freaking *job* was security, he shouldn't be bested by a cat. Speaking of which, he was itching for Avery to get home so he could get Poof.

He opened the app on his phone to check that the cameras were working, and was glad to see the resolution was really good. Now maybe he could catch the little bugger in action. He was still checking the camera angles when his phone vibrated in his hand. Erin, his assistant, was texting him. Odd.

He opened her message.

> Please call me when you have a minute

His brow creased. Erin almost never texted him, and when she did, it was short and to the point. No mysterious "call me" messages like this.

He hit the button to dial her number.

"Hey. Hang on a sec." Her voice was hushed.

He heard what he assumed was a door closing, and then she came back on the line.

"I'm so sorry to bother you on a Sunday."

"No, no. Is everything okay?" He suddenly remembered she'd been out for a doctor's appointment a couple of weeks prior, and hoped it had nothing to do with that.

"I hate being vague, but when you get home, could we talk? In person?"

Now he was worried. "I came home this morning. There was a situation with—never mind, I'm home, so yeah, of course."

"Can we come over?"

"Yeah, sure."

As soon as they hung up, he wondered who "we" was. And why she wanted to come to his apartment.

Half an hour later, his intercom buzzed and he hit the button to let her in the building. He opened the door to his apartment and watched the hallway until the elevator dinged and Erin, along with her boyfriend, Greg, emerged. Her large leather purse was wedged under her arm.

She looked up and down the hallway before hurrying to his apartment. "This is going to sound crazy, but is there any way we might be overheard?"

"No." Of that, he was certain.

She wrung her hands.

"Do you want something to drink? Have a seat." Inside, he was freaking out a little bit. Erin was always calm and steady. He'd never seen her so agitated in the six years he'd known her.

"No, no, this won't take long."

"Are you okay? Did something happen? Are you sick?"

Her eyes snapped to his. "Sick? Oh, goodness, Alex, you're sweet. No, I'm fine. Sorry, I didn't think you'd worry like that.

I'm fine. But… I wanted to tell you in person that I'm going to resign."

The wind whooshed out of his lungs. "Oh, no." Erin was amazing, and he didn't even want to think about losing her. But why the secrecy and nervousness?

"And you should consider it, too."

He dropped onto the couch, grateful it was immediately behind him so he didn't land on the floor.

Erin perched on the far end of the couch. "I'm sorry, I know this is out of left field." She fumbled with her purse, and he saw her hands trembled.

"Erin?"

Her boyfriend, Greg cleared his throat. "It's not my business, but I hope this doesn't leave your apartment."

Alex had met Greg a couple of times, and had always liked him. He looked back and forth between the two. Greg was looking at Erin, his face all concern. Erin was looking into her purse. What was going on?

She pulled out a file folder and swallowed hard. She gripped the folder with both hands. "I know you and Dean are friends, and if you want to just fire me, I understand."

"Fire you? Why would I do that?"

Her eyes reddened, like she was about to cry.

"Erin? Please. What's going on?"

"Dean's stealing from the company." She shoved the folder at him. "These were on the printer. I probably shouldn't have looked, but I did, and when I realized what this was… Dean was in a meeting, so I made copies and put them in my own papers and then put the originals back like I hadn't touched them."

Alex was torn. He'd suspected as much, but always hoped that he was wrong.

"I wasn't sure what to do. I was going to call you Friday

night, but I didn't want to ruin your vacation. Greg told me to wait until tomorrow, but I just couldn't stand it any longer. I'm sorry."

"No, Erin, stop." He tore his gaze from the folder he hadn't opened yet. "You certainly haven't done anything wrong."

Greg put a hand on her shoulder and squeezed.

"Let's, um, let's sit at the table so you can walk me through this, okay?" He was afraid to open the folder, to see what it held, because he knew it would change everything.

They all sat at the kitchen table. Greg pulled out a chair for Erin, then said, "Would you rather I left? I know it's not really my business."

Alex grabbed three cups from the dishwasher. "Doesn't matter to me. Erin?"

"At the risk of sounding paranoid, I'd rather he stayed."

"No problem." Alex filled the cups with ice, then water, and sat at the table. He couldn't avoid the folder any longer. "I'm not going to like this, am I?"

Erin shook her head. "No. You're not."

Greg settled into the chair beside her and sipped his water.

Alex took a deep breath, blew it out, and opened the folder. Inside was a stack of paper, probably twenty-five sheets. Whatever it was, Erin had taken a huge chance of being caught when she copied them.

He scanned the first page. An email from Dean to Mike Chancellor, the other part-owner. In it, Dean threatened to expose Mike for his part in the scheme. The next pages were copies of spreadsheets, outlining where money should have been going... and where it actually ended up, which was to Dean and Mike's personal accounts.

The next page of spreadsheet broke down each account. A smear of yellow highlighter caught his attention. His accounts. The hospital account. The arena account. The commission he should have gotten. The commission he did get... and the breakdown of the stolen commission that went to Dean and Mike. Assholes.

The next page was a printout of text message screenshots, where Mike wanted out. And older screenshots that clearly showed he was in just as deep as Dean. It looked like Dean might have been the mastermind, overpricing, overbilling, fudging the books to divert funds, and Mike didn't have a crisis of conscience until they started skimming commissions from the sales staff.

Alex flipped through the rest of the pages of emails and screenshots, not really seeing them. "I'll have to go through them again later, when my brain's not humming. This is just too much."

Erin nodded sadly. "I know."

He closed the folder and tapped it. "May I keep these?"

"Yes." She hesitated. "I made another copy that I'm keeping."

Insurance. Good idea.

"I'm going to call the police."

Alex met her eyes. "Can you hold off on that? A good friend of mine is a lawyer. She can probably give us some advice on the best way to proceed."

She glanced to Greg, then back to Alex.

"I'm not asking you not to say anything, I just think we might have a better outcome if we have a plan and some direction. I'll email her today, and if I don't hear back, I'll call her first thing Tuesday morning. I assume her office is closed for the holiday."

"Probably."

"I'm not sure I would have had the guts to stand there and risk getting caught making copies. You're amazing."

She let out a shaky laugh, "Yeah, well, I still want to puke."

"It'll be okay."

"I hope so." She stood and pushed her chair in. "I guess I'll see you Tuesday morning."

"Thanks, Erin." He led them to the door and opened it just as Avery came down the hall. "Oh, hey. Avery."

She paused and gave them a half-smile. "Alex."

"This is my assistant, Erin, and her boyfriend, Greg. This is Avery. She's not my girlfriend."

Avery rolled her eyes, while Erin cringed a little. Greg stared at a spot on the floor.

"I mean, she's my not-girlfriend."

Another eye roll, and Avery said, "I'm his neighbor. Nice to meet you."

Alex tried again. "It was a thing. Like ha-ha, not my girl-friend. Never mind." He lifted his hands in defeat. "I guess you had to be there."

Erin nodded. "Guess so. See you later." She and Greg walked down the hall and got into the elevator.

"I need to get Poof."

"Can I unlock the door first?" she shot back.

His first thought was to snap at her, to return her frustra-tion with his own, but it wouldn't do any good to argue with her. He just wanted his cat.

His cat.

A little voice in his head reminded him that if it wasn't for Avery, his cat would be sitting in a shelter right now, confused and terrified. And what would happen if Poof fell through the cracks during an understaffed holiday weekend? Not every shelter was a no-kill shelter. He bit down on his tongue. Avery had saved Poof, period. Lincoln hadn't. Jack hadn't. He hadn't. Avery had.

She unlocked the door and shoved it open, stalking inside and tossing her bag onto the couch. "He's in here." She went straight to the bedroom door and moved the chair she'd wedged under the knob so she could open the door.

Alex followed her. It felt odd being in her place because it was the same as his, only the mirror opposite. He walked past her bed, to the bathroom door, which was still shut. That was a good sign.

Avery twisted the knob and pushed open the bathroom door, then stood aside for him to go in.

Alex held his breath until he saw Poof, sprawled out on the counter, stretched over and licking a thin stream of water trickling from the faucet into the sink. "Do you have a leak?"

"Huh?" She came into the bathroom.

Suddenly, it hit him. He turned and looked at her bathroom door. "You've gotta be kidding me." He left the bathroom and walked through the living room to look at the front door. He smacked his palm to his forehead.

"What is it?" Avery was at his elbow.

Poof had followed her out of the bathroom and was rubbing against her legs, his tail winding around her calf.

"Houdini here. I can't believe I never figured it out. It's the knobs."

"Okay?"

"I realized it in the bathroom. Your faucet knobs are levers. My doorknobs are levers. They're not regular round knobs like yours. He can probably jump up and pull them down to open the doors."

Poof purred loudly, like he'd been waiting for them to solve the mystery. He paused to rub his cheek against her knee.

Alex inclined his head toward the cat. "He must know you saved his fuzzy butt." He reached back and rubbed his neck. "Thank you. I don't know how I'll ever make it up to you, but I really, really appreciate what you did."

"You'd have done the same."

"Sure, but I didn't. I mean it, Avery, I'm so grateful. I know Lincoln is, too. He was sure he was going to jail and it scared him half to death, which made it even harder for him to talk."

"Don't give me too much credit. If I hadn't met him the day we left, I wouldn't have known."

Any of the lingering annoyance Alex had vanished. In fact, he couldn't remember why he'd been annoyed at her in the first place. She'd put her own stuff aside–major stuff–and saved the day for him and Poof. And Lincoln. Right. Her own major stuff.

"How'd your meeting go?"

Her shoulders drooped. "The whole thing has been a disaster. Thanks to Jack, Rick was willing to talk to me, but it was way worse than Jimmy let on."

Chapter Twenty-Seven

Avery's head pounded. It had been the longest, shittiest day ever, and all she wanted to do was crawl into bed. She side-stepped the cat and went into the kitchen. Pouring a glass of water, she leaned her hip against the counter and popped a couple Advil. "Jimmy apparently told Rick that we weren't going to put up with customers essentially stealing from us."

"He said that?"

"I can't believe Rick agreed to come back. I'm not sure I would have given us another chance." She rubbed her temples. "Actually, I'm pretty sure I would have told me to go pound sand after something like that."

"I'm sorry you're dealing with this."

"Rick had one condition. That he never, ever has to deal with Jimmy again. I agreed, but I had to cross my fingers and hope it works out. It's not like Jimmy's in the store often, but when he is, holy crap can he screw stuff up."

Poof came over and wound around her legs again. He usually avoided her, so she thought he must truly understand she'd saved his sorry butt from a really, really bad weekend.

She reached down to scratch his fluffy head and was rewarded with a loud purr and a chirring, "Mrawr."

Alex said, "Thanks for everything. I know this was the worst possible day to deal with our stuff on top of your own."

"That's always the way, isn't it? When it rains, it pours." She wondered if she should go ahead and ask if he was getting back with Chelsea, just to put some crap icing on this crap cake of a day.

"I should take Poof home. Thanks again."

"No problem."

He scooped the cat up and walked to the door. "What are you doing tomorrow?"

"I plan to stay in bed with the covers over my head and move just enough that I don't get bedsores."

"Excellent plan. If you change your mind and want to hang out, let me know. I was thinking about going to the gym at some point. Then lunch? If you want?"

Okay, she couldn't let it go. "Won't that bother Chelsea?"

His eyebrows rose. "We're not together. We're not back together. We're not *getting* back together."

"Does she know this?"

"Seriously? Do you think I'd string her along?"

Avery held a hand up. "Stop. I'm just asking if you're both clear that there's no relationship, or if she's still trying to… whatever she was trying to do."

"No. She's not. We had a long talk after you left. It wasn't like she even wanted me, anyway."

That piqued her curiosity. "What do you mean?"

"She just had a bad breakup and had some rose colored glasses on about our relationship."

"Ah." She wasn't sure if that made her feel better or worse. "What if she had wanted you? Then what?"

"Then she'd still just be an ex, you'd still be my not-girlfriend, and I'd still rather spend time with you than just about anybody else."

"She's gorgeous."

"What am I supposed to say to that?"

Avery sighed. "I don't know."

"I don't get why she'd make you self-conscious or whatever."

"I don't know why, either, but she does. She's just so petite and cute and put together and polished I can't even do decent eyeliner half the time."

"Who cares about eyeliner?"

"I don't know, Alex. I guess I'm fixating on eyeliner because I'm exhausted and hangry."

"Do you want to get something? I'm hungry, too. Not quite hangry, but I will be soon." He shifted the cat in his arms. "I'll take Poof home and we can go?"

Avery thought about her empty fridge. It was either go to the store, go to eat, or starve. "Yeah."

A few minutes later, they were in Alex's car, heading to General Custard's. The place was busy, but not overly so. They stood in line at the food window and ordered. Alex paid for their food before Avery could get her money out. They waited near the pickup window until their number was called, then took their food out to one of the empty picnic tables.

Avery unwrapped her General Buster, a hot ham and cheese sandwich with lettuce, tomato, onion, pickles, and mayo. She bit into it and couldn't help but groan. "So good," she mumbled around the food.

Alex was inhaling his bacon cheeseburger. He nodded in agreement.

When the sandwiches were gone, they shared French fries and onion rings.

"I got some news today, too," Alex said.

She paused, mid-onion ring. "Good or bad?"

"Both. Mostly bad. Only good because I know I haven't lost my mind."

"Do tell." She was eager to talk about anything other than Rick, the store, her family, or Chelsea.

"Of course I have to give the standard disclaimer that this can't leave this table."

"Of course." She held up her hand. "It's in the not-girlfriend code of ethics."

"I got irrefutable proof that my commissions were stolen."

She dropped an onion ring into the ketchup and fished it back out. Anger on his behalf simmered under the surface, joining her own anger at everything else. "You're kidding. That's horrible. I mean, I guess we knew that, but it sucks that it's real."

"And that's just the tip of the iceberg. It's not just my commissions, and they're also overbilling clients. I put a call in to a lawyer friend of mine to see what she says I should do. I just want my money so I can get out of Dodge."

"I hope she gets back to you. I'd be going nuts trying to figure out what to do."

"Yeah, not just me, but Erin wants to quit and I can't blame her."

"I wouldn't want to stay, either."

"Same, but I don't want to deal with this alone."

Avery could relate to that sentiment. "I get that."

They finished eating and threw their trash away. Alex reached over for her hand as they walked back to the car. She gladly took it.

Chapter Twenty-Eight

Monday morning came, and Alex still couldn't figure out why Avery kept comparing herself to Chelsea and coming up short. He also couldn't figure out what possessed Dean and Mike to start stealing from their employees.

And for right now, he'd keep his mouth shut and go in to work as usual, at least for a few days. He'd updated his LinkedIn profile but that was the extent of any action. It drove him nuts, having his hands tied when he itched to do something. So instead of doing something about his career that was circling the drain, he decided to do something about his rotten cat.

As much as he hated to spend any money that he should probably be squirreling away for his inevitable unemployment, he knocked on Avery's door.

"Hey."

He gave her a half-smile. "Is this how you're spending your holiday?" He gestured to her pajamas.

"Yes. It's a holiday so I plan to take full advantage of it."

"I need doorknobs. I was going to run to Lowe's, and then I thought that would be crappy if it's something you carry."

She leaned against the door jamb and crossed her arms, pretending to scowl. "Wow, you're going to use your status as my not-boyfriend in order to shop at my closed store on a holiday?"

"No, I was going to wait until tomorrow."

"Come in." She moved aside and closed the door behind him. "Well, guess what. There *are* perks to not being my boyfriend. I can totally hook you up with doorknobs. But no discount, *and* you have to buy me lunch."

"Deal."

"Go secure your devil beast while I change into real clothes."

"You got it." He went to his apartment and locked Poof in the bedroom, wedging a chair under the knob so he couldn't escape.

"Mrowwr," Poof objected loudly from the other side of the door.

"Don't take that tone with me, mister. You can be glad you're not clinking a tin can across a set of iron bars right now." Alex shook the handle to make sure it was secure before joining Avery in the hall.

They took Avery's car to the hardware store.

"I feel like we're doing a heist."

Avery laughed. "Hardly." She unlocked the front door and closed it behind them, then punched a code into the security panel.

Alex paused and looked at it. "Not to sound like a salesman, but you might want to consider upgrading your system. If I'm not mistaken, the cameras probably aren't even HD."

"HD? Are you kidding? I'm pretty sure the system still records on VHS tapes."

He sucked in a breath.

Behind the counter, she touched something on the cash

register. "I'm kidding. It's not quite *that* ancient." She jerked her head. "This way to the doorknobs."

Alex followed her down the aisle to the knob display.

"We've got your exterior, which is actually what I'd recommend for your main door, even though it's not technically outside, and then these are what you'll want for interior. Color preference? There's brushed nickel, chrome, brass, and my favorite, the aged bronze that has a nice copper color showing through the distressed markings."

He touched the bronze knob. "That really is nice, but I think everything in the apartment is brass."

"Yeah, it is. I wonder why some of your knobs are lever-style. None of mine are."

He shrugged. "Last tenant must have changed them." He picked out an exterior set and three interior.

"You might want to get a childproof kit for the front door. Unless you're sure it's the lever thing."

"I'm not sure about anything these days." He picked the package off its hook.

"Need anything else while we're here? Tools to install the knobs?"

"Tools?"

"I'd recommend a power drill, nail gun, and circular saw."

"Wow, that's quite the upsell."

She laughed. "Okay, fine. All you'll need is a Phillips head screwdriver. I have some nice power options."

"I'm pretty sure I can get by with my manual set."

"Suit yourself." She scanned his purchases and ran his credit card. "Let me get your receipt." She bagged his items and put the receipt in the bag. "Thank you for shopping at Hannigan Hardware. Please come again."

"I'll be back on the Fourth of July and Labor Day. Maybe Christmas," he teased.

"Alrighty, let's get some lunch." She turned the register back off, armed the alarm, and locked the door behind them.

Alex held the bag up a little. "I really appreciate this. You didn't have to make a special trip for me, especially after you've already gone out of your way for me and Poof. So thanks. A lot."

"You're quite welcome. And don't take this the wrong way, but I'm kind of glad to deal with your mess for a bit. Keeps my mind off mine."

"I'm sorry both our messes ruined your vacation."

"And yours." She hit the button to unlock the car doors.

Alex slid into his seat and fastened his seatbelt. "We should try again in a few weeks when everything settles down."

"Just the two of us?"

"Yeah." He thought it was a great idea. Might as well have a nice vacation together since this one most definitely was not.

"Ocean City again?" She sounded hopeful.

"There, or somewhere else. Doesn't matter to me. We could do Outer Banks."

"That's pretty far. We'd have to fly home when Poof gets arrested again."

He laughed. "Hopefully changing the knobs solves that problem."

"I hope so. Where are we going for lunch?"

"Anywhere you want."

"Since it's your treat I'm picking the most expensive place I can think of. Lobster and seafood, here we come."

"Still trying to hold onto the ocean, huh?"

"The ocean, yes. That trip? No." She shook her head.

"Agreed. It was crazy, and I'm sorry for that. I wish we'd had a better time."

"It's okay." She pulled out of the parking lot and drove to Sonny's Diner.

"I thought you were going somewhere expensive."

"Eh, I'll go easy on you. This time."

They got out of the car and he reached over to grab her hand.

They had just settled into a booth when Avery's phone vibrated in her pocket. She pulled it out and looked at it. "Crap, I have to take this. Sorry." She swiped the phone to connect the call. "Hi, hang on a sec."

Alex watched her scoot out of the dining area and out into the parking lot. It didn't seem like she was saying much, just nodding and running a hand through her hair.

"Are you ready to order?"

"Oh. Not yet, but we'll both have iced tea."

The waitress gave him a nod and left. He turned his attention back to Avery. The call was short. She slid her phone back into her pocket. He watched her take a huge breath and let it out before he lost sight of her.

A few seconds later, she sat back down.

"Everything okay?"

"I'm not sure. That was my grandfather. He wants to meet with me this week."

"He didn't say what about?"

"Not a clue. Other than I'm sure it's about the store, of course."

"Sure."

"He's probably going to sit me down and tell me why Jimmy should have the store because even though I'm more qualified and will do a much better job, I don't have a penis."

"I hope that's not the case. Surely he's not that short-sighted."

"He's very old school. I don't have a lot of hope he's suddenly become enlightened."

"I'm sorry."

"Let's change the subject. Do you have any idea what you're going to do about your job?"

"Not a clue."

Chapter Twenty-Nine

Avery let Alex get the check, even though she'd only been kidding about making him buy lunch. On the way back to the apartment, she said, "Do you want help changing the doorknobs?"

"Sure, if you don't have anything better to do."

"Sadly, I do not."

Back at the apartment, Alex changed the knob to his front door while Avery changed the bathroom knob. He tested the keys to make sure they worked, then moved the chair and let Poof out of his prison.

Poof ran over and wound around Avery's legs, purring loudly.

"He's definitely had a change of heart about you."

Avery reached down and scratched his head. "He's still rotten." Truth be told, now that his sticky fingers – er, paws – were under control, he was much more lovable.

"Can't argue with that."

She tossed the old doorknob pieces into a plastic bag and helped Alex install the childproof sleeve over the front door knob. "Hopefully this fixes his escaping."

"I can't imagine how else he'd get out."

"He won't tell you how he does it."

"That's why I installed cameras."

"You did?"

"On the front door and the balcony door. And the door to Poof's room." He pointed up to the small square camera mounted on the wall facing the door.

"He has his own room?"

Alex flopped onto the couch and turned on a baseball game. "Of course he does."

Avery settled onto the couch beside him.

Suddenly, Alex sat up straight and pulled his phone out of his pocket.

She watched him curiously as he swiped, then grinned at her.

"I have an idea."

"Uh oh."

"It's a good one, I promise." He held out his phone to show her the screen. "Senators play at home today at four."

"Who are they playing?"

"Erie."

Avery couldn't remember who that team fed into, so she figured they weren't a big rival. She grabbed his phone and looked at the schedule. "Do you think we can still get tickets?"

"Yup." He took his phone back and tapped on the screen. A minute later, he said, "Done. We're even along the third base line."

"Nice." She hadn't been to a baseball game since she'd moved back to Hickory Hollow. The Harrisburg Senators weren't her favorite team by far (they fed into the Washington Nationals, who were a rival to her beloved Braves, after all) but it was a nice day, and sitting outside at a baseball game was the best way she could think of to spend the afternoon. "What time should we leave?"

"We can go now if you want."

"Yeah. Let me go over and change." She nudged Poof off her lap. He jumped to the floor and flounced away, offended.

Avery let herself into her apartment. It was almost two o'clock, and much warmer than they'd forecasted. She changed into a pair of shorts and, of course, a Braves T-shirt. She brushed her hair back into a ponytail and pulled that through the back of her Braves cap. Before she headed back out, she grabbed a can of sunscreen to take along.

Fifteen minutes later, they were getting into Alex's car for the forty-five minute drive to City Island, where the Senators played.

By some unspoken agreement, they kept the conversation light. No work, no family, no Chelsea. Mostly, they talked about baseball.

Chapter Thirty

Once they picked up their tickets, Alex followed Avery through the gate, where stadium personnel were handing out the freebie for the day–Senators T-shirts. Avery asked for a size small, so he knew she wasn't going to wear it herself. Not that he thought she would–she was much more diehard about her fandom than most people he knew.

They found their seats, which were thankfully in the shade, since there wasn't a cloud in the sky, and the sun was blaring down.

A beer vendor made his way up the aisle, and Avery's arm flew up, flagging him down. She paid for two beers and handed one to Alex. "I don't normally drink these, but I'm pretty sure it's a law to have at least one cold beer during a baseball game."

They clinked their cans together.

"Unless you're playing."

"Touché."

The game started with a bang. By the end of the first inning, the Senators were up 3-0. By the end of the fourth, they'd expanded their lead 8-2.

"YES!" Avery pointed to the big screen. The camera panned to three costumed characters racing onto the field. Mustard, ketchup, and a hot dog convened at home plate while the Senators mascot, Rascal, a giant, lovable, blue and red… something, pantomimed the race rules.

The mustard took off running toward first base, leaving ketchup and the hot dog behind.

"Go, hot dog!" Avery yelled, laughing.

"Come on, ketchup!" Alex joined in the fun.

The stadium roared with laughter and cheering for the characters. As expected, the mustard took a dramatic fall rounding second base, allowing the other two to catch up. The race from third to home was a back and forth, until the hot dog dove face-first onto home plate and then rolled over to make a dirt angel. Ketchup came in second, while the disgraced mustard came in last.

Alex's cheeks hurt from laughing by the time the players retook the field, mostly because Avery's laughter was contagious. She was determined to have a great time. For the hundredth time, he was glad he'd had the idea to come to the game.

During the seventh inning stretch, they snuck out to the restrooms and then got overpriced soda, hot dogs, and nachos. Back at their seats, Avery had just taken a huge bite of her hot dog and Alex had a mouthful of cheesy nachos when the Kiss Cam landed on them.

"Shmit," Avery mumbled around her hot dog. She waved to the camera and leaned toward Alex.

He tried to swallow his nachos and managed to give her a peck on the cheek while she gave the camera a thumbs up. The crowd cheered. Thankfully the camera panned away to another set of victims.

"That has got to be the worst thing ever," she said, shaking her head.

"No, the worst thing ever are the surprise Jumbotron proposals."

"Yes. You're right. One hundred percent." She shuddered.

At the end of the eighth inning the Senators were up 10-5. Alex leaned over and said, "Should we stay to the end or head out now to beat some of the traffic?"

Avery stretched her back. "I'm good heading out now."

They made their way to the parking lot. A handful of other fans had the same idea, and there was already a line of cars waiting to get off the island. Alex pulled into the line and they inched up the hill and onto the Market Street Bridge, where traffic flowed normally.

On the highway, heading home, Avery said, "This was the best idea ever."

"Next time, we'll do a major league game. Maybe when the Braves come to Baltimore, since that's an easy drive."

"That'd be awesome. We can make a day of it. Do the Inner Harbor, take a water taxi out to Fort McHenry, stop at the Cheesecake Factory."

"Sounds perfect." What sounded even more perfect than the details was making plans with Avery.

"Statue of Liberty." She pointed out the window at the miniature version of the statue that stands in the Susquehanna River. "Looks like she's got some company."

A flock of whiteish birds had descended on Lady Liberty and were perched on her torch, her head, and around her feet.

When they finally got back home, around eight, they rode the elevator in comfortable silence until it opened on their floor.

"Oh! I meant to give this to you earlier." She held out her

Senators T-shirt. "I got a small. I was hoping Sophie could wear it. Tell her it's from Poof as an apology for dragging you home and making her miss out on mini-golf with her favorite uncle."

Alex took the shirt from her. Emotion made his voice thick, so he cleared his throat. "Thanks. I really appreciate that. I know Sophie will love it."

Avery nudged him with her elbow. "If she doesn't want it, use it to line Poof's litter box."

Alex laughed. She was more fanatical about her baseball than he was, even though it had been his career. He wondered if she was also into football or soccer or hockey. He could easily imagine that going to any sporting event with her would be a blast.

"Thanks again for today. I had so much fun."

"Me, too. Good luck tomorrow."

She groaned. "You, too."

He hesitated, wondering if he should lean in, when she dropped her head down, fishing in her pocket for her keys.

"Night, not-my-boyfriend."

The moment passed. "Night, not-my-girlfriend."

It dawned on him that he'd really like that status to be updated.

Chapter Thirty-One

Tuesday was a madhouse at the store. By the end of the day, Avery's cheeks hurt from smiling and talking to all the customers. Jimmy had been there all day, but spent half of it in the office doing who knows what. Ginny and James were both on the floor all day, too.

Avery was glad it was so busy, because she wasn't in the mood to talk to any of them at this point.

Ginny locked the door and turned the sign off. "Thank goodness. What a day."

"Indeed," James agreed, stretching. His back cracked half a dozen times.

Avery opened the cash register and began counting the money.

Jimmy sauntered out from the office. "Whew, that was a really busy day, huh?"

Ginny shot him a glare. "What were you doing?"

"Uh, paperwork?"

"What paperwork?"

"Uh, like all kinds of stuff. You don't need to worry about it anymore."

"Yeah, right." Ginny yanked the bank bag out from under the counter and put it near where Avery was counting money.

"Oh yeah," Jimmy said, smirking at Avery, "We're going to start having two people count the money. And I think Avery needs to explain why she was giving more stuff away for free yesterday."

"What?" James raised an eyebrow and looked at her.

"I brought Alex in yesterday because he needed doorknobs for his apartment. The credit card slip is right here." She slapped the slip of paper onto the counter. "He bought three knobs and one childproof kit."

"How much of a discount does he get for sleeping with you?" Jimmy grabbed the receipt.

"Jimmy!" Ginny yelled. "Enough!" She whirled to James. "When are you going to put your foot down and stop letting your son treat your daughter like garbage?"

"Why are you yelling at me? I have nothing to do with this."

She crossed her arms. "You have *everything* to do with this. He says the ugliest things to her and I yell while you stand back and let me be the bad guy. What you don't realize is that you *are* the bad guy for your daughter because you never stand up for her." She spun back to Jimmy. "And you. If you want the money counted twice, do it yourself. Avery, let's go. The *manager* can figure out how to do the deposit and close up."

"What's going on here?" No one had heard Jamie come in through the back.

Avery stood beside her mom, feeling her seethe.

Jamie leaned on his cane and looked from face to face. "Well, since you're all here, we might as well talk now." Without waiting for a response, he turned and walked back to the small breakroom.

Avery nudged her mom's arm. "Might as well get it over with." She was the first one into the breakroom, where she sat across from her grandfather. Ginny, James, and Jimmy followed and filled the rest of the seats at the small table.

Jamie put a manila folder on the table and flipped it open. "You know I'm ready to be done with my part in this business. It's time for me to hand it over. You also know that it's always been my dream, and my clear intention, to build this business and hand it over to my son, who would then hand it over to his son."

Avery's jaw clenched. Here we go. This is it. The moment when Jimmy gets a business solely because of his penis.

"Well." Jamie cleared his throat. "I didn't build this business alone. Helen was by my side every step of the way. Without her, I would have failed a thousand times over. The first thing I'm going to do when I meet her on the other side is apologize."

Avery's head jerked up. *What?*

"I hope she'll accept my apology, and Ginny, Avery, I hope you'll both accept my apologies now. Ginny, I'm sorry. You're the backbone of this store. No way James could have kept it going on his own. Too doggone wishy-washy. Avery, you're cut from your mother's cloth. You came home when we needed you, and singlehandedly kept us from going bankrupt when your dad was sick."

"Hey." Jimmy's objection was pitiful.

Jamie's eyes swung to him, then back to Avery. "I'm sorry. I didn't give you the credit you deserve."

Avery couldn't speak. Who was this man? He looked like her grandfather, sounded like her grandfather, but those words didn't sound like him at all.

He tapped a finger on the stack of papers in front of him. "I had my lawyer draw these up. As soon as everything's signed, I won't own a single share."

Jimmy sat back and smirked.

"Wipe that smile off your face, boy, you aren't going to be happy about this."

Chapter Thirty-Two

"What's this all about?" Chip asked as he slid into the seat beside Alex.

"Beats me." Alex's palms were sweaty. The entire sales team, five of them in total, had gotten an email about a meeting in the conference room at five o'clock. Why it was scheduled at closing time, he couldn't fathom.

At two minutes after the hour, the sales team was antsy, and Mike finally hustled through the door. "Sorry to keep you waiting." He sat at the head of the table.

Dean came into the room and sat beside Mike. His face was tense, his mouth pursed and annoyed.

Mike tapped a stack of envelopes against the table top. "We called you all in here because we know you've had some questions about commissions lately."

Alex felt the heat crawling up his neck. What was going on?

"First we want to sincerely apologize. It was never our intention to short any of you. There were some accounting errors and funds were shifted into the wrong accounts and it affected your commission payouts. For that, we are sincerely sorry and sincerely hope you accept our apology."

Alex wished he could take a shot every time Mike said "sincerely."

Mike stood and walked around the table, handing each salesperson an envelope. "We've gone back through the accounting and cut checks for all the commissions you were shorted, plus a nominal amount of interest from the date you should have received the commission. We ask for your understanding and hope there are no hard feelings."

"What's to keep it from happening again?" Chip asked.

Mike held up a hand and resumed his seat. "You have my word. This was just a fluke."

You have my word? Alex managed not to scoff. Mike's word was worth nothing. He looked at Dean, who hadn't said anything since he came in. The muscle in his jaw clenched. Alex thought over the emails he'd read and reread and reread again. This was no accounting error. It was no mistake.

"If there's nothing else, you can go. We just wanted to make things right. You're the lifeblood of this company, and we appreciate all your hard work and your patience in this matter. Thanks for sticking around for this meeting."

Doreen stood up and said, "Thanks for making it right."

Alex stood as well, but said nothing as he filed out of the room with the rest of the salespeople. In his own office, he cut the envelope open and sucked in a breath. It was everything he was owed, plus the few dollars of interest. He grabbed his phone and searched the hours for the bank. They were open until six. If he hurried, he'd get there before they closed.

He hustled to the elevator. It slid open just as he took a step toward the stairwell. He rode to the lobby alone and scanned his badge to unlock the door and had to keep himself from running across the parking lot.

As glad as he was to have the check, it wasn't worth anything if it didn't clear.

At the bank, there was a limit of five thousand in cash. He took it, and deposited the rest into his savings account, where it would sit until it hopefully cleared.

He asked the teller, "When will I know if this cleared for sure?"

She smiled and tapped on her keyboard. "I can't give you information on this specific account, but what I can tell you is that if it weren't to clear for some reason, it would happen with tomorrow's business."

"So if it's still in my account on Thursday, it cleared."

"Yes."

"Okay, thank you." He pocketed the five thousand and crossed his fingers that the check wouldn't bounce in the next forty-eight hours.

Chapter Thirty-Three

Avery held her breath as her grandfather slid papers across the table to her. "What is all this?"

He tented his fingers and leaned toward her. "I'm giving my shares to you. As soon as you sign this, you will have controlling interest in Hannigan Hardware."

She swallowed hard.

"What!" Jimmy burst to his feet. "It was promised to me!"

Jamie stared his grandson down over the top of his wire-rimmed glasses. "I never, not once, promised to give you my shares."

"Dad said—"

"Your father made assumptions. Fair assumptions, based on things I've said or done, I won't argue that, but assumptions all the same. I've been accused of hanging on to the store too long, and I suppose I have."

"This isn't how it works, old man. You give your shares to Dad, then it's his decision. That's how it works." Jimmy jumped to his feet, fuming.

Avery sat still, watching her grandfather's eyes narrow.

"Your father didn't want control."

"Well, he does now," Jimmy shouted. "Tell him, Dad. Tell him you want the shares."

"Jimmy…" James began.

"Save your breath," Jamie snapped, cutting him off. "We've been over it a dozen times, and it's done. Avery."

She jolted upright, startled when the attention swung back to her. "Um."

Jamie slid a pen toward her.

"I, uh, obviously, I mean, thank you. I'm honored. Thank you, Grandpa. I need to read over these before I sign, in case I have any questions or anything."

"You stupid idiot!" Jimmy's face burned bright red. His eyes bugged. "He's handing you the store and you need to read it all over? What a slap in the face."

As much as Avery wanted to jump up and do just that–slap her brother in the face, she ignored his outburst.

"There's one condition." Jamie also ignored his grandson.

A rock plummeted into her gut. Of course there had to be a catch. And she'd guess it was a big one.

"You can't fire Jimmy from his managing position. He always has a place here."

Jimmy barked a laugh.

Tears stung the backs of Avery's eyes. "There is nothing I want more than to run this store and grow it and do you proud. I love you, and I love my brother, but he's incapable of successfully managing this store." She shook her head. Her hands trembled as she pushed the pages back toward her grandfather. "If the condition is that he always has a job, I'd agree. He can stock shelves for more money than he deserves. I could even live with sending him an allowance every month for forever. But no. If I own this store, he will not manage it. I'm sorry."

Jamie pursed his lips and straightened the papers.

"Avery, wait," Ginny said softly.

Before the tears could fall, or she could snatch the papers back and sign them, Avery jumped up and ran into the office. She grabbed her purse and made a beeline for the front door.

Chapter Thirty-Four

Alex pulled into his parking space and grabbed his bag of take out. He skipped the elevator and ran up the stairs, trying to burn off some of the nervous energy pent up in his gut. In his apartment, he was pleased to see that Poof was where he belonged, lounging on the back of the couch with no sign of escape or theft. He ate his burger and fries over the kitchen sink, but still felt unsettled.

He filled Poof's bowls with food and fresh water, then paced around the living room. Inspired, he changed into his gym clothes. Some time with the weights might help take the anxious edge off. He grabbed his gym bag with clean clothes and told Poof where he was going.

In the hallway, he pulled the door shut behind him. The elevator doors slid open. Avery stepped off and grimaced. He suspected she was attempting to smile, but it wasn't quite happening. "Rough day?"

She opened her mouth to speak, then snapped it shut. "I just want to punch someone. So, not the best conversationalist right now."

On impulse, he asked, "Wanna come along to the gym?"

"You know what? That might be good. You sure you don't mind me coming along?"

"Of course I don't mind. I wouldn't have offered." Mind? He was happy to have her go with him.

"Sure. Right. Come on in, it'll just take a minute."

He followed her into her apartment. She dropped her purse onto the floor beside the door and kicked it out of the way. After she walked into her bedroom, he picked it up and set it on the side table. He felt bad for her. She must have had a miserable day. Whether it was work itself or the family business drama, he couldn't guess.

A few minutes later, she came back into the living room in her gym clothes. "Ready." She slung her gym bag over her shoulder and closed the door behind them. In the elevator, she said, "Just to preempt any conversation, can you please not ask about my day?" Her chin quivered a little.

Alex put an arm over her shoulders. "Well, not-my-girl-friend, wait until you hear about *my* day."

When they were in his car, he started it and said, "They called a last-minute meeting for the sales staff for five o'clock, which was super weird. We never have staff meetings at five."

"Why would they call a meeting at closing time?"

"Exactly what I was wondering. So we're all in the conference room and nobody knows what's going on."

"How many salespeople are there?"

"There's five of us. The door opens and Mike comes in with a stack of envelopes. A minute later, Dean comes in, but he looks mad." He put his turn signal on and pulled into the gym's parking lot. "He doesn't say a word while Mike makes this huge apology and says there was an 'accounting error' and he hands out the envelopes."

"Was it your commission?"

"Yup. Every penny. Plus a nominal amount of interest as an apology for their 'mistake.'"

"That's what they're going with? An accounting error. Ooops, sorry we accidentally stole thousands of dollars from you, my bad, here you go, please don't sue."

"Pretty much."

"What are you going to do?"

"Right now, I'm playing it cool, like everything's fine. Meanwhile I'm putting out feelers to see what else is out there. I'm not doing anything else until the check clears, though. Don't want any red flags going up."

"Did you update your lawyer friend?"

"Yeah. I called her on my way home and left a message."

They got out of the car and crossed the sidewalk. Alex swiped his keycard to unlock the gym's door.

"Guess I didn't need to dig mine out." Avery slid her keycard back into the side pocket of her gym bag. "I'm going to hit the treadmill first, then the weight room. You?"

"Same. I'm going to hit the heavy bag for a while if you want to partner up."

"I'll take you up on that. Might help me get some frustration out."

Alex grinned. "I'll be sure to stand waaaay behind the bag. Just in case you swing and miss."

"I won't miss." She smiled back and jumped on a treadmill.

He took the one beside her and the conversation stopped. He eased into his run, but her feet pounded the treadmill next to his. He normally kept his eyes on the treadmill's data screen to avoid making eye contact with other gym-goers, but today he was glad for the wall of mirrors in front of them. He watched Avery's face, her determined stare locked on some spot in front of her. Her cheeks reddened with the exertion. Her lips pursed with each breath she blew out.

Alex slowed to a jog, then a walk. He wiped sweat from his forehead and said, "I'm heading over."

Avery's long ponytail bounced as she nodded. "Be there in a minute," she huffed.

The motion-activated overhead lights flicked on as Alex walked into the empty weight room. He gave the heavy bag a few half-hearted jabs while he waited for Avery. Something big must have happened, and while he'd respect her wish to not speak about it, he hoped she'd tell him soon.

The door clacked open, and Avery walked over, sweat dampening her hair and making little trails down her face and neck. She tossed her bag into the corner next to Alex's. Without a word, she pulled on a pair of gloves and eyed the bag. She circled it like it was a live opponent.

She found a spot she liked and bounced on her feet a few times, pulling her arms up. Her right arm shot out and she punched the bag, then her left. She punched again and grunted as she connected with the bag. Over and over she punched, giving motion to her anger. Alex was glad she wasn't mad at *him*.

Chapter Thirty-Five

Avery's arms shook, but she kept landing punches. It felt good to smash her fists into something. Would be even better if it was Jimmy's face, but she'd have to make do with the bag. Punch after punch after punch, her fists thumped against the bag. Her shoulders ached. Her upper arms ached. Her abs ached. Her legs ached from the treadmill. Her jaw ached from gritting her teeth. Her heart ached from the meeting.

She'd been prepared to watch her grandfather hand the store over to Jimmy. She'd been stunned when her grandfather gave the papers to her. And then given the one condition that was a slap in her face. It meant that he knew Jimmy was a fool and incapable of taking the store where it needed to go. But he'd still let Jimmy manage it into the ground. Because penis.

She punched the bag with all her might.

All the work she'd done was for nothing.

Punch. Punch.

Cleaning up her parents' mess with the computer system.

Punch. Punch.

Spending months reorganizing the entire business.

Punch. Punch.

Working with vendors to get better pricing.

Punch. Punch.

Doing her brother's job because his lazy ass wouldn't.

Punch. Punch.

Giving up her life in Atlanta. Foregoing her days off. Cutting her *one* vacation short. Cleaning up her brother's messes. Begging Rick not to pull his business.

Punch! Punch!

Nothing. In the end, it was all for nothing.

Punch! Punch! Punch! PUNCH! PUNCH!

Avery's swings flew wide. She squeezed her eyes shut against the tears scalding the backs of her eyes.

PUNCH! PUNCH!

She yelled, the frustration clawing its way up her burning throat. Her arms shook. She yelled out again, the last of her strength leaving her body. She grabbed the bag and leaned against it for support. She yelled again, but this time it was a sob. The tears broke free, streaming down her face, mingling with the beads of sweat.

She felt Alex pull her gloves off and heard the soft thud of them hitting the floor. He pulled her away from the bag and into his arms. "I got you, Ave."

She clung to him and cried until there was nothing left. He never moved, never wavered. Just held her until she let it all out.

Finally, she pulled back, suddenly aware of the sweat that soaked her clothes and hair. "Sorry, I probably don't smell great."

He chuckled. "Athlete, remember? I've smelled worse."

That made her laugh.

He pushed a loose strand of damp hair off her face. "Okay?"

"Yeah."

"Hit the showers?"

"Definitely." Her legs were shaky, but she grabbed her bag from the corner and headed for the women's locker room. She let the hot water soothe her muscles. She shampooed her hair– yay for travel sized toiletries. The suds washed away the sweat and grit from her hair. She soaped away the grime from the rest of her body and reluctantly turned the refreshing water off.

She felt much better as she toweled off and pulled on a clean set of clothes. She put on a pair of flip flops and gave her hair one last fluff with the towel before stuffing it into her bag.

Alex was fresh and waiting on the bench outside the locker room doors. He shoved his phone into his pocket and stood. "Better?"

"Much."

He picked his bag off the floor.

Her flip flops slapped against the tile as they walked to the exit. "I can't believe we had pretty much the whole place to ourselves. This was great."

"Yeah, usually I'm stuck with one of the crappy ellipticals because all the treadmills are taken."

"Elliptical machines are the devil. I hate them." She pushed through the exit door.

"I can't stand the stair machine."

"I actually like that one."

Alex hit a button on his key to pop the trunk open. They threw their gym bags in.

In the car, Avery put a hand on his arm. "I'm really glad you asked me to come along. I definitely needed this."

He put his hand over hers. "Good."

His touch sent a tingle up her arm. At least there was one bright spot in this crappy day. "And I'm glad you got your commission check."

"Me, too, but in some ways it makes it harder to know what to do in the long term."

"I can see that. It's easier to walk away when they've done you so wrong, but when they make it right, it's harder."

"Yeah." He started the car and drove out of the parking lot.

"Do you mind stopping at Sheetz? I was so upset I wasn't hungry, but now that I've gotten some of my rage out, there's room for food."

"Don't mind at all."

She knew from his sideways glance that he wanted to ask what was going on, but he was respecting her request that he not say anything about it. How sweet was that? "You've probably guessed that I didn't have the greatest ending to my day."

"I suspected." He reached over and squeezed her hand. "I'm perceptive like that."

She laughed and returned his squeeze. "Right at closing time, Grandpa came into the store with some papers. We all sat in the break room and I was sure he was signing everything over to Jimmy."

Alex pulled into the Sheetz parking lot and turned the car off.

"That's not what happened, though. He apologized to my mom and me for being sexist, and said he knew the store wouldn't have survived without us. Even said he was going to apologize to Grandma when he sees her on the other side." She pulled in a deep breath. "He had his lawyer draw up the papers to sign all his shares over to me."

Alex shifted sideways in his seat, to face her. "Avery, that's great!" Then he frowned. "But?"

"But there's one condition. I would have to keep Jimmy on as manager. Forever." It felt like her voice was coming from somewhere else, detached from her.

"After he almost single-handedly ruined the business. What stupidity is that?" Alex's outrage comforted her.

"I gave the papers back." She let her eyes drift shut. Had she just made the biggest mistake of her life? She didn't think so, but sliding those papers back across the table was one of the hardest things she'd ever done. "I said I'd keep Jimmy on the payroll if I had to, but he would absolutely not be my manager."

"Whoa. That must have been so hard."

"Did I make a mistake?"

Alex took both her hands in his. "Look at me."

She looked into his bright blue eyes.

"It would have been easy to agree and deal with the consequences later. Saying no wasn't just the right thing, it was brave, and I'm really proud of you. It took guts, Avery, and if that doesn't convince your grandfather that you've got the balls to run the business, then he's a shortsighted fool."

She looked down at their clasped hands and ran her thumbs over his fingers. "Part of me thinks I should have taken it and fired Jimmy later anyway. I mean, it can't really be enforceable, can it? Like, if Jimmy was stealing, I'd have the right to fire him." She let out a heavy sigh. "But I just couldn't do it."

"That's called integrity."

"I suppose." She gently pulled her hands away from his. "I better get some food before I get hangry."

"We would not want that."

They got out of the car. She didn't mind when Alex reached over to take her hand as they crossed the parking lot. In fact, she liked it. So much so that when they were leaving with her big salad and mega fountain drink, she–with zero subtlety– grabbed his hand for the walk back to the car.

Chapter Thirty-Six

Alex squeezed Avery's hand. He didn't miss the way she'd reached over to hold his hand as soon as they'd gotten outside. He also didn't miss the way his heart raced a little at her touch, or the warm fuzzy feeling he had watching her damp hair swing loose as she got into the car. Or how protective he felt when she was sharing her burdens with him.

As he pulled out of the parking lot, Avery took a long sip of her soda. "My arms are going to be jelly tomorrow."

"Drink lots of water."

"Yes, sir. I promise I will stay hydrated." She smirked at him over her cup.

"Hey, those muscle cramps are no joke. I've had more than my share over the years."

"Me, too. I remember one time we had this tournament and we played literally all day long. Afterwards, we went out for some celebratory drinks and had a few too many, which was really stupid, and I swear I was one big cramp from head to toe. Even my hair cramped. I thought I was going to die."

"Been there a time or two."

"Training camp?"

Alex laughed. "Nooo, never. We were practically Boy Scouts in training camp."

"I believe that like I believe there are little green men on Mars."

"Well, I've never been to Mars, so there's a chance there could be little green men there. There could also be little green men in Poughkeepsie, since I've never been there, either."

"If that's the criteria, there could be little green men in the trunk right now, because we're not there."

"Whoa. It's like Schrödinger's Little Green Men."

Avery laughed and twisted a lock of hair around her finger. "Speaking of Schrödinger, how was Poof? Foiled by the new knobs?"

Alex pulled into his parking space at the apartment building. "So far, so good, but I honestly don't think he's even tried getting out."

"Maybe he got scared straight. Like those kids they put in jail for a few days to show them what it's really like."

Alex held the building's door open for her. "I know you're kidding, but I honestly think that might have happened with him."

"Let's hope so."

They crossed the lobby and Avery hit the button for the elevator. The doors slid open and Alex felt Avery lean into his side.

"Good evening," Mr. Barrow said to Avery's chest, then glanced up at Alex. "I hear you're harboring a *cat burglar*." He snickered at his own joke.

Alex adjusted his gym bag to create a little extra distance between the creeper and Avery. "Yeah, well, we got that all straightened out."

"Is the cat on your lease?"

He bristled. It wasn't any of this guy's business. "Of course he is. Now if you'll excuse us." He stuck his hand on the elevator door so it wouldn't close.

Mr. Barrow inched out of the way. Avery slid behind Alex and into the elevator.

"Certainly. Have a nice evening." He directed his comment to Avery's chest again.

The door slid shut and Avery did a full body shudder. "Ugh! That guy gives me the creeps on like a thousand levels."

"I'm only creeped out on a hundred levels, and that's plenty." Alex slipped an arm around her. "You should carry pepper spray or something."

"Baseball bat? Maybe you could hook me up with one."

"I'd be happy to outfit you with an authentic Louisville Slugger."

"They should have a special line of self-defense bats."

She laughed, but Alex didn't. The idea of Mr. Barrow making her uncomfortable bothered him a great deal. "I still think you should call the police."

"Alex." She looked up at him. "You really don't get it. He's creepy and gross. He stares at my chest when he talks. But he's never made a threat or uttered any inappropriate words. He's never touched me, or even tried to. I can't stand the guy. He makes my skin crawl. But being a creep isn't illegal."

She was right, but he didn't like it.

The elevator opened on their floor.

Alex said, "Enjoy your salad."

Avery pulled another long sip of her soda. "I will. After which I will drink a ton of water to hydrate myself, doctor." She juggled her gym bag and food bag to find her keys. "But first, these nasty gym clothes are going in the washer."

Alex reached over and grabbed her bags so she could get to her keys without dropping anything. "Let me know how everything goes tomorrow."

"Oh, I can tell you now. Jimmy will gloat and do zero work. My mom will be furious with him but not say much because of the customers, and my dad will pretend everything's just peachy. Meanwhile, I will be working my butt off. Or maybe I'll just do the bare minimum. I'll decide when I get there."

"It's like you're psychic."

"If I was psychic, I'd have stayed in Atlanta," she grumbled darkly.

"Would you?" He leaned against her door jamb.

"No. I still would have come home to help while Dad was recovering. But I might have just taken a leave of absence and not given up my apartment. I could have stayed with my parents for a month or two and gone back." Her voice was low, contemplative.

"Well, *that* would have been very unfortunate."

She looked up at him. "It would?"

He reached over and tucked her still-damp hair behind her ear. "Because then you wouldn't have an amazing not-boyfriend and I'd just be a sad and lonely cat guy."

"Oh. That *would* be a shame." She leaned closer to him.

"It would."

She rested her hand on his chest. "I'd be lost without my not-boyfriend."

"I'd be lost without my not-girlfriend." He inclined his head ever so slightly. *Is this really going to happen?*

She moved her arm so her soda cup was no longer between them.

Alex ran a tongue over his teeth. How was his breath? He thought it was okay, but it would have been great to brush his teeth before this.

Avery's hand slid up his chest to rest on his shoulder.

Alex flexed his fingers, then lightly touched her waist. He held his breath and focused on her mouth. Her lips were slightly parted. *Yes. This is happening. Right now. I'm going to kiss Avery. Right. Now.*

He felt her breath against his mouth and swallowed hard. *Oh, crap, did she hear that?*

"There! That's him!" Mrs. Simmons shouted.

Alex jerked back, as did Avery.

A police officer followed Mrs. Simmons down the hall toward them.

"Um, can we help you?" Alex asked.

Mrs. Simmons crossed her arms. Her eyes shimmered with tears.

"Oh my gosh, what happened?" Avery took a few steps toward Mrs. Simmons and put a hand on her arm.

"My necklace! My amethyst necklace is gone. It's a purple heart on a gold chain. My husband gave me that necklace on our wedding day."

"Oh, no."

Alex bristled. He could see where this was going. "Mrs. Simmons, I'm so sorry, but Poof hasn't been out since the incident over the weekend."

Officer Pennick shook her head.

The elevator dinged again and another uniformed officer stepped out, a large man in a greenish outfit. *Oh, no.* The realization hit Alex. Animal Control.

Avery gasped. "Mrs. Simmons, are you sure you didn't misplace your necklace? I know with everything that happened, this is a logical assumption, but Alex is right. Poof hasn't been out."

"You can't know that for sure." Mrs. Simmons wrung her hands. "And my necklace is *gone.*"

"I'm here to take the cat," the Animal Control officer announced loudly.

"He hasn't done anything." Alex's heart pounded in his chest.

The burly officer scratched his ample belly. "That's what we're going to find out."

Alex snapped, "So you're taking him in for questioning?"

"I'm gonna need you to get the cat."

Alex looked to Officer Pennick.

She nodded once.

Avery's hand circled his forearm. "It'll be okay."

His hands shook, jangling his keys. "He hasn't done anything."

The elevator dinged again. A second police officer and Mr. Barrow stepped out. "My, my," he said. "This is why we shouldn't have pets in the building."

His comment raised Alex's hackles. How on earth did he know what was going on? This wasn't even his floor. Creep.

"I'm sure they'll find your necklace, Mrs. Simmons."

Officer Pennick jerked her head toward Alex's door. "The cat, sir."

Alex's vision swam as he unlocked the apartment door. He considered slamming it shut in the officers' faces, but guessed they'd just break the door down.

The Animal Control officer followed him inside, quashing that notion. He scrawled something across a paper on a clipboard. "I'll need you to sign here."

Alex read down over the paper. "No. I'm not relinquishing custody and I'm not signing anything saying I am." He caught a glimpse of Poof, hunkered under the couch, his eyes wide and taking in the situation.

In a hot second, Poof bolted. He streaked out the door and into the hallway.

"Poof! Stop him!" Alex shoved past the Animal Control officer.

In the hallway, the second policeman bent and grabbed for the cat, but missed. Poof wildly clawed the carpet, picking up speed. He flew straight, then flashed right, into the elevator. Alex ran, but the doors slid shut.

"No!" He smacked his palms on the silver doors.

Avery dropped her gym bag and cup. The lid popped off, sending a cascade of ice across the carpet. She ignored it, sprinting for the door to the stairwell. "Alex!"

They pushed through the door, Alex taking the steps two, three at a time.

The elevator dinged at the second floor. Alex crashed through the stairwell door and rounded the corner. The doors were sliding open. His heart pounded as the doors opened to reveal a frightened cat. He dove to his knees and snatched Poof off the floor. Poof yowled and dug his claws into Alex's shoulders, clinging to him.

The doors slid shut and delivered them to the lobby, where Avery waited, panting. "Oh, thank God he's okay." She held the elevator door with one hand as the call button lit up. She jammed her foot against the door so it wouldn't close. Fumbling, she yanked a key off her keyring. "Here." She shoved it at him.

Alex looked. Avery's car key.

"I'll go back up and do what I can."

He held Poof tight. For half a second, he debated.

Avery stepped into the elevator and hit the button for each floor, then let go of the door. "Go."

Poof mewled again, a pitiful, terrified sound.

Decision made. He ran for the parking lot and jumped into Avery's car. He pulled the door shut. Poof jumped onto the passenger seat and curled himself against the back of the seat, trembling. Alex fumbled with the key. It was only when he dropped it that he realized Avery's Rav4 had a push-button start. He left the keys on the floor and started the car, then backed out of the space, his heart pounding. *Does this make me a fugitive?*

He pulled out and drove to the highway, careful not to speed, checking his rear view mirror every few seconds. He expected sirens any second.

Poof was hunkered down, his eyes big and his tail wrapped protectively around his body.

Now what?

He could only think of one place to go. Stopped at a red light, he reached around to pull his phone out of his back pocket. Empty.

Oh, no.

"It's okay, buddy." He reached over and touched Poof's head. It alarmed him how much the cat was shaking. "We're almost there."

When the light turned green, he eased forward, earning an impatient horn blast from the car behind him.

Ten minutes later, he turned down the long driveway to his parents' house. The garage door was open, and the hatch on the back of his parents' minivan was up. His dad straightened from picking something up out of the back and turned. His mom came around the side of the van, looking curiously at the strange vehicle coming down their driveway.

Alex pulled up to the third garage door and rolled the window down a crack.

His dad's expression changed into a wide smile.

"Can I park in the garage? Please?"

"Sure." Bert motioned to Dolly, and a moment later, the third door slowly rolled up. Alex watched in the rear view mirror, expecting the police to show up any second. He eased into the garage and said, "Please hit the button."

His mom gave him a strange look, but hit the button to lower the garage door. "What's going on? Who's car is this?"

"Avery's. I'll explain in a minute."

Bert shrugged and grabbed an armload of stuff to carry into the house.

"Mom? Can you put the other door down? Please? I have Poof and I don't want him to get out."

"What on earth?" She gave him a puzzled expression that clearly said an interrogation was forthcoming, but closed the garage door.

When the exits were closed, Alex scooped Poof off the passenger seat and carried him into the house. He needn't have worried about Poof trying to escape, because he just clung to Alex's shirt. At least the trembling had subsided.

Dolly pointed to a kitchen chair. Alex dropped into it while she put leftover food from the beach house into the fridge.

A few minutes later, Bert came into the kitchen and said, "I started the first load of laundry." He turned to Alex. "What the heck's going on?"

Alex sighed and stroked Poof's fur. "I think we're in trouble."

Chapter Thirty-Seven

Avery got her breathing under control as the elevator lifted to the fifth floor. The doors opened to four curious faces. "He's, um, looking for the cat."

Officer Pennick shook her head. "Okay, well, Mrs. Simmons, let's go back to your apartment and we'll ask a few more questions, okay?"

Mr. Barrow scowled at Avery's chest. "We'll get that thieving cat out of here, one way or another."

Avery's skin crawled. Not just from his leer, but from the venom in his words. This man was on a mission. "Poof's on the lease."

"He's a thief."

She wanted to respond, but decided it was probably best to disengage and not talk to him at all.

Officer Pennick handed Avery a card. "When he gets back —" she gestured to Alex's apartment, which was still open, "— have him call me."

The Animal Control officer stood in Alex's living room, looking around.

"Hey, um, the cat's not in there, so, how about you come out so I can close the door."

He grunted and wiped his nose, then came out into the hallway. "Let me know if he finds the cat."

"Yeah."

Mr. Barrow interjected, "I'll be sure to call as soon as I see it."

Avery went into Alex's apartment and closed the door. "Oh, crap." Alex's phone and keys were on the coffee table. Now she had no way of getting in touch with him. Not knowing if he had a spare key, she slipped his keys into her pocket. After a moment's hesitation, she checked the hallway. Thankfully, everyone was gone. She scooped the melting ice back into her cup and picked up her gym bag. Her salad was probably gross by now.

In her own apartment, she found a piece of paper and scribbled a quick note to let Alex know she had his keys. She threw an old towel down over the spilled soda to sop up the wetness then taped the note to Alex's door.

As she'd suspected, her salad was wilted and not particularly appetizing. But it was after nine o'clock, and there was no way she was going back out. Oh. She couldn't even if she wanted to because Alex had her car.

She kept checking her phone, even though there was no way Alex could reach her. Unless he'd memorized her number. Which was highly unlikely. Did people even do that anymore? Avery hadn't memorized a number in a decade.

She finished what she could stand of her sad salad and changed into yoga pants and a tank top. At eleven, she heard a soft knock on her door. She leapt off the couch and ran to yank the door open.

"Hi." Alex's sister, Holly, stood in the hallway.

"Hi, come in." Avery stood aside and closed the door behind Holly. "How's Alex?"

"A little frazzled and convinced he's going to prison, but otherwise he's fine." She held up the note from Alex's door. "I was hoping you were still up. Sorry to bother you so late."

"No, no, it's fine. I'm just glad to know he's okay. I wasn't sure if he had a spare key, so I figured I shouldn't lock the door with his keys inside."

"Speaking of keys, here's yours. I hope you don't mind, but I drove your car here so I could swap with Alex's. He didn't want you to be without your car while he's on the lam." She snickered. "I shouldn't laugh, but this is so absurd. What, they're going to throw a cat in jail?"

Avery took her key and handed over Alex's. "I know. The whole thing is bananas." She wanted to ask where Alex was, but assumed he was with his family if he'd sent Holly on this mission.

"That brother of mine gets into some crazy situations. Thanks for sticking your neck out for him. And his rotten cat." She chuckled and reached for the door.

"He is a little beast, isn't he?" Avery laughed. "Let me know if there's anything else I can do. Oh, and Alex's phone is on his coffee table."

"Ah. That explains a lot. He used my phone to text his. He thought you might see the notification pop up."

"No, I didn't."

Holly opened the door and stepped into the hallway. She held up the keys. "Thanks again. Bet you didn't expect to be helping a cat run from the law when you met Alex, did you?"

Avery couldn't help but laugh. "Nope, did not see that one coming."

"Not to rush off, but this is past my bedtime." She turned to leave.

"Mine, too."

Holly turned back and said, "Hey, I hope everything's getting straightened out at your parents' store. It's a shame you had to leave early."

"I know. It's still a mess that I'm not sure will ever get sorted out."

"I probably shouldn't tell you this, but you should know that Chelsea thought it was an opportunity, but Alex shut that down and she left not long after you did."

Warmth bloomed in her chest. "That's pretty much what Alex told me happened." It was nice to have the unsolicited confirmation, though.

"He's a good guy." She took a step back and pointed over her shoulder to the elevator. "Thanks again. I'll be sure to get Alex's phone to him." She yawned. "See? I'm too old to be up this late. I'll be locking myself in my office on a 'conference call' tomorrow." She made air quotes and laughed.

"Excellent plan. Good night, Holly."

Avery closed her door and turned the lock. It was a few minutes after midnight when her phone dinged with a message from Alex.

> We're OK, thanks for everything.

> No problem. We'll talk tomorrow.

She set her phone back on the nightstand and managed to fall asleep.

In the morning, Avery felt like she had a hangover. Her entire body ached. The combination of a hard workout and a lack of sleep and forgetting to hydrate was not fun. She groaned and rolled out of bed, then shuffled to the bathroom, hoping a hot shower would help ease her aches.

It didn't.

On the upside, thinking about Alex's mess took her mind off her own drama. Until she unlocked the store and turned off the alarm code.

A few minutes later, Jimmy arrived. He stopped in front of the counter and scowled at her. "You just can't think of anyone but yourself, can you?"

She paused in counting the money for the cash register. "Excuse me?"

"Everything would have been fine. You should have just signed the papers."

"And agreed to keep you on as manager? Are you crazy? You're the last person in the world I'd let manage a business I owned. Besides, now that I turned it down, Grandpa will probably regret trying to break tradition and you'll get your shares."

"No, idiot, he's thinking about outside investors."

She nearly dropped the cash bag. "What?"

"Oh yeah, after you made your little scene and left, Dad asked if he was going to sign it over to me and he said no. He said he'd have to rethink things, and maybe even bring someone in from the outside."

Avery knew, this time at least, that Jimmy wasn't lying or even exaggerating. She almost felt a little pang of sympathy for him. He'd been expecting Grandpa's shares, and got nothing. Of course, if he had a modicum of self-awareness, he shouldn't have expected to get the shares, but still. It had to hurt.

"We'll figure something out," she offered.

"Bite me, Avery. You'd have me out on the street."

Her anger and frustration boiled over. "I'd have you *do your job* and not act like an entitled man-baby loser with no responsibilities!"

"Better than a bossy, shriveled up old hag who doesn't know her place," he fired back.

"Chauvinist."

"Bitch."

Her fingers curled around the bank bag. Before she could respond, the door opened and the first customer of the day walked in. Jimmy claimed the victory and smirked as he walked toward the office.

Avery breathed in and put a smile on her face. "Hi, can I help you find anything?"

The man came over to the counter and handed her a screw with a star-shaped head. "Do you have any screwdrivers that fit these?"

"Absolutely. Right this way." She came around the counter and led him to the screwdrivers. She selected one of the mid-priced options and handed it to him. "There are a few other styles here, but this is what you need. This one is ratcheting, which is a bit easier to work with, and it comes with a few different-sized bits."

"Great, thanks."

"Anything else?"

He huffed a little laugh. "Yeah, a good contractor who'll actually return my calls. This house is breeding new projects every time I turn my back."

"Absolutely. I have a card up front."

He followed her back to the counter. A rack of business cards hung on the wall behind her. She selected a few cards. The first she gave him was Rick's. "I can personally recommend these guys. Rick is a general contractor who does amazing construction work on all sizes of projects, and he returns calls. If you have plumbing issues, use Bill for sure, and Miguel is who you want for any HVAC work."

His voice was enthusiastic. "That's great, thanks. Maybe I can get some of these projects off my honey-do list. Do you happen to have a recommendation for driveway resurfacing?"

"Absolutely." She grabbed another card and handed it over. "DJ's Paving does excellent work. They just redid my parents' driveway last year."

She rang up his purchase and took his cash. Handing him his change, she said, "Do you need a bag?"

"Nah." He picked up the screwdriver set.

"Have a great day."

"You, too."

The customer headed for the door.

"Avery."

She startled and jerked her head toward the far end of the counter where her grandfather stood. He continued, "Come with me."

The door opened and more customers came in.

"Grandpa, this isn't a good time."

"It's the perfect time." He turned and walked toward the office.

"Hey, Avery, can I tack this on your bulletin board?" Grover Murdoch, one of their regulars, held up a sheet of paper.

"Sure." She tacked the page without looking at it, then followed her grandfather to the office.

In the doorway, Jamie barked, "Jimmy. You have customers."

"I'm busy with this stuff."

Jamie whacked his cane across the door. "You. Have. Customers."

Jimmy sniveled as he slid off his chair and slunk out the door, past Avery.

"Grandpa, I'm not sure I'm ready to talk about what happened last evening."

He motioned her into the office and closed the door. "Nor am I." He sat in a chair beside the desk and pointed at the security monitor. "I wanted to observe."

Observe, they did. Jimmy's incompetence made itself clear in under a minute, when he took a customer to the wrong aisle for loose screws and nails. Then again, when he ran the wrong amount on a customer's credit card. And yet again, when he said they didn't carry light switches.

For some bizarre reason, Avery felt the urge to defend him. "I mean, it's really busy, and the manager technically doesn't usually work the floor."

Jamie's eyes swung to hers. "Do you believe what you just said?"

"Uh…"

"Are you looking for another job?"

Where did that come from? "Not yet."

"Good. As of right now, you are promoted to manager/operator of this business. What is the first thing you plan to do?" His arm made a sweeping motion to encompass the office.

She blinked and glanced around the room. Jimmy had piles everywhere that would take her forever to sort. Her gaze landed on the grainy security monitor. The door opened and more customers filed in. "The first thing I'm *going* to do is help our customers." She stood. "I appreciate the position, but I honestly don't know how long I'll be staying."

His shrewd eyes held hers. "Understood."

She hurried back to the front of the store, her customer service smile bright and welcoming as she rescued her floundering brother. She threw herself into assisting her customers, her grandfather and his eagle eyes forgotten.

Chapter Thirty-Eight

Alex spent the day with his office door closed. He obsessively checked his banking app, which told him the money was still in his account, and social media, checking to see if he was popping up on any "most wanted" lists or anything.

He'd left Poof at his parents' house, after a stealth midnight run to Walmart for food and litter. He'd given strict instructions not to let him out of the basement. And if anyone asked, Poof wasn't there.

Five o'clock couldn't come soon enough. Erin was at her desk, still antsy about the whole theft thing, and every time she buzzed him, he jumped, assuming the police were there to arrest him.

At two minutes before five, he nearly fell off his chair when someone knocked on his office door. Swallowing hard, he walked over and opened the door. He breathed a sigh of relief when it was Erin.

"Do you have a minute?"

"Of course." He stepped aside and let her in.

She surprised him by closing the door. That wasn't a good sign.

He sat back at his desk and waited while she situated herself on a chair across from him.

"What's up?"

She held an envelope in her hand and dread settled in his belly. He guessed she was quitting the same time she said, "I'm resigning."

"Erin…" He didn't know what to say.

"I know. Even with them cleaning up the commissions, they still overbilled clients and probably stole more than I even know about. I can't keep working here. I'm giving you my two weeks' notice, but make sure you understand that's for you, and not the company."

"I appreciate it. Truly. Did you find another job yet?"

"Not yet. I have some savings, and my parents and Greg offered to help me out until I find something. I just can't stay here."

"I will obviously write you a glowing recommendation. And if I come across anything, I'll let you know."

"Thank you."

"I'll do what I can to get you some kind of severance."

"I'm not even holding my breath for my final check, to be honest. I heard some more rumors from Accounting. Just… be careful, Alex."

"My eyes are open, believe me. I'm just waiting for my commission check to clear before I make any moves."

"Hey, you can put in a good word for me wherever you end up." She gave him a big smile and stood. "You're a good boss."

He stood and reached across the table to shake her hand before she walked away. Losing Erin would probably make a bigger dent in the company than when he inevitably left.

Because leaving was his only option. He couldn't hang onto this job *and* his ethics. It was just a matter of making the right move at the right time.

And not ending up in prison over his cat.

He grabbed his laptop bag and left the office, checking over his shoulder the whole way to his car. He paid extra attention to the speed limit as he drove to his apartment to get fresh clothes. So this was life on the run. Sort of.

Okay, not quite. But it was not fun.

He turned off his car just as Avery pulled into her space. Immediately, his spirits lifted and he jumped out of his car. "Hey."

"Hey yourself. How's life on the lam?" she asked as they reached the sidewalk.

"Not funny. It's been a miserable day."

She wrapped her hand around his. "How's Poof?"

He looked around to make sure no one else was around. "He's fine."

She stage-whispered, "In a safe, undisclosed location?"

"You're poking fun."

"Not really. I'm glad you're both okay."

In the elevator, he put his arm around her shoulders and pulled her against him. "How was your day?"

"More eventful than I like. And I have something to show you."

He sighed. "I'm sorry. I don't have much time. I just came to get clean clothes and then head back to—" he looked up at the camera in the corner of the elevator. "—the undisclosed location."

"Oh." She sounded disappointed.

"Are you busy? Why don't you come with me?"

The elevator opened and they walked to their apartment doors.

She nodded. "Yeah. Why not. I'll be ready in like ten minutes?"

"Perfect."

Fifteen minutes later, they were back on the road, and ten minutes after that, they pulled into his parents' driveway. "I told Mom you were coming along. She can't wait to see you."

"Aww, that's sweet."

He led Avery inside and waited while his mom gave her a big hug, then whisked her off to the kitchen.

"I'm going to see Poof," he said, even though no one was paying him any attention. He hurried down the steps to his parents' finished basement. Poof was stretched out on the sofa, surrounded by piles of new toys, living his best life. Alex sat on the couch and relaxed for the first time all day.

Until his phone vibrated. He jerked it out of his back pocket and answered. "Sandy, hi, how are you?"

His attorney friend answered, "Alex. What have you gotten yourself into?"

He sat upright, one arm nervously stroking Poof, and then he launched into the tale, starting with the first theft. "I don't know what to do. Do I have to turn him over? How much trouble am I in? What am I going to be charged with? I mean, Poof's my cat, will they charge me with theft? Aiding and abetting? Harboring a fugitive? Am I going to prison?"

"Alex. Slow your roll. I happened to have lunch with the DA today, and we had a chance to talk about your situation. We're both in agreement. Neither the police nor Animal Control had any authority to ask you to surrender the cat. You do not have to turn him over. I drew up a strongly worded letter and emailed it to you. Just print it out and hand it to them if they try to take him again. You haven't broken any laws, not even by proxy."

Alex wilted with relief. He sank back against the couch and squeezed his eyes shut.

"Sandy, thank you so much. I really owe you."

Her warm laughter filled the air. "You probably won't be so thankful when you get my bill. One last thing."

He nodded, even though she couldn't see him. "Of course. What?"

"You need to stop binge watching Law & Order." She chuckled, then cleared her throat, back to serious business. "Now, about your work situation."

Chapter Thirty-Nine

Avery tiptoed back up the basement steps, feeling a little guilty about eavesdropping, but so thankful Poof and Alex weren't in trouble. And yes, the thought had crossed her mind that if Alex was in trouble for escaping with Poof, she'd probably be in trouble for providing the getaway car.

Back in the spacious kitchen, she told Dolly, "He's on the phone with his attorney."

"Okay." She handed Avery a pair of salad tongs. "Would you toss while I drain the pasta?"

"Of course." Avery gladly tossed the salad, a colorful, fresh display of yumminess that made her stomach growl.

Steam hissed in the sink as Dolly poured the water out of her pot.

Bert came in just as a timer rang. He stopped the beeping, then pulled garlic bread out of the oven. "Nice to see you, Avery. How's the hardware store?"

"Nice to see you, too. It's an adventure, that's for sure."

Footsteps thumped and a second later, Alex appeared in the doorway, a wide grin on his face. "Good news. I'm not in any trouble, and neither is Poof, so we can go back home."

Dolly looked a little smug. "See? I was right."

Bert snickered. "Never question your mother."

Dolly had mixed sauce in with the penne pasta and dumped it into a serving bowl. "Let's eat," she said, carrying the bowl to the table.

Avery set the salad beside the pasta while Bert put the basket of garlic bread down. Alex rummaged in the fridge and produced parmesan cheese.

Dinner was warm and comfortable, but Avery was itching to talk to Alex alone. She felt a little bad about being so glad when dinner was over. "Can I help with the dishes?"

Dolly waved her away. "Nope. Bert'll put the leftovers in the fridge, and all this will go in the dishwasher." Despite her weak objections, Alex and Avery loaded the dishwasher.

Alex leaned over and kissed his mom on the cheek. "I hate to run, but I'm going to take Poof home."

Back in the car, with Poof in a carrier on her lap, Avery pulled a crumpled paper out of her back pocket.

"My attorney, Sandy, is who I was talking to before dinner."

"Yeah, sorry, I kind of overheard a little bit when you were talking about Poof. Your mom sent me down to tell you dinner was ready. I wasn't trying to eavesdrop or anything."

"You could have come down." He reached over and touched her arm.

"I didn't want to butt in. That's great about Poof, though. And that she sent you a letter to use if you need to."

"She also agreed that I should probably leave my job as soon as I can. Erin gave me her resignation today. I want to get her as much as I can, as far as any earned PTO or sick time, before I give my own resignation."

"About that. I have something you might be interested in." She unfolded the paper and smoothed it along the top of the carrier while Alex pulled into the apartment parking lot.

"Oh?"

"Do you know Grover Murdoch?"

"Yeah. He sells security systems. A little more old school than what I do, but he's a nice guy. Why?"

"I'll show you when we get upstairs."

He took the cat carrier from her. Poof made a little yowl of protest, but settled in the elevator. When they got inside the apartment, Poof ran around, inspecting everything in his domain. Probably to make sure no one had touched his stuff while he was away.

Avery held the flyer out to Alex. "Grover brought this in today for the bulletin board. I didn't even pay attention to it at first, but when I was closing up tonight, it caught my eye."

"He's retiring?"

"Yup."

"I'm not really interested in buying his inventory."

"Alex. Think about it. Not the inventory, but what if he's open to selling the *business*?"

He looked up from the paper.

"I know it's a little lower tech. For now. He's the one who installed the system in my store. You'd have existing clients to service, and you could start there with upgrading, as well as adding new clients and maybe expanding into event security like you talked about."

"This… Avery, this could be something."

"Call him."

Alex grabbed her into a bear hug. "You're amazing."

She breathed in his scent and relished the feel of his arms around her. "Yeah, I kind of am. I'm going home. Call Grover and keep me posted."

She gave him a squeeze and let go.

If only her problems could be solved by a flyer on a bulletin board.

Chapter Forty

Alex hung up with Grover, stunned. Not only was Grover willing to sell Alex the business, he was willing to do it for a steal. He was also willing to sit down with Alex on Saturday and bust open the books and show him everything about the business before anybody made any decisions.

He explained the situation to Poof, who approved.

He also knew who would make the perfect business partner. Which might make things a little awkward. Before he made another phone call, he padded out into the hallway and tapped on Avery's door.

"Hey, that was quick." She let him in.

They sat on the couch and he told her all about Grover's offer and their meeting Saturday. "There's just one thing."

"What's that?"

"The business is bigger than I expected, and I would need a partner."

She sat up straight.

"I think Erin would be a great partner in a business like this." He held his breath, hoping he hadn't offended her.

"Oh, thank goodness." She put a hand over her heart.

"You're not upset that I'm not asking you?"

"I'm relieved. I know my situation is messed up right now, but my grandpa just promoted me to manager, and if we can work around the Jimmy situation, it might work out."

"Wait, he promoted you? When?"

"This morning." She filled him in on the talk with her grandfather.

"Avery, that's great."

"I'm trying not to get my hopes up, but I really do love that store. I want it. I've earned it."

"You have." He hoped her grandfather saw it as clearly as he did.

"Sounds like you have another phone call to make before it gets too late."

A few minutes later, he was in his own apartment with Poof curled up on his lap. He held his phone and tapped Erin's number. He wasn't sure how to start.

"Alex? Is everything okay?"

"Hey. Erin. Are you busy Saturday?"

There was a long pause. "Um, why?"

"You know Grover Murdoch?"

"Yeah."

"He's retiring and selling his business. If everything goes well, he's selling it to me. Or, if you're interested, he's selling it to us."

"Us?"

"How would you like to be my partner in Gold Star Security?"

"What kind of investment are we talking?"

He gave her a number. "But here's the thing. Grover's willing to do a payment plan. So if you don't have cash up front, we can structure it so your half comes out of payments from your share of the profits. I'm just spitballing here. How about you come with me on Saturday, and if it's something you're interested in, we can talk to an accountant or business attorney or whatever. It's a bigger company than I expected, and there's a lot of room for growth. The best part? Grover said he'd be willing to do a six-month transition where he's basically on call when we need him."

"Wow. That's a lot to think about."

"I know." Alex hoped she'd be on board, but it was a big ask. And heck, maybe she was done with the security business.

"I'll think about it. I'll go along on Saturday, just so I can make a totally informed decision, and we'll talk after the meeting."

"Absolutely."

"We'll also have to have a discussion about roles and responsibilities. If we're equal partners, we're equal partners. I'm not going into this to be a glorified secretary and keep track of your stuff like I do now."

"I know. Believe me, I understand that right now you're my assistant, but in this venture, you would be my partner. Once we talk to Grover on Saturday, we'll have a better idea of what gets done, and we can start thinking about who will take care of what. I know there are employees we'll have to deal with as well."

"How many?"

"Two? Three? I'm not exactly sure."

Erin's familiar noise of contemplation came across the line. "Okay. Well, you've given me a lot to think about tonight. I'll see you tomorrow."

"TGIF."

"This week has been reeeeeeally long."

"I'll see you tomorrow. And Alex?"

"Yeah?"

"Thank you."

Once he hung up, he texted Avery.

Erin's thinking about it.

Avery texted back the crossed-fingers emoji.

He felt bad that they hadn't had time to talk about her work situation. He hoped her grandfather came around and did the right thing. Not just for Avery, but for the store.

Chapter Forty-One

Friday was thankfully uneventful, until Jimmy strolled in just before closing time.

James was stocking paint. Ginny was sweeping, and Avery was at the counter, ringing up a customer.

"Would you like a bag?"

"YOU'RE a bag!" Jimmy shouted. "You stole my job out from under me, you *bag*."

The customer grabbed her purchase and made a beeline for the door.

"Are you drunk?" Avery asked, aghast.

"What if I am? What are you going to do, call Grandpa? Maybe he'll take my car, too, like he took my job."

"Your car? You *drove* here?"

"Screw you. You're not my boss." He hiccup-laughed. "Oh. Wait. I guess you are." He held his arms out wide. "Myyyyyy sister, now my *boss*. My bitch boss. How's it feel having every-thing handed to you on a golden platter while the rest of us have to *work* for everything we have?"

Avery's mouth hung open. Jimmy was delusional. And completely wasted.

"You." He leaned across the counter, poking his finger toward her face. "You ruined my life."

"That's enough." James came alongside his son and put a hand on his arm. "Come on, Jimmy, let's get you some coffee."

Jimmy glared. "Coffee," he spat.

Ginny stood at the mouth of the aisle, clutching the broom handle, looking like she was about to cry.

"This place sucks anyway." Jimmy reached out and swiped a display of metal garden stakes onto the floor. They clanged against the cement floor and scattered. James immediately bent to pick them up.

Jimmy laughed and took two giant steps to the key machine where they made duplicate keys. He grabbed the edge of the pegboard key display and yanked it down, sending hundreds of blank keys skittering across the floor and into the aisles and under the shelves.

"Get out." Avery came around the counter and stood toe to toe with her brother.

"Or what?"

"Or I'm calling the cops."

"Avery—" James began, but Ginny cut him off.

"Jimmy, go in the back with your father and get some coffee."

"I don't want coffee," he growled.

"NOW." Ginny stepped in front of Avery and pointed back the aisle to the break room.

He took two steps and stumbled into the shelving. A row of mason jars crashed to the floor, shattering and spraying glass. Two jars on the small local honey display on the endcap teetered and plunged to the floor as well, adding an amber goo to the mess. Great.

Jimmy burst into laughter. "You should see your faces! I'm outta here. Screw you all." He lurched toward the door.

Ginny grabbed his arm. "You're not driving."

He yanked his arm from her grasp and barreled out the door, shouting, "You don't tell me what to do!"

He jumped into his car as James followed him out and grabbed the door handle, wrenching the door open. Wild-eyed, Jimmy cranked the engine and threw the car in reverse. He slammed the gas and the car lurched backwards.

Directly into a pickup truck that was pulling into the parking lot.

Avery's scream was absorbed by the sickening crunch of metal. The owner of the truck jumped out, cursing.

Of course.

Rick Lauder.

Chapter Forty-Two

Alex read the paper HR had given him that outlined the severance package for Erin. It was one of those things buried deep in the employee manual that nobody ever asked for, because nobody ever really read the manual. Because of Erin's job grade, she was entitled to her accrued PTO, sick leave, plus two weeks' salary if she left under good terms.

As her direct supervisor, Alex gladly scrawled his signature on the page, approving the amount. And as far as he was concerned, she was leaving on good terms even if she set the building on fire on her way out. Okay, not quite, but almost.

He hand-delivered the page back to HR and went back to his office. "Severance package approved," he told Erin as he passed her desk.

"Thanks. I'll see you tomorrow at Grover's." She stood and grabbed her purse. "I'm looking forward to it."

"Me, too." He really was. He could already see the ways they could update the business and hopefully turn that into bigger profits.

Whistling, he left his office for the day and on a whim, swung through Dunkin' Donuts. He ordered Avery's favorite iced coffee and a flavored iced tea for himself. He slowed as he approached the hardware store, hoping he'd be able to see if Avery was still at work, or if she'd headed home.

What he did not expect to see was two police cars, a damaged pickup truck, and a car being loaded onto a tow truck. Avery and her parents stood huddled by the front door.

Alex threw on his turn signal and pulled into the far side of the parking lot. He hesitated, not wanting to get in the way, but he wanted to make sure Avery had his support during whatever was going on.

He got out of his car and trotted along the sidewalk until he reached Avery. As everyone does at an accident, he watched the scene playing out, and before he could ask what was happening, he recognized Jimmy in the back of the police car.

Wait. They don't haul people away in police cars for plain old fender benders. His curiosity was in overdrive, but he kept his mouth shut.

Avery's shoulders were slumped. Her face was tight. She ran a hand over her hair and tugged at her ponytail, something Alex noticed she did whenever she was stressed out. He put his hand on her back.

"We have to go see what we can do," James said.

Ginny snapped, "We have to clean up his mess."

Avery reached over and squeezed her mom's hand. "I'll clean up the mess."

Alex was lost. Wasn't Jimmy's mess on the way to the police station?

A man was near the pickup truck with the dented front end, animatedly talking on the phone.

Avery's mom started to quietly cry, but her mouth was set in a scowl, just like his own mother cried when she was very, very angry. She turned away from them and composed herself.

When she turned back, she said, "You clean up enough of his messes, Avery."

"We have to go," James said.

"Mom, I've got it. Really."

"I'll help." He had no idea what he was signing up for, not that it mattered much. If Avery needed help, he'd be there.

Ginny hesitated, then followed James around the corner of the building.

Avery pulled open the store's door. "After you."

He stepped inside and stopped. Chunks of glass lay all over the floor, a goopy mess of something yellowish blobbed in one area, and was that a key? He looked to the right. It wasn't just a key, it was probably a hundred keys from the overturned display. What the heck happened here?

Avery let out a massive sigh. "I'll grab the dustpan and…" she waved her hand at the yellow goop, "something to clean that up."

She took an aisle to the left, presumably one that didn't have shattered glass. Alex spied a broom laying on the floor halfway down the aisle with the glass. He took the same aisle Avery had taken and came around to get the broom. He picked it up and swept slowly, nudging the glass onto a pile.

Avery set the dustpan on a shelf behind him and said, "I'm going to start picking up keys."

"Where's the trash can? Behind the counter?"

"Yeah, hang on, I'll put a different bag in it." She disappeared down another aisle, came back and went behind the counter. A minute later, she set a trash can, lined with a heavy-duty bag, near the end of the aisle.

"Are you okay?"

"I'll be fine." She gestured to the keys on the floor. "I'm glad you're here."

"Me, too."

He maneuvered the pile of glass onto the dustpan and dumped it into the trash bag, then used an entire roll of paper towels to clean up what turned out to be honey. With its own glass chunks, of course.

Avery piled the keys on the counter and began sorting them into piles.

"Is there a dust cloth or something? I want to wipe down these shelves in case any of the glass flew up."

She pressed a hand to her face. "I didn't even think of that."

"Hey." He came behind her and wrapped his arms around her middle. She turned and leaned on him. "It's okay."

Her shoulders shook. "It's not okay. A customer's kid could have—"

"Avery." He said her name sharply and immediately felt bad, but he wanted to get her attention away from that negative place. "Stop. Sweetheart, listen to me."

Her blue eyes held his.

"We've got this. We'll get everything cleaned up and good as new. Okay?"

She nodded.

"We've got this," he repeated, softly. "I've got you."

Something shifted in her gaze. Slightly, ever so slightly, she lifted her chin.

Alex tilted his head. Her breath was warm against his mouth.

And then, it happened. Their lips met somewhere in the middle, their first kiss so soft and sweet it squeezed his heart.

Avery's hands splayed across his back.

One hand touched her face, while his other arm circled her waist, holding her tight against him.

He was the first to pull back, just a little, and pressed his lips to her forehead.

She let out a long breath, this one calm and maybe even a

little happy. After a long moment, she whispered, "We should finish cleaning up so we can get out of here."

He nodded and stepped back, not wanting to let go of her. "Hey. I have something for you. Hang on."

Her brow furrowed, curious, as he grinned and ran out to his car. A minute later, he came back inside, holding her iced coffee and his tea.

"Alex!" She grabbed the coffee and pulled a long sip. "Oh my gosh, you are the absolute best." She gave him a wide smile.

"Caffeine to get us through, right?"

"Yes. Let me grab you a cloth." She disappeared down the aisle again, and a few minutes later came back with a spray bottle of cleaner and a microfiber cloth. "The spray will help catch some of those little shards."

He took the items from her and leaned in, planting a kiss on her lips.

She put her hands on the sides of his face and kissed him back.

"Mmm, iced coffee flavor."

She giggled. "It should be a lipstick."

An hour later, the shelves and all the items on them were wiped down. Avery had fixed her pegboard key display and sorted all the keys and hung them back up. Alex had gotten on the floor and used the spray to clean up the last of the honey residue.

"I'll be finding stray keys for years. I bet in fifty years when this shelving unit gets moved, we'll find a bunch of them."

Alex laughed. "I bet you're right." He wanted to ask what had happened, but he didn't want to bring the mood back down.

Avery planted her hands on her hips and looked around, taking in every detail. "I'm going to do a quick mop of this area, then I'm calling it done." She glanced over at him. "Five minutes, tops, then I'm ready to leave."

He heard her stomach growl. "How about you mop, and I'll pick up food and meet you back home?"

"You're amazing."

"I know."

She laughed and shoved his shoulder. "And so modest."

"It's hard to be humble with this much greatness." He patted his stomach.

As he'd hoped, she rolled her eyes and groaned. "Go, before I have to mop up vomit."

Laughing, he twirled his keys on his finger and said, "See you at home."

Chapter Forty-Three

Avery rolled the mop bucket from the back and squeezed the string mop in the strainer, then mopped the floor in front of the counter, and in the aisle where the glass had broken. She carefully mopped the spot where the honey had fallen.

Satisfied, she stuck the mop in the bucket and rolled it back through the break room and into the maintenance closet. She'd worry about dumping it tomorrow. Right now, she was beat. All she wanted was food, a shower, and bed.

And maybe another kiss or two.

She smiled at the thought and pressed a fingertip to her mouth. Okay, she knew it would be amazing to kiss Alex, but she hadn't expected her entire brain to go quiet and her heart to thump so loud.

She took one last look around, set the alarm, and locked the door behind her. Her car was like a thousand degrees inside. She rolled down the window and pulled out, anxious to get home. The weight of the day was going to come crashing down, she knew it. And she wanted to be at home when it did. Preferably in her pajamas.

She pulled into the apartment complex just as Alex was

getting out of his car. He had two plastic bags of food, which he held up with a grin. "I thought for sure you'd beat me home, but Sonny's wasn't very busy when I stopped."

She sucked in a happy breath. "You got from Sonny's? You are seriously in the running for the best not-boyfriend ever."

He chuckled and followed her to the elevator.

On their floor, he said, "Your place or mine?"

"Mine, please. I'd really like to grab a quick shower." She looked longingly at the bags of food. As hungry as she was, she didn't want to handle food when she was this grungy and sweaty.

"You got it."

She found the right key and slid it into her lock.

"Alex?" a voice called from down the hallway.

"Oh, no," he said under his breath.

They both turned to see Mrs. Simmons hurrying from her apartment at the far end of the hall.

"Mrs. Simmons."

"Alex. Hello, Avery. Alex, I need to speak to you, please. It'll just take a moment."

"Um, sure."

Mrs. Simmons clasped her hands in front of her and pulled in a deep breath. "It's not easy to admit when one is wrong. I… I misplaced my necklace." Her eyes grew watery. "I was too quick to blame you. Well, your cat. I'm very sorry. I called the police to let them know I found it. I hope you'll… I hope you'll forgive me."

"Of course."

Avery took the bags from Alex. He gave the older woman a hug.

"I'm very sorry."

"It was an honest mistake. I'm sorry my cat had gotten in your apartment in the first place."

Mrs. Simmons produced a tissue from the pocket of her housedress and wiped her eyes and nose. She chuckled. "I once had a cat who got trapped on the roof of our house for two days. We called the fire department and wouldn't you know, the little bugger shimmied onto a tree limb and got himself down."

Alex laughed.

Avery smiled, awkwardly trying to stay out of the conversation.

"Anyway." Mrs. Simmons flapped her hand. "I do apologize, and I hope your cat is alright."

"He's fine. And your apology is accepted."

She sniffled and patted his arm. For the first time, she looked directly at Avery, then back to Alex. "You're good kids. You make a nice pair."

With that, she turned and walked back toward her own apartment.

Avery shoved the door open and looked at the bags. "Changed my mind. No way I can shower first. I'm going to starve to death."

"Ditto."

They washed their hands, then unloaded the bags on the table.

"Oh, man, you got pizza fries." Avery pulled the clear lid off the French fries covered in pizza sauce and melted mozzarella cheese. "You really are the best."

He pushed a foil-wrapped sub to her. "And a cheesesteak sub."

"My favorite."

"I know."

They devoured the food in companionable quiet, barely leaving a crumb. Avery spied two more foam containers. "What's that?"

He grinned. "Fresh strawberry pie."

"Noooo." She groaned in delight. "I am going to exhibit an amazing level of self-control and take a shower before I eat dessert."

"Me, too. I'll put these in the fridge and be back over in a bit." Alex stood and put the containers in the fridge.

Avery took a quick shower, eager to just get the grime washed away from her skin and hair. Fresh and clean, she tugged on a T-shirt and yoga pants and let her wet hair hang loose to air dry.

She gladly answered the knock on her door.

Over pie, she told Alex the entire story of Jimmy's meltdown and that thankfully he had good insurance that would cover Rick's truck repairs.

"He seemed to understand that the problem is Jimmy, but I'm still afraid he'll pull his business. That's a lot of drama, and I'm not sure I'd keep shopping with us. But at least now that I'm manager, I have the authority to deal with whatever happens." She snuggled next to Alex. "I'm glad today's over. And I'm glad you're here. You're the best not-boyfriend in the whole world."

"So. About that."

Her heart skipped a little. "Yeah?"

"We should drop the 'not.'"

"You don't not want me to not be your not-girlfriend?"

"I do *not* want you to *not* be my girlfriend."

"Wait. That's too many double negatives for my tired brain to untangle."

"I would very much like to be your boyfriend. No nots at all."

Avery shifted so she could look up into his bright blue eyes. "I would very much like you to be my boyfriend."

Epilogue

Sixteen months later
   Labor Day Weekend

Avery held her arms out, her face tilted up to the sky, the sound of the ocean and the smell of the salt water surrounding her. The water rushed over her ankles. It flowed away, pulling the sand from under her feet.

Paradise.

"We should probably get the suitcases out of the car now," Alex chided with a laugh.

"I had to get my feet in the sand."

"Want me to grab the beach chairs?"

"Nah, we can do that after lunch." She turned and reached out for him.

He wrapped his arms around her and she breathed in the scent of him and the ocean air. Perfection. Their home for a week was the tiny beach cottage behind them, a wedding present from Alex's parents. It was similar to the real new home they'd purchased a month ago – a small ranch house with all new doorknobs. No lever handles for them, ever. Poof loved his new digs, especially the living room wall they'd covered with carpeted shelves so Poof could go as high as he needed to survey his new domain.

It also had a huge back yard. Alex had already started building a mini-golf course for the nieces and nephews, but let's be real, he was doing it mostly for Sophie.

They'd both been glad to leave apartment life behind, even though the drama was cheaper than cable. Months ago, Mrs. Simmons's apartment had been broken into yet again, only this time the culprit was Mr. Barrow, caught red-handed on the new hi-def security system Alex's company had installed. When the police searched his apartment, they not only found jewelry and stolen money, they found a stash of inappropriate photos of unsuspecting women. It had been rather satisfying to see Mr. Barrow being escorted out in handcuffs.

Avery still couldn't quite believe that forty-eight hours earlier, they'd exchanged vows in a small ceremony in her parents' backyard, followed by a barbecue and dancing and lawn games, topped off with fireworks. Jack had officiated, putting his online ordination to good use. The kids – and some adults – ran around barefoot, having a wonderful time. Completely informal. Completely perfect. Completely *them*.

And twenty-four hours ago, they'd been in Philadelphia, screaming themselves hoarse as the Braves shut out the Phillies. Afterwards, they'd made a mad dash for the car because there wasn't much "brotherly love" for people supporting the away team.

This time, their beach vacation went off without a hitch. Jimmy texted once every evening to let Avery know her store – that she was now 100% owner of – was doing great. Yes, Jimmy. After his "accident," he had a dramatic awakening. Avery assumed he'd hit his head, because he'd done a complete 180. He got a full time job, moved out of their parents' house, and had even been dating a nice woman who took zero crap from him. When his job was downsized, Avery had hired him back, with a great deal of skepticism and plenty of firm boundaries. But his about-face seemed permanent, and without the nonsense, he was a good Assistant Manager.

Gold Star Security was in the capable hands of Alex's partner, Erin. They'd built on Grover's solid business foundation and were slowly and steadily expanding. They'd even picked up a number of their previous company's clients after that company was shut down when Dean and Mike were arrested for embezzlement and fraud.

Poof was probably spending the week terrorizing Lincoln, who was house- and cat-sitting. The whole situation with Poof had so frightened Lincoln that he bit the bullet and started therapy for his severe anxiety. He told them it was because he never wanted to be in another situation where he couldn't speak, especially to the police. Avery suspected it was more because he wanted to date and most women expected conversation. Whatever his motives, she was proud of him for taking the huge step of getting help.

On the last evening of their stay, Avery and Alex lay on a blanket on the beach, staring up at the stars.

"Did you see it?" Alex pointed to the sky. "Falling star. Make a wish."

Avery closed her eyes and opened them again. She traced Alex's jaw with her fingertip. "What more could I possibly wish for?"

He turned and softly kissed her lips. "That's what I was just thinking."

Enjoyed this trip to Hickory Hollow? Keep those warm fuzzy feelings going and dive straight into Book 6 in the Hickory Hollow series, Mending Fences.

Chandler has her fairy tale happily ever after. House in the country, two kids, white picket fence, the whole nine. It hasn't always been easy, but her marriage has weathered every storm that's come their way. Until a Category 5 in the form of a vindictive mother-in-law roars through and leaves a trail of lies, misunderstandings, and broken trust in her wake. (NOTE: Chandler and Oren were first introduced in Caller Number Nine.)

Hickory Hollow. Get comfy, stay a while!

You don't want to miss news of upcoming books, events, and behind-the-scenes sneak peeks! Sign up for my newsletter today at carriejacobs.com!

Acknowledgments

Inspiration comes from the most random places. Remember Drunk on a Plane? It was inspired by a song. Cat Burglar was inspired by a news article my friend and fellow writer Stacy Whitmore shared. It was about a cat who was caught on camera stealing clothing from all over his neighborhood. Nellie Batz, the third fellow writer in our little group chat, replied with a note to the effect of: *ha ha, Carrie, this could totally be a meet cute in one*

of your books! Boom. Here we are. Thanks, Velociposse! RAWR!

As always, Jen & Laura – MWAH! Your support and friendship on this ever-changing journey keeps me sane. Ish.

Huge thanks to Magan from Court of Spice Editing for helping me polish this book! She was so thorough and found so many errors I missed in the 7,000 times I combed through this book. Need an editor? Visit Magan at courtofspice.com.

Thank you to Rebecca Allman from Hot Tree Editing for her insightful beta read!

Michelle – Thank you for letting us crash your store with our laptops and snacks! Cupboard Maker Books is a *must* if you're in central Pennsylvania. Books and cats, y'all! cupboardmaker.com

As always, my biggest thanks go to my husband Scott.

And thanks to YOU, dear reader, for picking up this book and reading this far. I hope you enjoyed Avery and Alex's (and Poof's!) story as much as I enjoyed writing it!

About the Author

Carrie's love of storytelling began in early childhood and never wavered as time marched onward. She reads in pretty much every genre imaginable, but found her writing happy place in small town contemporary romance and romantic comedy.

From that love came Hickory Hollow, a mashup of her hometown and places she's either visited or would like to. Her favorite part of Hickory Hollow? The residents don't have to drive an hour to get to Target, like she does in real life.

Carrie lives in beautiful central Pennsylvania with her family and very spoiled furry editorial assistants.

Connect with Carrie through her newsletter or social media!

Website: carriejacobs.com

facebook.com / writercarriejacobs

instagram.com / carriejacobsauthor

goodreads.com / carriejacobs

www.ingramcontent.com/pod-product-compliance
Lightning Source LLC
Chambersburg PA
CBHW061610190726
48288CB00007B/2264